LETTER FROM A CAVE

ALSO BY CHRISTA POLKINHORN

NOVELS

The Italian Sister
The Wine Lover's Daughter, Book One

Finding Angelo
The Wine Lover's Daughter, Book Two

Fire in the Vineyard
The Wine Lover's Daughter, Book Three

An Uncommon Family
Family Portrait, Book One

Love of a Stonemason
Family Portrait, Book Two

Emilia
Family Portrait, Book Three

POETRY

Path of Fire

LETTER FROM A CAVE

Christa Polkinhorn

Bookworm Press

Bookworm Press
1223 Wilshire Blvd., #1054
Santa Monica, CA 90403

Cover design: Diane Busch
Cover images: György Károly Tóth, Pixabay

ISBN: 978-0-9600135-6-2

Printed in the United States of America

For Risayra and Muriel

Prologue: December 10, 1943

My beloved Bella,

I made it! I arrived. I'm exhausted, full of scrapes and bruises from the climb, but I'm here free and safe. What a relief! I just wish you were with me, my dear Bella. I miss you so much. At the same time, I'm grateful we decided for you not to make this difficult journey. It would have been too strenuous, especially in your present condition. There was a pregnant woman with us, but she had to turn back. It was too hard on her. So, we just have to be patient. Our friend will bring you along as soon as possible. I just hope and pray that this terrible war will be over soon.

Anyway, I'm not going into any detail about our trek just in case this letter gets into the wrong hands, which I don't think will happen with all the precautions we took, but you never know. So here are just the basics. Aside from the strenuous hike, the weather changed all of a sudden and it began to snow heavily just as we neared the border. It was a terrible storm. I was afraid we'd get lost and end up in an abyss. But Guido, the guide, (not his real name to protect his identity) was fantastic. He brought me safely through the horror of the storm.

Unfortunately, we got delayed because of the bad weather, and when we finally arrived, it was dark. The Swiss guide, who was supposed to bring me to the valley on the Swiss side, was no longer there. Guido assured me that this happened occasionally. He brought me to a cave that he and his fellow guides had set up as a refuge for people who got stranded. It's quite cozy in here with blankets, water, dry food, and firewood. I'm going to spend the night here and wait for the Swiss guide to come back tomorrow to take me to the village. If for some reason he doesn't show up, I can make it down to the valley on my own during daytime.

I'm exhausted, but I couldn't go to sleep without writing to you. I'll mail this letter from the village, so you know I'm safe. Take care of yourself, my dear Bella, and take care of our little girl or boy. I hope it's going to be a girl and that she is as beautiful as you are. But as long as you and the baby are safe and healthy, and we'll soon be together again—that's all that counts.

I miss you, my love. *Molti baci.*
Joshua

Chapter 1: Spring 2018

Andreas gasped. He sat up in bed, tightening his fists as his heart hurt with longing. It had been another one of his dreams about Karla, his wife, who had died three years before.

"Where are you now?" he whispered with a sob.

He pushed the comforter back, slid his legs to the edge of the bed, and put his feet on the throw rug. Planting his elbows on his knees, he covered his face with his hands, then brushed the tears away. He got up with a groan, rubbing his lower back. It was one of the mornings he became aware of his seventy-year-old body. He walked to the window, slid the sheer curtains aside, and opened it.

Outside, it was gloomy. Clumps of dark clouds obstructed the view of Piz La Tschera and the other surrounding mountains that were visible on clear days from the village of Andeer in the northeast of Switzerland. The air smelled musty of wet leaves and grass.

Karla had died in a car accident in the south of Switzerland where they lived at the time. She'd been a careful driver, but it had snowed heavily the night before. Andreas hadn't wanted her to drive, had offered to go to the store himself. She'd waved him off, saying, "I'll be careful. Go on with your work." He'd been in the middle of a large sculpting project for an upcoming exhibition and was fully focused on his work. So he let her go. Feelings of guilt still haunted him three years later.

The road toward Locarno, a city in the canton Ticino, had been well plowed, but there were patches of ice. They found her car at the bottom of the hill at the edge of the Maggia River.

Her body lay halfway down the hill beside a tree stump. The police surmised she'd been thrown from the car against the stump, snapping her neck.

"It happened fast. She didn't have time to suffer," the police had assured him. The memory tightened his throat and new tears flooded his eyes. He'd done the suffering for her.

He picked up her photo from the chest of drawers. It slipped out of his hand, dropped on the hardwood floor, and the frame cracked. His jaw clenched as he carefully pulled the photo out and slammed the broken frame into the wastebasket. He let out a harsh breath, trying to squelch the rage rising from the pit of his stomach. An angry sob escaped. The picture could be fixed but not her life. It was so unfair.

He stepped into the bathroom, and took a hot shower, letting the water soothe his stiff shoulders, then shaved for the first time in days. Back in the bedroom, he dressed in a pair of jeans and a long-sleeved green cotton shirt.

As he walked out of the bedroom, he heard the sound of the coffee grinder downstairs. *Karla?* A flash of irritation cursed through him. "Of course not, who the hell ...?". He hesitated, then walked downstairs, the smell of freshly ground coffee beans wafting toward him. His anger faded when he stepped into the kitchen and saw his son, Tonio, putting a cup under the spout of the espresso machine.

"What are you doing here?" Andreas asked.

"Well, hello to you too, Papa." Tonio scrutinized him, lifted an eyebrow, then turned back to the coffee machine.

Andreas gave a quick smile. "Just surprised. I didn't expect you." He put his hand on Tonio's shoulder.

Tonio pressed the button on the espresso maker. The scent of coffee intensified in the kitchen. He handed his father a cup, then put an empty one under the spout.

"Thanks." Andreas took a sip and observed his handsome son, the finely chiseled face, the dark eyes framed by long eyelashes, the shiny black hair with natural reddish-blond highlights that showed a few solitary gray streaks. Tonio was forty-two years old but looked younger.

The slightly bitter, full-bodied coffee woke Andreas' senses. "So, what's going on with you? I thought you were in Milano." Tonio and his boyfriend, Mario, owned two fashion boutiques, one in Lugano in the south of Switzerland and the other one in Milano, Italy. They lived in Lugano but spent a lot of time in Italy at their other business.

"I just got back yesterday. I reserved our rooms in Tuscany." Tonio put a colorful brochure on the kitchen table. It showed an estate with several vineyards, meadows full of poppies, houses and farm buildings in a town called Vignaverde in Tuscany. They were going to spend two weeks of vacation there. It was a present from Andreas to his youngest daughter, Emilia, who had completed her studies as a veterinarian. Andreas had first refused to go with them, saying he would be bad company. Emilia's siblings—Laura, his older daughter, and Tonio—had convinced him, however, that Emilia would be very disappointed if her father didn't go along, so he finally relented.

Andreas picked up the brochure and paged through it. "Looks nice. I still feel you'd have more fun without your old father."

Tonio rolled his eyes. "You're not that old and it will be good for you to get out and do something fun for a change instead of moping around the house and missing Mother."

"You're probably right." Andreas forced a smile.

Tonio looked around the living room. He walked over to the rustic fireplace and touched the granite mantel. "How do you like your new place?"

11

"I like it a lot, and I enjoy being near Emilia."

"Good." Tonio checked his watch, then picked up the rest of the vacation brochures. "Is Emilia home or is she at work? How is she doing by the way? I haven't talked to her in a while."

"She's at the practice. She loves her work. She keeps bringing home pictures of dogs and cats for me." Andreas chuckled. "She feels I should have a four-legged companion."

"Not a bad idea," Tonio said. "You could use some companionship. I mean it won't replace Mother, but still."

"I'll think about it. It would be nice to have someone to take along on my walks."

"Talk about walks. You're still going on extended hikes?" Tonio peered at him. "Staying out overnight?"

"Yes, I still go on long hikes. No, I try not to stay out at night."

"I heard otherwise," Tonio grumbled.

Andreas gave a snort. "Emilia worries too much, but I've been trying to call her when I'm out for longer hikes."

"See that you do. It's not fair to make her worry. Laura and I worry too."

"All right. All right. I got the point." Andreas tried not to sound irritated. He knew his children meant well, but he felt they treated him like an old man or a child. He wasn't senile yet. He pointed at the brochures. "You can leave these here. I can give them to Emilia."

"Okay, I'll call her from home." Tonio checked his watch again, an elegant and expensive one, as Andreas could see. His son loved fashion and beautiful things in general.

"I need to scoot." Tonio picked up the empty coffee cups and put them into the kitchen sink, then gave his father a quick hug. "Take care of yourself and read the vacation material. That'll cheer you up."

"Thanks, Son." Andreas walked Tonio to the door, watched him saunter to his sports car and drive away, giving a small wave. Andreas smiled. "Fast cars, every young ... or middle-aged man's dream."

He pulled the local newspaper out of the mailbox, stepped inside, and sat in the rocking chair in the den next to the living room. He paged quickly through the paper, then put it down and looked around his home. He loved the rustic style of his house: the hardwood floors, the exposed beams on the ceiling, the carvings along the wooden staircase that led to the upper floor. He had furnished the place in the typical style of the area with rustic furniture made of Swiss stone pine wood, a chest of drawers with carvings, wooden tables with slate tops, and chairs with carved backs. There was always the scent of wood in the house, which he liked.

He sighed. *Karla would've liked it too.*

Chapter 2

A few months before, Andreas had moved to Andeer, a village in the Rhaeto-Romanic area of the canton of Grisons in Switzerland. Emilia, his youngest daughter, had found her first job as a veterinarian in a practice in Andeer. Andreas sold his home in the Maggia Valley in the south of Switzerland because he felt too depressed and lonely after Karla's death. Emilia wanted to buy a small house and Andreas helped her with her down payment. He bought a cottage next to hers and rented a workspace nearby. He occasionally worked on a sculpture but without much enthusiasm.

One morning, after a night without disturbing dreams of Karla, he decided it was time to clean out his wife's belongings. He had avoided it, knowing it would be painful. He got up, showered, and made himself a cup of coffee, then went over to Emilia's place.

It was a Saturday in June, a day off work for Emilia. When Andreas knocked on the door, Emilia opened it, giving him a warm smile.

"Just in time. I'm making breakfast. Want some?"

"That would be great. I need sustenance." Andreas hesitated. "I decided to go through Mama's things today."

Emilia looked at him surprised. "What a great idea. I'll help you if you want me to."

"I don't want to take up your free day."

"I don't mind. Let me help."

"Okay, if you want to. I'd appreciate it." Andreas was relieved. He didn't trust himself to go through this alone.

Emilia's home, like Andreas' house, was built in the rustic style of the region. It had hardwood floors, which she had covered with a few colorful throw rugs, and a ceiling of exposed wood beams. The living room, kitchen, a breakfast nook, and a bathroom were on the ground floor. From the living room, a wooden staircase led to the upper floor with a bedroom, a bathroom, and a den.

They sat in the breakfast nook next to the kitchen and had a leisurely brunch of soft-boiled eggs, freshly baked bread from the local bakery, butter, locally made cheese, marmalade, and coffee. A fire burned in the fireplace. The early mornings in June could still be quite cool in the mountains, though on sunny days, it warmed up in the afternoon.

"How is work, and how are the animals doing?" Andreas asked while spreading marmalade on his buttered bread.

"Great." Emilia's blue eyes lit up. Andreas marveled once again how different his youngest daughter looked from the rest of the O'Reilly family. Whereas her older brother and sister had inherited their parents' dark hair and her mother's dark eyes and skin that tanned easily, Emilia had the slender figure, blue eyes, fair skin, and blond hair of her maternal grandmother.

"The rabbit with the broken leg Peter found in his backyard and nursed back to health was well enough to go out into the wild," Emilia said.

"Oh? Did the little guy leave?" Andreas asked.

"You should've seen him. First, he sat there in the grass and looked around, seemingly confused, but then he hopped away and was gone." Emilia laughed. "Peter said he didn't even say goodbye or thank you."

"Peter is funny, isn't he?" His daughter became quite animated whenever she talked about her veterinary partner. He suspected she was a little in love with him. "Do you know anything about his family? I heard his parents have a farm. Does he have siblings?"

Emilia picked up a piece of dark, crusty bread, then hesitated and put it back on her plate again. "He doesn't talk much about his family. He did mention his mother, his brother, and his sister with whom he seems to be close." She slathered butter and marmalade on the bread. "I don't think he has a good relationship with his father, though. I once asked him if he'd ever thought of taking over the farm. He said no and then something to the effect that he couldn't stand working together with his dad."

"Oh, I see. Sounds like they don't get along."

"I know his younger brother plans to take over the farm once his parents retire," Emilia said. She looked out the window, then faced Andreas. "I really like Peter. He's very kind, but sometimes he seems sad. He gets this forlorn look."

Andreas waited for her to continue, but she didn't. "Perhaps you'll find out what that is when you get to know him a little better."

"Yeah. Probably." Emilia put her hand on his. "We better start with your project."

Andreas exhaled deeply. "I guess so."

Emilia gave him an encouraging smile. "It'll be okay. You'll feel better once it's done."

Back in Andreas' house, they went through the closet where Andreas kept Karla's clothes and boxes of her other stuff. Emilia watched her father with a heavy heart as he took a few of Karla's dresses from their hangers and held them against his nose.

"I can still smell her lavender perfume." His dark, gravelly voice broke. He looked at her with his green eyes that used to be so expressive but now had lost their luster. His face was

16

lined and furrowed. He was still a handsome man, tall, athletic, and muscular with unruly salt-and-pepper hair.

They began to sort through the clothes and shoes, trying to decide what they wanted to donate and what to keep. Andreas picked out a blue summer dress and showed it to her. "Want to try this on?"

Emilia narrowed her eyes and examined the dress. "I don't think it would fit, and it's not really my style."

Andreas stroked the dress gently, then put it on the pile for the thrift store. He let out a deep, long sigh as he touched each of Karla's belongings, her dresses, shirts, trousers, and pants, some still splashed with dried paints. Her mother had been a well-known artist.

"Are you all right?" Emilia gave him a concerned look. "Shall we stop?"

"No, let's check out one of the boxes." They went through a carton full of her jewelry, shoes, purses, and other accessories.

After about an hour, Andreas got up from the floor with a groan and sat on the bed. "I'm already exhausted. This is hard."

Emilia sat next to him and put her arm around him. "I know. Let's take a break. We can continue later."

Andreas nodded. "Good idea."

Emilia looked around the room. There were piles of clothes, some old jewelry, knickknacks, and shoes ready to give away. "We got quite a bit done," she said.

Andreas got up. "What I need now is a long hike in nature."

"But don't stay away too long again." Emilia felt alarmed. Her father had developed a habit of taking extensive hikes in the mountains and sometimes stayed out all night.

"Take your phone with you … and make sure it's charged."

Andreas smiled. "Yes, I will. Please don't worry about me. You know hiking always makes me feel better."

Emilia watched as he got his backpack ready with a bottle of water, a small thermos of hot tea, a few granola bars, a flashlight, and a light thermal blanket. He lifted his phone to show her that it was charged and put it into his backpack.

"Don't sleep outside again," Emilia told him.

He smiled. "Don't worry. I'll try to make it back in time."

They hugged and Emilia watched him walk away, a tall man with a lumbering gait and a slight stoop. After a while, however, he stood tall and walked with more energy. She knew that hiking in nature was an elixir for his mind and emotions, but she couldn't help being worried. She watched him until he turned a corner and was out of sight, then went back inside.

One of Andreas' favorite places was the area of the Splügenpass close to the border with Italy. As he walked through Andeer, his heart felt lighter. He loved this picturesque village with its stone and wooden houses typical of the area, the meadows full of wildflowers, the bubbling streams and tumbling waterfalls, as well as the surrounding mountains. Andeer was also known for its thermal baths. After a long, strenuous hike, Andreas sometimes relaxed in the pools there.

Past the village, Andreas walked along Via Spluga, the old route of the pack drivers and tradesmen who used to cross the Alps to transport their goods from north to south. He hiked past the foaming Roffla waterfalls, then crossed the highway and entered the calm of the spruce, pine, and oak forest. He finally reached the village of Sufers. From there, he walked through fields and stopped a few times to take in the breathtaking panorama of the surrounding mountain peaks.

He inhaled the fragrance of wild herbs along the mule tracks. After hiking for several hours, he sat on one of the rocks to rest for a while, drinking sips of water.

Above the mountains in the north, he spotted banks of dark towering clouds. He checked his watch. Since he'd gotten a late start, he wondered if he had enough time to hike back before it began to rain. As if nature answered his thoughts, he heard thunder in the distance and soon felt the first raindrops on his face. He grabbed his backpack and looked around, wondering where he could spend the night. With the approaching rain, he needed shelter. There were a few vacation homes with covered patios that were empty since the guests hadn't come up from the cities and valleys for vacation yet. He had spent the night on patios before and had always managed to avoid detection. He went to one of the places that looked boarded up and since it was quite late already, he didn't expect the owners to arrive for the night, and he would be gone early in the morning.

Sitting on the wooden floor of the covered patio, he watched the storm brewing in the distance. He pulled out his phone, remembering to call Emilia. "No connection," he murmured. He got up and walked around the house, but there were still no bars on the display. He would try again later. He went back to the patio and sat down.

As usual, when he was alone, thoughts of Karla were never far away. He remembered their common walks in the mountains when they searched for beautiful stones. Sometimes, they ate a picnic outside and spent the night in a mountain cabin. While Andreas gathered a few unusual stones, Karla snapped photos of the landscape which she would use later for her drawings or paintings.

The sound of the wind howling around the corners of the house pulled Andreas out of his melancholic musing. Soon, it poured hard. Thunderclaps filled the air and fiery arrows of

Christa Polkinhorn

lightning shot across the sky. He leaned his back against the wooden patio wall and wrapped the blanket around him. He took a sip of hot tea from his thermos and gazed at the shadows of the trees swaying in the wind. After some time, the rain diminished. Listening to the wind, less violent now, and the rain drumming on the roof of the patio, he managed to fall asleep.

Chapter 3

"Where did your father go?"

"Hiking in the mountains, as usual," an exasperated Emilia said. She was at the police station in Splügen, a village fifteen minutes by car away from Andeer. Andeer itself didn't have a police station, just an office that was open a couple of hours one day a week.

Karl, the police officer, smiled at her. "Well, it wouldn't be the first time he stayed out late. But he always seems to find his way back."

"Yes, but with the storm this afternoon ... and it's supposed to get worse." Emilia looked out the window at the trees flailing in the wind. The rain came down in buckets now. "He promised to call me whenever he couldn't make it back the same day. What if he fell, hurt himself, and is stranded somewhere outside? I'm really worried."

"Do you know where he normally hikes?" Karl asked.

"In the mountains around the Splügenpass. He usually hikes along Via Spluga." Emilia gave a deep sigh.

The door opened and Franz Suter, the police chief, stepped out of his office. "Emilia," he called out. He was tall, athletic looking despite a slight beer belly. His short brown hair was cut in military-style fashion, but his strict, authoritarian demeanor was tempered by his warm brown eyes.

"What are you doing here?" He raised an eyebrow. "Not your dad again?"

Emilia nodded, tears welling in her eyes. She and Karl filled him in on Andreas' disappearance.

Franz had gone to school with her older sister, Laura. When Emilia found her job in Andeer and Andreas moved there as well, Laura remembered her former schoolmate, and so Emilia, Andreas, and Franz became friends as well. The police chief worked in the village of Splügen but lived in Andeer.

Franz walked to the window, his forehead creased, then glanced back at Emilia. "He's such an experienced hiker. I don't think he'd do anything stupid during this storm. He may have decided to find shelter. And you know phone connection is spotty at best in the mountains. But then again ... well, okay." Franz glanced at his watch. "It's too late now to do something about it today. If he doesn't come home tonight or you don't hear from him, call me at home. We'll start a search party early tomorrow."

"Thank you so much. I'm sorry about this. He shouldn't just leave like this. It's irresponsible. But ever since Mama died ... he hasn't been the same."

"Yes, I know. He'll come around though. He knows his family still needs him. He wouldn't do anything stupid."

"I hope so, Franz."

"Does he have provisions with him, do you know?"

"He always takes his backpack with water, food, a sweater, and rain gear."

"Okay. In spite of his often-adventurous outings, he is an experienced hiker. Don't worry too much, Emilia. I bet you anything he'll turn up tonight." Franz put his hand on Emilia's shoulder and accompanied her to the door. "Drive carefully and get home safe." He gave her an encouraging smile, then went back into his office.

All evening, the storm raged, blowing the rain against the windows of Emilia's home. She stared into the approaching night, her phone in her hand, worrying about her father who must be stuck outside somewhere. She kept trying to call him, but it was impossible to get a connection. Unable to relax, she walked around the living room, then went into the kitchen to make herself a cup of chamomile tea to calm her frazzled nerves. She sat down next to the fireplace. Her eyes fell on one of her mother's paintings hanging on the wall. She looked at the few family photos on the shelf above the fireplace. Emilia's worries about her father's well-being gave way to sadness and longing. She missed her mother so much right then, her comforting and reassuring presence.

With her mother gone, Emilia felt responsible for her father's well-being. She was around him more than her siblings, since her brother lived in Italy part of the time, and her sister and family were away in England.

Now, it was too much. Tears flooded her eyes; she began to weep, shaking with sobs. She realized that ever since her mother's death, she had tried to comfort her father and hadn't allowed herself to truly grieve. Now, she couldn't hold it back anymore. She cried for a long time.

All of a sudden, her phone rang and to her great relief, the display showed her father's number.

"Papa, where are you for heaven's sake?" She tried not to scream at him.

"I'm here. I'm fine. Don't worry, honey, I'm okay. I'm on the mountain above the village of Sufers. I had no connection on my phone all afternoon, perhaps because of the storm. I have connection now, but it's spotty and I don't know for how long. I just wanted to tell you, I'm all right. It's too dark and it's raining, too dangerous to hike back tonight. I'll be home tomorrow morning."

"Oh, thank God. I was so worried," she said, her voice muffled by a sob.

"Are you crying, honey?"

His loving voice brought on a new flood of tears. "I was just worried about you being out so late ... and I miss Mama so much." She tried not to cry but couldn't help herself.

"Oh, sweetheart, I know. I miss her too."

"I just wish I wouldn't have to worry about you so much," she said.

A pause, then his dark, compassionate voice. "I'm sorry, Emilia. I know I've been very selfish with my grief. It's not fair and I'll change. I love you a lot, and I'm grateful for you being here for me. But I need to be here for you as well and I will. Okay?"

"Yes," she said. "Where are you staying tonight?"

"Don't worry. I found ...."

"What did you say?" Emilia shouted.

"I think I'm losing you. Don't worry, sweetie. I'll be home tomorrow morning, okay?"

"Hello? Papa?" But there was no answer. Emilia disconnected the phone. "Thank God." Then she called Franz Suter at home to let him know her father was all right.

"I'm so sorry, I didn't mean to waste your time."

Franz laughed. "Don't worry about it. I had a feeling you'd hear from him. I'll have to have a serious word with him, though."

"Good," Emilia said. "He needs to hear it from you. Perhaps he'll listen to you." She hesitated. "Well, he's getting a little more responsible. At least, he called me now."

"Okay. You have a good night. Don't worry. The old man will show up."

The following morning, on her day off, Emilia got up to make coffee. She stood by the window, looking at her father's cottage. The sky above was a deep blue. The only signs of the storm of the night before were a few tree branches in the grass next to the house. It promised to be a quiet and sunny day. She had just taken a sip of coffee when she heard the noise of a door opening and someone coughing next door. It was her father. He waved at her as she stepped outside.

"Sorry I was gone so long." He rubbed the back of his neck.

"Where did you spend the night?" Emilia asked.

"Well … I found this porch on one of those abandoned summer cottages." When Emilia rolled her eyes, he added quickly. "It was quite cozy, really."

"Jesus, Papa, a patio of someone else's house? No wonder, you look like a bum." Emilia pressed her lips together, but her relief at seeing her father back safe was stronger than her anger at his recklessness.

"Yeah." Andreas brushed his hand through his unruly hair and scratched his two-day old stubble on his chin. "I need a shower."

"I'll make you some breakfast," Emilia said.

"Don't bother, sweetie. Just some coffee is enough."

"You need to eat, Papa."

"All right." He smiled. "I'll be over in a few minutes."

Andreas took a shower, shaved, and dressed in clean jeans and a light pullover. He stepped outside and glanced at the now clear blue sky. It was still nippy from the rainstorm the night before, but he enjoyed the warmth of the sun on his face.

Walking up to Emilia's house, he wrinkled his nose and smiled. The smell of freshly brewed coffee welcomed him through the open door. Emilia was preparing a large pot of oatmeal with banana and blueberries. Andreas realized he was famished.

"What's the occasion for such a rich breakfast?" he asked.

Emilia gave him a stern look. "Well, you slept outside. You need something solid."

Andreas smiled, put his arms around her, and kissed the top of her head. "Are you feeling better again?"

She nodded.

He held her tight. "I'm sorry for being so selfish. I was only thinking of myself. That's immature and unfair."

"It's okay, Papa. All I want is to know where you are when you go on long hikes. I know that hiking makes you feel better."

"I will. I promise." He stepped back and smiled at her.

"Okay, it's ready," Emilia said. "Can you get the coffee, Papa?"

Andreas brought cups of coffee to the breakfast nook while Emilia put two bowls with oatmeal, topped with a dash of cinnamon, on the table.

"A breakfast for a king," Andreas remarked.

"More for a peasant, I think," Emilia said. "Where exactly have you been and where did you spend the night?" She pointed an accusing finger at him. "And be honest."

Andreas chuckled. "I'll show you on the map. First, I wanted to come back, but the weather really turned fast, so I had to look for shelter." Andreas told her how he spent the evening and the night *al fresco*, as he called it.

Emilia grinned. "What would Mama have said to this? You sleeping on someone's porch?"

"Oh, she would've liked it." Andreas dipped his spoon into the oatmeal. "We used to go hiking together and spent a few nights outside, well at least in some modest mountain hut."

Emilia sighed. "You're probably right."

Chapter 4

Early in the morning on a muggy day in July, Andreas was sitting on a rock above a cliff, contemplating suicide. It would be easy to just let himself drop down into the abyss. On this day everything had gone wrong. He had slept poorly, dreamed about his wife's accident again. When he tried to work, he felt paralyzed. In the past, the rocks and stones he carved used to inspire him; he saw their inner form before he started to work. He would chisel away the parts that kept the form trapped. He used to see himself as liberator of the spirit already inherent in the stone. Now, the stones appeared dead. He knew that it was he who had changed, not the rocks, but he couldn't rekindle the creative fire that had been part of his work and art.

He knew he wouldn't do it, throw himself down the mountain, but there were a few times he had been close to it. He had resisted in part because of his love for his children, in part out of shame, feeling like a coward. Karla would've been furious.

As usual when depressed, he'd filled his backpack with some essentials and had gone hiking. He'd taken the bus, called *Postauto* in German, to Splügen and then after about an hour of a steady climb along Via Spluga, he'd stopped at a flat rock where he sat now and stared into the distance. The world around him seemed to have lost its radiance. The usually vivid colors—the green of the trees and bushes, the yellows, blues, and reds of the flowers along the path—now appeared muted, even dull. The top of the Sorettahorn and the other surrounding mountains were shrouded in mist. The sky was a faded blue with large gray clouds towering over the Teurihorn, signs of a possible thunderstorm. The valley below was covered by a blanket of fog. The muggy air gave him a headache. He wiped a few drops of sweat from his forehead.

With a sigh, Andreas pulled out his phone to send Emilia a message to let her know where he was. He tried to be more considerate of her feelings. Her breakdown and the tears the other day had made him aware that he had indulged his grief in a most irresponsible way.

After pressing the Send button on the phone, he heard a strange sound like the whimpering of a child. He got up and looked around. Halfway down the hill, he saw a furry bundle that seemed to move slightly. He narrowed his eyes. A dog? The little creature must have fallen and hurt himself. Forgotten was his depression, his thoughts of throwing himself into the abyss. Instead, he searched for a place where the drop-off wasn't as steep. He let himself slide down to the small stone platform where the dog was lying.

It was a young dog, possibly a Jack Russell terrier with something else mixed in. His short-haired fur was dusty, but Andreas could tell that it was a pretty pattern of black, brown, and white. The dog was trembling, and Andreas talked to him in a low soothing voice. He kept gently stroking his back. The dog lifted his head, then tried to stand. He was weak but after a few attempts, he stood. He seemed to have hurt one of his hind legs. He flinched when Andreas touched it. After making sure that the dog didn't have any serious injuries, he carefully picked him up—it was a male, as he noticed. With the dog in one arm, he reached for protruding rocks with the other hand and hoisted himself up the hill, thinking how ironic it was that now he tried hard not to fall down when just minutes before he was contemplating throwing himself off some mountaintop somewhere. "You may have saved my life," he murmured.

At the top, Andreas took his water bottle and a small bowl he carried with him out of his backpack. He poured the dog some water, which the little guy lapped up greedily. The dog ate a small piece of a beef jerky but seemed too weak to eat fully. After gently stroking the animal for a while to reassure him, he put his stuff back into the backpack and carried the dog in his arms. "I know exactly where to take you. I know just the person who can help you."

Andreas walked down the mountain, his mood improved, his gait more energetic again.

He arrived at Emilia and Peter's practice in the late afternoon. Emilia was busy handing back a cat to her owner. The woman hugged her kitty with tears in her eyes. "I thought I'd lost you." She turned to Emilia. "Thank you so much. I'm so grateful."

Emilia tenderly stroked the cat. "Make sure to give her the medicine for a week." She handed the woman a small paper sack. "And if anything unusual happens, if she doesn't want to eat, just give us call. But she should be fine now."

After the woman left, Emilia looked at Andreas. "Oh, my, who do we have here?" She gently touched the dog's head. "What happened?"

Andreas told her how he had found the animal at the bottom of a cliff. "I think his rear leg is hurt."

Emilia checked his leg. "It's not broken, probably just strained. I wonder how long he was down there." She hugged the little dog who licked her hand.

Peter Walser stepped into the room. "Hi there, Andreas. And who is this?" He gently touched the dog's back.

"Papa found him on his walk," Emilia said. "He must have fallen down a cliff and hurt his leg. He looks like a Jack Russell mix. Probably part fox terrier, according to the beautiful coloring of his fur." She kept stroking the dog's back.

29

"He doesn't seem to be badly hurt but he looks somewhat dehydrated. We'll check him out carefully. Why don't I keep him overnight to watch him," Peter said to Emilia. Andreas knew that Peter's apartment was above the practice.

"We'll have to find out who he belongs to," Emilia said. "He has a collar and a tag but without an address or name on it. He may have a chip. I'll check the website for missing dogs. Aside from having possibly spent a couple of days or so without food and water, he seems well-cared for, which makes me think he does belong to someone. Where exactly did you find him?"

"Up in the mountains near Splügen where I usually hike. There is a hamlet not too far away, I think, a small mountain farm. I could ask there."

"Let's go together once the little guy feels better again. In the meantime, I'll try to find out something about his owner."

"I'd love to keep him," Andreas said. "I already got used to him."

"Well, we'll see. If he does have an owner, I can help you find another dog."

"Yeah." Andreas didn't feel convinced. He had to admit; he was already in love with him.

The following day when Andreas arrived at the practice and stepped into the examination room, he saw that his friend had recovered quite nicely. He'd had a bath and now his black, brown, and white fur was shiny. The dog welcomed him with a joyous bark. One of his back legs was bandaged, but that didn't prevent him from hopping on three legs toward Andreas, who picked him up and hugged him. "Hi there, buddy, you must be feeling better."

Peter, who had carried the dog into the room, laughed. "He had a good night's sleep, and he was up at the crack of dawn." He rubbed the dog behind an ear.

Emilia took off her lab coat and turned to Peter. "You're sure you don't mind if I leave for a while? I want to help Dad look for the owner."

"Sure, no problem. We don't have many patients today. Take your time." Peter winked at Andreas. "I heard you don't really want to find the owner."

Andreas sighed. "Yes, I've grown fond of him, but of course I want what's best for him." He cradled the dog in his arms and kissed his head.

"You may be lucky," Emilia said. "So far, I haven't found anything about a missing Jack Russell. But I don't want to get your hopes up. Remember, if you decide to get a pet, there won't be any shortage of little critters who are looking for a forever home. We can help you find one."

"I know. Thanks. We'll see what happens. Ready for the search party?"

Andreas and Emilia drove to Splügen where Andreas had last hiked. They parked the car and hiked up Via Spluga, then walked across the meadow toward the small farmhouse Andreas had seen the day before. The rain during the night had cleansed the oppressive air. It was still a little misty, but the sun had burned away the heavy fog. It smelled of fresh soil and a touch of fertilizer.

When they arrived at the hamlet, a man, perhaps in his sixties, stepped out of the barn. He saw them and rushed toward them.

"Oh, my God, we thought we'd lost him. I just reported him missing," he called out. Andreas' heart dropped as he realized he would have to give the dog back to his rightful owner.

"When did you report him?" Emilia asked.

"Yesterday evening," the man said.

"I checked the website," Emilia said. "It must not have been listed yet."

"Where did you find him? I'm Reto by the way."

Andreas told him how he found the dog at the bottom of a steep hill.

"Here is the little devil," an excited voice said. A sturdy-looking middle-aged woman, her brown hair in a messy bun, stepped out of the house. "God, we searched everywhere. I'm Linda." She invited them to sit on the patio where Reto explained that the dog had been given to them by a friend who left the country for overseas and couldn't take him along.

"My friend had been heartbroken, so we promised to take care of Pietro." Reto scratched the dog's ear. "Problem is we have enough animals already," he said, "and he is young and energetic, so he needs a lot of attention. Dogs are attached to their owners and though Harold had owned him for just a few months, Pietro may have run away, looking for him."

Andreas cleared his throat. "Would you consider leaving him with me? I have to admit, I got really attached to him. I'd love a companion, and I would have the time to take care of him."

Reto and Linda looked at him surprised, then at each other. "That would be wonderful," Linda exclaimed. "Pietro needs more than we can give him."

"Great." Andreas felt his face stretch into a smile.

"I'll get the papers ready, so we can transfer ownership," Reto said.

"Let's have something to drink in the meantime," Linda offered. "We have fresh homemade lemonade, or would you prefer something else?"

"Lemonade sounds good," Emilia said. She bent down and rubbed Pietro's ears. "He is so sweet."

"He is a good little dog, but I warn you, he's active." Linda winked at Andreas.

"Just what I need, something to keep me engaged." He petted Pietro, who obviously indulged in all this attention. "So, you're coming home with us?" Pietro acknowledged it with a short bark. "I guess that means yes."

Linda and Reto brought glasses of cool lemonade. They all sat at the garden table, enjoying the view and the refreshing drink.

"This is a beautiful place." Andreas motioned at the house and barn. "I see some goats hopping around over there." He pointed at a corral, where a bunch of active goats were jumping and playing.

"Yes, and look at the sheep," Emilia said. In a pasture nearby, sheep were grazing. "And there is a dog."

"That's Barri, our Bernese mountain dog. He's old, but he still does a good job keeping his herd safe. He's still the boss." Reto laughed.

Andreas pointed at the door of the house. "I see from the sign that you sell cheese and vegetables."

"That's right," Linda said. "This is our main income. All our products are organic. We sell them from our home as well as at the weekly market in the valley and at local stores."

"Great. I'd love to buy some cheese," Andreas said. He and Emilia followed Linda into the small store where an assortment of cheese as well as yogurt and other dairy products was laid out on the table and in the cooler. There was also a basket full of vegetables—broccoli, cauliflower, carrots, spinach, onions as well as a dish of fresh raspberries.

"From your garden?" Emilia asked.

Linda nodded. "Yes, we're almost self-sufficient."

Andreas paid for the food they bought. Linda added several additional cheeses and vegetables to the bag. Andreas and Emilia thanked her for her generosity and stepped outside.

"Boy, a real old-fashioned farm," Andreas said. "How wonderful. There aren't many of them left."

"That's true," Reto, who brought a few sheets of paper with him, added. "It's hard work, always a struggle to keep our heads above water financially, but we love it."

After the papers were signed, Andreas and Emilia took leave of their new friends. Andreas picked up Pietro and a bag with his favorite toys Reto had collected, while Emilia carried the bag with the food.

"Thanks again for everything," Andreas said. "I'll probably see you again on one of my hikes in the area."

"You're always welcome to stop by again and rest," Linda said. Reto waved goodbye and Andreas and Emilia walked the small path through the meadow, then down the hill to their car. Andreas carried Pietro so the dog could rest his back leg.

"He hardly seems to hurt anymore," Emilia said, gently touching his leg. Pietro licked her hand. "I'm so happy you get to take him home." She put her arm around Andreas' waist.

Cuddling Pietro in his arm, Andreas smiled. "So, Pietro is it? All right, we'll keep your name. No need to confuse you with a new one." Andreas kissed the top of the dog's head.

Chapter 5

Andreas had been working on one of his sculptures with more enthusiasm than he had been able to muster in a long time. Pietro, his new companion, was sitting at the door to his workshop, giving a short whimper and wagging his tail.

Andreas raised a brow. "You want attention, don't you? Ready for a walk?"

The answer was a brief bark and more tail wagging. Andreas put away his carving tools. He went to his cottage nearby, grabbed his backpack with his essential survival gear and added two small bowls, some dog food and water. When Pietro saw him take down the leash from the hook, he could barely contain his happiness. He jumped up and down and turned in circles.

"Hey there, calm down. You're going to wear yourself out before we even start." Andreas fastened the leash to the dog's harness, then sent a text message to Emilia at the veterinary practice. He walked to the bus stop and took the bus to Splügen. He wanted to hike along Via Spluga toward the Splügenpass. After about five minutes, his phone beeped.

Take Pietro and your charged phone with you and don't spend the night on someone else's porch again

Andreas smiled and texted: *Pietro is here phone is charged have a good day*

He walked briskly, realizing he got a late start, but it also allowed him to avoid the worst heat. It had been unusually hot the past few days. On the solitary mountain path, he let Pietro run free for a while. The little dog was his usual energetic self. He enjoyed himself, chasing birds and sniffing at every corner of the path, digging in a field occasionally, looking for possible mice or other underground creatures. Eventually, he slowed down and, in the end, Andreas carried him.

At the highest point on the Splügenpass, Andreas sat on a rock, feeling content, his canine friend lapping up water from a small bowl next to him. Pietro was a great companion; he made him feel less lonely.

He admired the view of the valley that led down to the Italian side of the mountain as a sudden breeze kicked up. He had planned to hike past Montespluga to Isola, the village on the Italian side, but the weather looked ominous. In the north, dark clouds gathered and soon they were rushing across the sky. He heard thunder in the distance. Checking his watch, he realized he may be stranded out there and needed to look for shelter if he didn't want to get soaked.

The Berghaus Splügenpass, an inn nearby, was closed that day. It was near sunset but because of the clouds, it was getting dark fast. He decided not to try to hike back. He pulled his phone out of his backpack—fortunately, he had reception—and called Emilia. She didn't answer, so he left a message. "A storm is brewing, it's too dangerous to hike in the dark, so Pietro and I will stay put. Don't worry about us. I'll call you tomorrow morning. Bye, sweetie."

He smiled and felt proud for having remembered to call her. He really tried hard not to worry her. Of course, he knew she'd prefer if he didn't go on such long hikes and spend the night out in nature. Andreas, however, enjoyed sleeping under the stars on a warm summer night, but now, he needed to find shelter. He remembered the cave he had come across on one of his former hikes. It was quite comfortable, and they would be able to spend the night there.

Once inside the longish cave, he unpacked his sandwich, took out two small bowls, filled one with water and poured dog food into the other one. The two of them ate and enjoyed the quiet before the storm, but a storm was definitely brewing farther north.

The wind picked up, and after a few minutes the temperature dropped, and the floodgates opened. It poured; the storm whipped the rain almost horizontally. Andreas and Pietro retreated more deeply into the cave so as not to get rained on. Fortunately, Pietro didn't seem to mind the thunder and lightning too much. Andreas hugged him close and was glad to feel that he wasn't trembling.

After eating and drinking his fill, Pietro went exploring the cave. After a while, Pietro seemed to have found something. He gave a brief bark and growled a little. Thinking the dog may have found a mouse or other animal, Andreas pulled his flashlight out of his backpack and walked to the back of the longish cave. "What is it, Pietro?" He saw the dog pull on what looked like a piece of cloth. "What do you have here, my friend?"

In the corner in the back, Andreas pulled on the cloth his dog had found. It belonged to something that was covered with dirt and stones. Once he extracted it, he saw that it was a very old backpack. The cloth was stiff and the color a dirty green. He opened it and to his great surprise he found several items.

On top, there was an envelope with an address in Italy. It was unsealed. Andreas opened it and pulled out a piece of thin paper with writing on it. He put it aside, then pulled out the rest of the items. He was stunned to find an old Italian passport with the picture of a young man. The name in the passport was Giovanni Rota. There was also a sepia-colored photo of a beautiful young woman and some old Italian money as well as some men's clothes and underwear, a pen, and a flashlight with corroded batteries.

Andreas picked up the paper again. He had to handle it carefully because it almost fell apart, it was so old. Trying to read the faded writing, he discovered to his shock that the paper was a letter to a woman by the name of Bella. The text was in Italian. What surprised him even more was the date on the letter, December 10, 1943, over seventy years ago, during the Second World War. Although the writing was faded, he was able to read it.

My beloved Bella,

I made it! I arrived. I'm exhausted, full of scrapes and bruises from the climb, but I'm here free and safe. What a relief! I just wish you were with me, my dear Bella. I miss you so much. At the same time, I'm grateful we decided for you not to make this difficult journey. It would have been too strenuous, especially in your present condition. There was a pregnant woman with us, but she had to turn back. It was too hard on her. So, we just have to be patient. Our friend will bring you along as soon as possible. I just hope and pray that this terrible war will be over soon.

Anyway, I'm not going into any detail about our trek just in case this letter gets into the wrong hands, which I don't think will happen with all the precautions we took, but you never know. So here are just the basics. Aside from the strenuous hike, the weather changed all of a sudden and it began to snow heavily just as we neared the border. It was a terrible storm. I was afraid we'd get lost and end up in an abyss.

But Guido, the guide, (not his real name to protect his identity) was fantastic. He brought me safely through the horror of the storm.

Unfortunately, we got delayed because of the bad weather, and when we finally arrived, it was dark. The Swiss guide, who was supposed to bring me to the valley on the Swiss side, was no longer there. Guido assured me that this happened occasionally. He brought me to a cave that he and his fellow guides had set up as a refuge for people who got stranded. It's quite cozy in here with blankets, water, dry food, and firewood. I'm going to spend the night here and wait for the Swiss guide to come back tomorrow to take me to the village. If for some reason he doesn't show up, I can make it down to the valley on my own during daytime.

I'm exhausted, but I couldn't go to sleep without writing to you. I'll mail this letter from the village, so you know I'm safe. Take care of yourself, my dear Bella, and take care of our little girl or boy. I hope it's going to be a girl and that she is as beautiful as you are. But as long as you and the baby are safe and healthy, and we'll soon be together again — that's all that counts.

I miss you, my love. Molti baci.
Joshua

Andreas blinked back tears. The longing in the letter, a letter composed many years before, during the Second World War, triggered his own sadness. It also made him aware of how much worse this couple must have had it. What destiny! Having to flee, being separated just when your wife was pregnant. Not knowing if you'd ever see her again. Well, she didn't get the letter; it wasn't mailed. What happened to the young man? Why didn't he send the letter? The name in the passport was an Italian name but the letter was signed with

Joshua, a Jewish name perhaps. Was this to hide the identity of the writer? Or of the person it was addressed to?

So many mysteries. Pietro licked his hand. He was obviously ready for action. "Thank you, buddy, for finding this. I want to know what this is all about."

Andreas slid the letter carefully back into the envelope, then collected the other items and put them into his backpack. He settled down with his thermal blanket he always carried. Pietro cuddled up to him. It was quiet now, the storm having passed. Andreas, however, was unable to fall asleep. His mind was on the love letter and on the unknown destiny of the young man, his wife, and child. After a while, he got up and stepped outside.

The sky above was full of stars and in the east a moon peeked over the mountain. The air smelled of wet grass, the musty scent of summer after a thunderstorm. Andreas felt his dog rubbing against his leg. "Can't sleep either, Pietro?" The dog gave a brief snort. "All right, you don't want to be alone. Let's try and get a few winks."

He went inside and lay down again. Feeling Pietro's warm body pressed against his, he finally fell asleep.

The following morning, Andreas felt a wet nose on his cheek. When he opened his eyes, his little friend looked at him expectantly. "You're up already? All right, I better get going too." He sat up with a groan, rubbing his aching back. He pulled a face. "My kids must be right. I'm getting too old for these outdoor adventures."

He stepped outside and stretched. The storm of the night had left the sky a deep blue. The sun was rising, coloring the mountains and fields of wildflowers golden. The grass in the fields was still wet. He breathed in the scents of pine, sage, and other wild mountain herbs and plants. While Pietro ran around, marking a few spots next to the rocks, Andreas admired the view. He poured water and dog food into Pietro's bowls, then ate a granola bar.

After sending Emilia a brief text message, Andreas called Pietro who was exploring the neighboring meadow. The two of them began the descent toward the valley with Pietro running back and forth, chasing the occasional crow that settled on the grass and then took off again. Andreas, deep in thought, pondered the love letter, eager to uncover its mystery.

Chapter 6

"Oh, my God, this is so sweet ... and sad," Emilia said after she had read the letter Andreas had found in the cave. She looked at the photo of the young woman. "Is that the wife?"

Andreas nodded. "I'm pretty sure it's her."

"She is beautiful. I love these sepia photos." Emilia gently touched the picture, then checked out the passport. "But why is the letter signed with Joshua, but the name in the passport is Giovanni Rota?" she asked. "Were there two men in the cave?"

"The name in the passport may be a fake one. He may have been a Jewish refugee and perhaps he had a false passport in case he got caught by the Nazis, so he couldn't be identified," Andreas said.

"Why a Jewish refugee?" Emilia's forehead creased.

"Well, look at the date. This was toward the end of World War II."

"Gee, you're right. I didn't know there were Jewish refugees from Italy," she said.

"It's not a well-known fact, but yes, I read something about that. Mussolini and Hitler were allies, but the people in Italy suffered under the German occupation. Jews were in danger and many of them deported."

Emilia read the letter again. "Where *is* Joshua? Why didn't he send the letter?"

"I don't know. But I really want to find out what happened." Andreas' eyes sparkled.

Emilia handed the letter back. "You should show this to Franz Suter," she said, referring to the Chief of Police.

"I'm planning to. Perhaps there is some kind of record from that time of someone who arrived here and disappeared." He rubbed Pietro's tummy. The dog was lying on his back, enjoying the massage.

"Very mysterious." Emilia's excitement grew. "I'll have time this afternoon. I'd like to come along."

"I am going to call Franz," her father suggested. "Perhaps we can meet him after work. It would be more relaxing than if we have to take up his time at the station."

"Good idea. I've already taken up more of his time than I should, what with all my calls about my missing father." Emilia gave him a stern look.

Andreas smiled. "You're such a worrywart. Can you make a copy of the letter? That way I don't have to handle the original too much. It's already falling apart."

"Sure." Emilia took the letter, went to the den and printed a few copies on her printer. She put the original and the copies into a plastic folder and gave them to Andreas.

In the evening, Emilia and her father met Franz in one of the inns in Andeer called Weisses Kreuz. The cozy restaurant was furnished with beautiful wooden tables and chairs. It served hearty as well as elegant meals and was also a place where locals came for a glass of beer or wine and to play cards.

Emilia, Andreas, and Franz sat next to the window. The waitress, a hefty woman, came over and slapped Franz on the back. He flinched a little and grinned at her. "Susie, my dear. You almost knocked me out."

"Oh, come on Franz, you're the top cop. Where is your fighting spirit?"

"For what?" Franz laughed. "All I do is take care of a few stranded tourists with twisted ankles, illegal parking, and every once in a while the occasional break-in."

"Well, thank God, it's a peaceful village," Susie said. "What can I get you?"

While the men ordered beer, Emilia opted for a glass of wine. "And bring us some of your excellent Salsiz, some Bündnerfleisch and cheese," Franz said. Salsiz was a dry-cured hearty sausage; Bündnerfleisch was smoked, dried beef. Both were typical of the region.

With the waitress gone to order their food, Andreas showed Franz a copy of the letter, the passport, and the photo of the young woman as well as the pouch with old Italian money. Franz stared at the items, frowned, then read the letter. His eyes widened. "Amazing … and where did you find these things?"

Andreas told him about his hike, his looking for shelter in a cave when a storm broke, and how Pietro, his new companion, dug up the backpack. "It was in the very back under some dirt and stones that must have accumulated and covered it over the many years. That's probably why nobody ever found it."

Susie came with their order. Once they were alone again, they toasted each other and took a sip of their drinks.

Franz narrowed his eyes and scratched his chin. "This is so long ago. I'll have to check the archive to see if we have anything." He hesitated. "Of course, he could've just left without his wife."

"Read the letter again." Andreas pointed at the sheet of paper. "Was this written by someone who would leave his wife and unborn child behind voluntarily?"

"Probably not," Franz admitted. "Can I keep this for a couple of days? I'll have to do some research."

"No problem."

"And in the meantime, you could go and check with my daughter Marianne," Franz suggested. "She is one of the librarians at the local library in Thusis. She may be able to help you find information from that time. The libraries are all connected with the Internet these days and she often works from home." He glanced at his watch. "In fact, she may be home by now. If anything is mentioned in one of the local newspapers from that time, she would be able to find it."

"Let's do that," Emilia said, all excited. "I got Marianne a kitty the other day. I want to check how they're doing." She turned to Andreas. "I can introduce you."

"Great." Andreas said.

"And while Marianne searches the library, I'll check the archive. If anything unusual happened near the Splügenpass around that date, it may be listed. Of course, I can't guarantee anything, but it's worth a try."

They finished their food and drink, then left the inn. Franz waved goodbye, and Emilia called her friend on her phone.

Marianne, a young woman with wild wavy chestnut-colored hair and piercings in her nose and ears, opened the door of her apartment in one of the beautiful stone houses with blooming geraniums in window boxes. Cradling a black-and-white kitten in her arms, she greeted Emilia and Andreas with a big smile. "Hi there, Emilia."

"Hey, Marianne," Emilia said. "How's Susie?"

Marianne kissed the kitten's head. "I adore her. She's so cute and playful."

"Good," said Emilia. "This is my father, Andreas. We wonder if you could help us with something. We're doing research, or rather my dad is."

Marianne nodded at Andreas. "Hello. Great to meet you. And of course, I'll help." She waved them inside. "Can I offer you something to drink?"

"Not for me, thanks," Andreas said.

"I'm fine," Emilia said. "We just came from the White Cross inn. We met your father there and he suggested we talk with you."

"Oh, really?" Marianne put Susie down and asked them to sit on the sofa in the living room. Susie, not wanting to be left out, jumped on Emilia's lap and began to purr.

"Oh, my." Marianne tittered. "She still remembers you." She looked at Andreas who pulled out a copy of the love letter and showed it to her. "Your father is looking at the police archive. I wonder if there was anything mentioned perhaps in the local papers of that time." He sighed. "I know that's a long time ago. It's probably like trying to find a needle in a haystack."

"Read the letter," Emilia said to Marianne who did just that.

"Oh, my God. This is so romantic." She gave a huge smile. Then her forehead furrowed. "But where did you find it?"

Andreas gave her a quick overview of how he discovered the letter.

"What happened to these people?" Marianne asked.

"That's what we're trying to find out," Emilia said. "Something must have happened to the husband since the letter never got mailed."

Marianne kept on staring at the letter, then looked up. "I can certainly try. This is so fascinating," she said, all excited. "I'll check at the library, and I can also do some of the research from home. I don't want to get your hopes up though, but I'll try to find out more." She glanced at the letter again. "He arrived not too far from here, obviously. And then what?" She gazed out the window as if deep in thought. "Can I keep this for a while?" She held up the copy of the letter.

"Yes, of course, I have more copies," Andreas said.

"Okay," Marianne said. "I'll get right on it. I feel like a detective ... or a spy." She laughed.

Andreas and Emilia got up. "Thank you so much for trying," Andreas said.

"Let me give you my phone number." Marianne grabbed her phone. I'll let you know as soon as I find something."

"Great, thanks," Andreas said. "Here is mine." They exchanged phone numbers. "You can also call Emilia."

"Yes, of course," Emilia said. "We'll have to do something together once again. A movie perhaps or happy hour."

"Sounds perfect." Marianne accompanied them to the door.

Outside, Andreas chuckled. "She doesn't look like a librarian or the daughter of a police chief."

Emilia laughed. "I know. She is a modern and quirky young woman. But she knows her stuff, and she loves doing research. If anything exists in the library, she'll find it. Well, I better scoot. I'll have to check on the animals at the practice before I go home."

"This will be interesting." He gave Emilia a quick hug. "See you at home."

"Bye." Emilia looked after her father. He seemed energized and had a spring in his step she hadn't seen in him in a long time. She felt relieved. It looked as if Andreas had found a new interest, something worthwhile to pursue again.

When she arrived at the practice, there was only one person with a dog in the waiting area. It was a friend of Peter's who had brought Owen, an Irish setter puppy, for his first vaccination.

"He's so cute," Emilia exclaimed. She lifted him up onto the examination table. But Owen had other ideas. He refused to hold still. He wiggled and jumped off the table, ready to bolt. At that moment, Peter came inside and laughed.

"Irish setters are among the most active breeds. Let me help you." They caught the puppy and Peter held him while Emilia vaccinated him.

"Good boy," she said. "That wasn't so bad, was it?"

She lifted him down, then gave him a treat. Owen wolfed it down, then looked at her expectantly. "Oh, well," she said and gave him another one.

"Ah, that's why our treats are gone so fast." Peter snickered.

"How did your research go?" he asked after Owen and his owner had left. Emilia had told him of her father's mysterious find.

"We met with Franz Suter and with his daughter, Marianne, the librarian. They're going to look into it. We'll see if they can find anything.

"This sounds exciting." Peter brushed through his reddish-blond hair. "Like a mystery novel."

Chapter 7

A few days later, Andreas was up early. After returning from walking Pietro, he received a voicemail message from Marianne. "I found something." At the same time, his phone pinged with a text from Franz, "found something."

Andreas smiled, seeing the identical phrases. "Like father, like daughter," he murmured, then got excited. He called Franz who asked him to meet him at the police station in Splügen. Then Andreas got a call from Marianne. "I sent you an email with what I found," she said. "Did you get it?"

Andreas confirmed it. He read the short note in one of the local papers of that time:

The body of a young man was discovered at the bottom of an abyss. A search of the area didn't provide any clues as to what happened. It looks like an accident. It had been snowing heavily the past few days. He could have slipped on the ice and fallen. The absence of any identification and the area where the body was found led the police to believe he could have been a refugee from Italy.

"Oh, my God," Andreas murmured. "Could this have been Joshua? The date is close, December 12, 1943, two days after the date on the letter." Slowly his hopeful excitement gave way to sadness. "If that was the man," he said to Marianne, "then he died. He was never able to mail the letter. His wife never heard from him again."

"I know. Isn't it awful?" she said.

Andreas let out a harsh breath. "I wonder … I wonder if there is a way to find his wife or at least her child. She was pregnant."

"But it was so long ago. Would they still be alive?" Marianne said. "That was over seventy years ago."

Andreas nodded. "Yes, but they sounded like a very young couple. They were expecting their first child. Perhaps Bella is no longer alive. She would be in her nineties. But perhaps her son or daughter would still be around. He or she would be in his or her seventies, about my age." He hesitated, then gave a quick smile. "I'm going to meet with your dad. He seemed to have found something as well."

"Oh, good," Marianne said. "Let me know what he found."

"I will. Thank you so much for your help."

"It's my pleasure," the young librarian said. "I just wish it was a more hopeful message."

Andreas printed out the email, then got ready to leave. Pietro was standing by the door, wagging his tail in hopeful anticipation of another walk.

"Sorry, Pietro. You'll have to stay home this time. I'll be back soon." A quiet whimper was the answer and a disappointed Pietro stretched out in his basket.

"Hello, Mr. O'Reilly," Karl, the policeman at the station in Splügen, greeted him. "Have you been hiking lately?" He winked.

"I've been good," Andreas said. "I'm really trying to let Emilia know where I am."

Karl laughed. "Good to hear."

"Is Franz in? Is he busy?"

"He's in his office. Just go ahead." Karl pointed to one of the doors down the hallway.

Andreas thanked him and walked to Franz' office. The door was ajar, so he knocked and pushed it open.

"Ah, Andreas, come on in." Franz pointed at the chair opposite his desk.

"I got something from Marianne," Andreas said as he put the short article in front of Franz. "Your daughter has been very helpful."

"Good. Yes, she knows her way around," Franz said. He proceeded to read the article from the library. "Wow. Interesting. This seems to match with what I found." Franz showed Andreas a single sheet of paper from that time, an old police report, indicating that the body of a young man of about twenty-five years, slim, with dark curly hair and a short beard had been found at the bottom of a gorge. The area was near the cave where Andreas found the letter. Nobody ever claimed it. It was noted as a possible accident. The assumption was that he fell to his death during the heavy snowfall. The body was discovered on December 12, 1943.

The two men looked at each other quietly. "This seems to be the man," Franz said. "The dates correspond, and this is the only death noted during that time at that place." He rubbed his forehead.

"Yes," Andreas agreed. "And the physical description in the report fits the photo in the passport. This couldn't be a coincidence."

Franz nodded. "He must've written the letter, spent the night in the cave, then left for some reason, thinking he'd return shortly. Perhaps he slipped on some ice and fell down the gorge." He gave Andreas a questioning look.

"Yes, that would make sense. How terrible. He survived the trek across the mountains and then, just as he thought he was safe ...." Andreas took a deep breath. "I'd love to find the woman or the family, to give her the letter. It must have been awful not knowing what happened to her husband. How sad."

"That would be an enormous task." Franz pointed at the envelope. "You wouldn't be able to find the wife at the address here. It's a post office box in a town called Quercia."

"I know," Andreas said. "But I can at least try. She may not even be alive anymore, but her daughter or son might still be around." He rubbed his forehead. "What about the passport? Could this help to trace someone?"

"This is clearly a fake passport," Franz said. "The only true thing is his picture and with only a seventy-year-old photo … I don't know how much that would help. But I'll try to investigate some more."

"Thanks, Franz. I really appreciate it." Andreas got up. "I'll be in Italy for a two-week vacation. We're celebrating Emilia's graduation and first job as a veterinarian. I won't have time to really search, but perhaps I can make some inquiries."

"Okay, yes. And if you are in Italy and find the town, perhaps the post office can help you with the mailbox. It can't hurt. Let me know what you find, and I'll see if I can find anything more from here." Franz got up as well. "So, Emilia likes her work with Peter?"

"Yes, she loves it. They get along really well. Last time I talked to him, he was very happy with her work."

"Peter is a great person and an excellent vet," Franz said. "Being the only one in the area, he was overwhelmed with work, so I bet he's really grateful having Emilia help him."

"Yes, now he can concentrate on the larger animals and the farms in the area while Emilia takes care of the pets," Andreas agreed. "Well, see you later and thanks again."

"Glad to be of help." Franz lifted his hand in a goodbye gesture.

At home, Andreas began to work on a sculpture in his studio. Although he was more enthusiastic about his art again, he kept thinking about the letter and had a hard time focusing. After working for a while, he put the chisel down, wanting to take a break. He went home, poured himself a cup of espresso, then called Tonio in Milano. He had told him about the mysterious letter earlier and now they talked at length about the possibility of trying to find Bella. "I know it's a crazy plan, but why not try?" he said.

"Yes, it's crazy," Toni said, "but so what? The worst that can happen is you won't find her, but at least you tried."

Andreas smiled at Tonio's enthusiasm. His son was always ready to start something new, in particular when it came to his business. "Well, I'm glad you're not thinking I'm losing it."

"No, in fact I haven't heard you so upbeat in quite a while. That's good," Tonio said.

"You're right. I do feel better, more energetic again. Talking about that, I need to get back to work."

"That's the spirit." Tonio laughed. "I'll talk to you soon."

Later that afternoon, Andreas decided to cook dinner once again. He had been eating a lot at Emilia's but felt guilty for always letting her feed him. He called her and invited her for dinner at his place. "I'll fix something simple," he said.

Emilia accepted gratefully, so Andreas went to the grocery store to buy veal cutlets, prosciutto, fresh vegetables, lettuce, tomatoes, and peppers. He wanted to prepare saltimbocca. Tonio was right. He did feel a lot better.

He pounded the veal cutlets with a mallet, seasoned them with salt and pepper, dredged them in a little flour, and browned them in a frying pan. When the meat was cooked, he put it aside, added some flour to the pan, stirred it together with the oil, then poured in white wine and bouillon, letting it simmer until the liquid was reduced by half. He topped the cutlets with a slice of mozzarella, then a sage leaf and a slice of prosciutto, put them back into the pan with the sauce, covered the pot with a lid, and let it simmer some more.

In the meantime, he cooked the pasta, then added olive oil and Parmesan and kept the dish warm in the oven.

"Oh, it smells wonderful." Emilia came inside carrying a bottle of wine. "Wow, you said a simple meal. This is fancy." She put the bottle on the kitchen counter.

Andreas set the veal on a plate and removed the pasta dish from the oven. "Can you bring in the salad? I think we're ready to eat."

They sat on the wooden benches in the dining nook. "I cheated with the dessert," Andreas said. "I bought a hazelnut cake."

"Ah, my favorite," Emilia said. "And it's not cheating; it's being smart. Our baker's cakes are to die for." She tried a piece of the veal. "This is such a treat. Perfect."

"I'm glad you like it," Andreas said.

"I try to eat healthy." Emilia picked a few pieces of penne with her fork. "But when I work all day, I'm tired in the evening, so I just grab what's available rather than prepare a full meal."

"I should cook more for you. I have the time." Andreas poured the wine and handed Emilia a glass. "And I actually enjoy it."

"Well, you're hired, Papa." Emilia raised her glass. "By the way, any news about Joshua?"

While eating, Andreas filled her in about Marianne and her father's findings as well as his plans to make some inquiries while on vacation in Italy.

"That's so exciting," Emilia said. "But how would you go about doing this? We don't know anybody in Italy, and we'll only be there for two weeks."

"I know." Andreas took a sip of wine. "All I can hope for is to get some general idea how to go about researching this. I most likely will have to go back some other time when I have more solid information." He chortled. "The whole thing sounds crazy, doesn't it?"

"It sounds like an adventure; you should go for it," Emilia said.

Chapter 8

Emilia gazed out the window of her train to Milano while eating a sandwich and sipping a cup of coffee. She was on the way to visit her brother, Tonio. Letting the landscape of northern Italy pass before her eyes—the fields, lanes of cypress trees, small farms, and towns—she thought of her job and of Peter, her partner. She had been working with him for half a year.

Emilia had always loved animals; she couldn't imagine a life without a dog or a cat. She remembered how happy she'd been when her parents gave her the first young dog, a golden retriever and Labrador mix. She had been born late into her parents' life and after her older sister, Laura, and brother, Tonio, moved out, she felt lonely. Skippy, her dog, became her perfect companion and ever since then, she was convinced she wanted to work with animals. Skippy had died of old age after a happy life, but Emilia had been heartbroken by the loss. Even as a child, she had decided to become an "animal doctor." That wish had never left her and here she was, surrounded by animals she tried to help. It wasn't an easy job. There were moments of heartbreak when she couldn't save a dog or a cat. More often, however, she was able to successfully treat an animal and hand it over again to the happy and grateful owner.

She also enjoyed working with Peter. He was about five years her senior, an enthusiastic and already successful vet. His family owned a farm, and his grandfather had been a veterinarian. That's where Peter got his first "training," as he called it, "holding that struggling calf" while his grandfather vaccinated it.

Yes, she liked Peter, and the longer she worked with him, the more attractive he became to her. He was tall and sturdy, not handsome in an elegant way, definitely a farmer's boy. He had a kind, sometimes mischievous smile when he teased Emilia, who could never get used to holding a cat by the scruff to stabilize it. She felt he liked her too, at least as a friend, and she knew he respected her as a fellow veterinarian in spite of her youth and limited practical experience. After work, they sometimes went out for coffee or a beer, to talk about all kinds of things. He was entertaining, always full of ideas and had plans to expand his clinic, adding an animal rescue area. "You could manage it; you'd be perfect," he had said the other day.

The longer she worked with him, the more attractive he became. She knew of course that a workplace romance was risky. If it didn't work out, it might endanger their working relationship. Emilia turned her attention to her visit to Milano and her brother's boutique. He owned it together with his boyfriend, Mario. They specialized in men's and women's clothes and accessories with an emphasis on young and modern fashion.

Outside, fields and woods disappeared as the landscape turned into the ugly industrial centers at the outskirts of the city of Milano. When the train entered the station, Emilia grabbed her overnight bag and purse and climbed out of the train.

Tonio, who was already waiting at the end of the track, waved at her. "Hey there, my favorite sister. How are you?" He hugged and kissed Emilia.

"Don't let Laura hear that. She might get jealous," Emilia said.

"Well, you know me. I'd say the same thing to her. You're both my favorite sisters. How was your trip?"

"Good. I love train rides. So much more relaxing than driving a car through this crazy city."

"Yeah. I understand. Besides, you're just a mountain girl taking care of goats. Just like Heidi."

Emilia laughed. "No goats yet. Sorry."

While Emilia was trying on pants, shorts, skirts, and tops as well as some summer dresses at Tonio and Mario's boutique, Mario himself, a man in his late forties, walked in and hugged her. He had curly black hair and brown eyes. Tall and elegant, he was fashionably dressed in slim white pants and a tailored colorful shirt. "My favorite woman," he exclaimed.

Emilia chuckled. "Wow. It's my day of being a favorite. I'm flattered."

"I'm serious. If I wasn't gay and committed to your brother, I'd marry you."

They chatted and joked around for a while, then Tonio asked in a more serious tone, "How's Papa?"

"A little better," Emilia said. "He still goes on long hikes and comes home disheveled, but he did start on another sculpture after months of doing nothing. And he actually called me a few times on his phone when he was hiking and got delayed. So that's progress. And he loves his new dog."

"He'll come around," Mario said. "I mean let's face it, the love of his life died only three years ago. That's not very long if you consider they were together for ... how long?" He looked at Tonio.

"They were married over forty years," Tonio said.

Mario lifted an eyebrow. "My mother was grieving for a long time after Dad passed. And they didn't even have such a great relationship."

"You're right. Perhaps we asked too much of Papa," Tonio said. "I was just worried about the way he'd let himself go in general. And he forgets things. He finally agreed to be tested for dementia, but the report came back negative. The doctor felt that his symptoms and behavior were related to grief."

"Well, as I mentioned, he has improved." Emilia held up a pair of shorts. "And I told you about the letter he found. He now wants to track down the relatives of the family in Italy."

"Yes, Tonio told me about that," Mario said. "What a mystery."

"And it's something that takes his mind off his grief," Emilia said.

"This upcoming vacation will be good for him," Mario said. "He can have some new experiences. Perhaps he'll even find an attractive Italian woman."

"Ha, I doubt it." Tonio laughed. "Well, you never know."

The three of them had dinner at one of Tonio and Mario's favorite restaurants that specialized in seafood dishes and pasta. They ordered a bottle of wine and enjoyed the leisurely evening, talking about their plans for the future. Tonio and Mario tried to decide if they wanted to stay in Milano for good or move back to Switzerland.

"We both love Italy," Mario said. "The boutique here is more profitable, but the economic situation in Italy is always volatile."

Tonio took a sip of wine, brushing his longish hair out of his face. "That and the bureaucratic nonsense in Italy."

"So, would you sell the boutique here?" Emilia asked.

"No, but we're thinking of leasing it," Mario said. "We have someone in mind. He is an Italian citizen and a lawyer, someone who knows his way around the complicated and often corrupt legal system here as well as the business side.

And he loves fashion. We're getting old and tired of the constant back and forth."

"Old? Speak for yourself, Grandpa." Tonio chortled. "But it's true, the fashion business isn't easy in Switzerland either, but compared to Italy, there are advantages. And to be honest, as exciting as Milano is, being closer again to our families would be great." Tonio put his arm around Mario. "And your mom would love it too."

"Yeah," Mario said, "she'd be happy about it."

Emilia smiled. "I'd love to have you nearby again. I miss your company." She hesitated. "Besides, I wouldn't have to worry about Papa on my own. Papa would love it too."

Tonio pulled her close and hugged her. "I feel guilty about being away so much. And Laura and Stefano have spent a lot of time in England. That's another reason I'd like to be closer. It's not fair that you have to be the only one to care for him." He kissed her. "But you do know that I would be there for you immediately if there was an emergency. And so would Laura."

Emilia nodded. "I know and besides, I tend to worry too much. As I said, he seems to be doing much better."

Chapter 9

"Good news." Andreas greeted Emilia with a hug. He had just come back from the police chief's office. "Franz found one of the guides on the Swiss side who helped refugees from Italy during World War II."

"Oh really?" Emilia said. "After such a long time? Who is it?"

"His name is Flurin Pitsch. Franz is friends with his grandson. That's how he found out. I'm going to see him this afternoon. Want to come along?"

"Sorry, but I have to work today. But tell me all about it."

"I will," Andreas said. "How is work going? And how is your charming vet?"

"Work is good. Peter is as charming as ever." Emilia blushed. "Anyway, I'm off. See you this evening."

"Okay. I'm really curious what I can find out."

In the afternoon, Andreas and Franz got ready to see the man who secretly led refugees from the Italian-Swiss border to the village of Andeer in Switzerland. Flurin Pitsch lived with his grandson and family in a house on a hill a little outside of the village.

When Franz knocked on the door, Andreas opened it, holding Pietro by the collar. The little dog was wagging his tail furiously, most likely hoping for another outing.

"You'll have to stay home this time, buddy." Andreas scratched Pietro behind an ear. "I can't take you with us, but I'll be back soon. Come on, stay. Be a good boy."

Pietro looked at him with sad eyes and gave a brief whine. Andreas pointed at the dog basket. "Stay." The dog, trying his best to make Andreas feel sorry for him, slunk toward his basket, looking back once more before lying down.

"He obeys pretty well," Franz said.

"Yes, he does. He was fairly well trained when I got him."

Since it wasn't far to their destination, they decided to leave Franz's car parked in Andreas' driveway and walk. At the outskirts of the village, they hiked up the short but steep hill. It was a sunny and breezy day. Andreas felt cheerful, having finished the first sculpture in a long time the day before. Ever since he got his new companion, his mood and creativity had improved. He felt more joyous and energetic again. Besides, the mystery of the letter in the cave occupied his mind and pushed away gloomy thoughts of Karla.

At the top of the hill, Franz stopped, exhaled deeply, and wiped away pearls of sweat from his forehead with his handkerchief. "God, I need to do something about exercise." He groaned. "This is getting ridiculous. I get winded walking up a small hill." He stuffed his handkerchief into his pants pocket. "Too much office work and too many beers, I guess. When I was a regular cop on the beat, I got a lot more exercise. But now …" He touched his slightly protruding belly.

"You should come on hikes with me." Andreas slapped Franz' arm. "Although my midsection isn't as slim as it used to be either."

"Well, I may take you up on the offer," Franz said. "But your adventurous hikes and sleeping outside might be a little too much for me."

"Oh, you don't know what you're missing. But honestly, I've slowed down quite a bit. Pietro here tends to wear himself out and then I have to carry him. So now my strenuous hikes have turned more or less into walks."

"Here we are." Franz motioned at the large house in front of them. It looked old but well-kept with eggshell-colored walls and deep-set windows with red shutters. Up and down the walls and around the windows were delicate carvings. In front of the house was a cleanly mowed lawn and a flowerbed in the corner with an assortment of colorful flowers—yellow and white daisies, blue cornflowers, and red geraniums. At each end of the lawn, a tall birch rose into the sky as if standing guard, with small light-green leaves glittering in the sunlight.

When Franz rang the bell, a tall, slim, middle-aged man opened the door and greeted them. "Tschau Franz."

Franz turned to Andreas. "This is Bruno, Flurin's grandson."

"Thanks for coming," Bruno said. "Grandpa is in the den. "Would you like something to drink? Coffee, tea, mineral water, or a beer?"

"No beer for me." Franz wiped another drop of sweat from his forehead. "I'll stick with mineral water."

"Water would be great. Thanks," Andreas said.

Franz and Andreas followed Bruno through the hallway to a small room adjacent to the living room. The interior of the house showed the familiar interior design of the region. The ceiling had wooden beams. The cabinets along the walls were decorated with carvings. Andreas inhaled the smell of wood he'd come to like so much.

An old man was sitting by the window that looked out onto the meadow and a cluster of pines and firs.

"Grandpa." Bruno raised his voice a pitch. "The men are here." He turned to Franz. "He's a little hard of hearing."

Flurin Pitsch stood, holding on the edge of the table for support.

63

"Oh, Herr Pitsch, you don't need to get up," Franz hurried to say.

Flurin faced him with a humorous glint in his eyes. "Young man, I may be old, but thank God I can still get out of my chair without help."

Flurin was a spry ninety-five-year-old man with a full head of white hair and clear blue eyes that exuded mental alertness. He gave Andreas a probing but friendly look.

"Thank you for agreeing to talk to me," Andreas greeted him.

Flurin gave a quick smile. Bruno came back with a bottle of mineral water and three glasses, which he set on the coffee table. "I'll get your tea, Grandpa." He added a few words in a language Andreas recognized though he didn't speak or understand it.

"That was Romansh, wasn't it?" Andreas said. He knew that it was the original language of that part of the canton of the Grisons. It had almost died out but the communities in the Rhaeto-Romanic region as well as teachers and linguists made an effort to keep it alive and teach it to the younger generations as well. It was recognized as one of the four official languages of Switzerland along with French, Italian, and German.

"Yes, it is. Grandpa still speaks it occasionally, and I try to practice it. We don't want to lose it altogether."

"Sure," Andreas said. "I read somewhere that it descended from spoken Latin."

"That's true, but it has some other influences as well," Flurin said. "But please sit down." He pointed at the chairs across from him, then turned to Andreas. "I heard you have some questions for me about the war?"

Andreas nodded. "I found something so amazing that I just had to look into it." He pulled out a copy of Joshua's love letter and showed it to the old man. "It's in Italian. I can translate if necessary."

"I understand Italian." Flurin took a pair of reading glasses, put them on, squinted a little, then perused the letter, wrinkling his forehead.

"I found the original in a cave up in the mountains near the border to Italy where refugees supposedly had come into the country," Andreas said. "It was in an old backpack covered by dirt and stones in the very back of the cave. I saw my dog pull on something and that's when I discovered it. Aside from the letter and envelope, there was an old passport, a photo of a young woman, the wife, most likely, and some other items." He opened a folder and pulled out the passport and photo and gave them to Flurin. "The name in the passport was different from the name he signed the letter with, a fake one, most likely. That made me suspect he was a refugee."

"We're just wondering if you remember anything about a refugee that perhaps you were supposed to meet and either never showed up or disappeared," Franz added. "I know it sounds vague."

Flurin looked at the letter for a long time, then checked out the passport and the photo. He put the items down. "You realize this was over seventy years ago. I picked up many refugees."

"I know," Franz said. "We don't expect you to remember. It's just such an incredible coincidence that Andreas found this letter that this man, Joshua, wrote and wasn't able to send. He made it across the border, but it looked like he fell down a cliff to his death. We found reports about a body that was found in the abyss near the cave. The dates of the letter and the report match. It could very well have been this refugee, Joshua."

Flurin rubbed his forehead, then looked up. "Now, that you mention it, yes, I do remember that there was someone I was supposed to meet who didn't show up. It didn't happen very often. Usually, if they got delayed, they waited in that cave." He glanced at Andreas. "This was indeed a temporary shelter in case I couldn't pick them up the same day for whatever reason. There were times in the winter when the weather was bad and they didn't make it in time, or sometimes they didn't make it at all. But normally I found out later from the Italian guides if something happened that made the refugees turn back.

"The reason I remember this incident is the report you mentioned about a body that was found in the abyss near the cave. I read about it at the time, and I've always wondered if that was the refugee who didn't show up. Of course, I couldn't investigate or ask the police. What we did wasn't exactly legal. We couldn't draw attention to ourselves or to the refugees."

He pointed at the letter. "Now, it seems very likely that this was Joshua. How sad. He survived this dangerous journey, made it here, and then fell to his death."

"Did somebody ever come looking for him?" Franz pointed at the letter. "He was married and if this wife survived, she might have tried to find him, perhaps after the war."

"I don't remember anything about that. But I left right after the war and went to work in the city."

"I'd love to find the woman the letter was addressed to or her family," Andreas said. "She was pregnant. Her son or daughter may still be alive even if she herself isn't. She could be in her eighties or nineties."

"Well, that would be quite an undertaking," Flurin said. He studied the letter and the envelope again, then handed it back to Andreas.

"I'll be in Italy for a while, on a vacation," Andreas said. "Who knows, perhaps I can make some inquiries. I'd like to try."

"I wish you the best of luck," Flurin said. "Do me a favor. Let me know if you find out anything."

"I will," Andreas said.

They talked for a while. Flurin told them a few stories of his time as a guide during the war and his work as a carpenter after the war. Andreas told him about his sculpting work. They talked about life in Andeer and their favorite hikes in the mountains. After finishing their drinks, Andreas, Franz, and Flurin said goodbye. Bruno accompanied the visitors to the door.

"What a story," Bruno said, brushing his hand through his curly brown hair.

"Did your grandpa ever tell you about that time, about what he did?" Franz asked Bruno.

"My mother, his daughter, told me a few stories," Bruno said. "The family suspected what he was doing although he'd never told them. When I asked him personally, he just said that he and others helped a few people out, but he always dismissed it. He never felt like a hero. In fact, this is the first time he opened up about his role at that time."

"He's very modest," Franz said. "A good man."

"Yes, that he is," Bruno acknowledged.

"What a generous soul," Andreas said as they walked down the hill. "I think we know a little more now. It looks very much as if Joshua is the man who fell to his death."

"Yes," Franz acknowledged. "The notices in the archive and the newspaper and now Flurin's statement make it more likely. Such a tragedy. He survived this horrendous trek, evaded the Nazis, made it into Switzerland, and then fell to his death."

"Just doesn't seem fair, does it?" Andreas pressed his lips together. "Thanks, Franz, for helping me with this."

"It's my pleasure. I'm curious as well. I'll try to find out more. But in the meantime, enjoy your vacation." He slapped Andreas' shoulder, got into his car, and drove away.

Andreas waved goodbye, then murmured to himself. "I definitely want to try to find Bella."

Chapter 10

"I already miss him," Andreas mumbled as he drove the mountain road from Andeer to Splügen.

Emilia tapped him on the shoulder. "He'll miss you too at first, but you saw how happy he feels with Peter."

"Yeah, I know, but still ... ah, your father is getting to be an old softy."

Andreas and Emilia were on their way to Milano and from there to Tuscany for their vacation at Vignaverde. After a lengthy deliberation and with a heavy heart, Andreas had decided to leave Pietro behind. The dog would be better off staying with Peter who knew him well and whom Pietro loved rather than being dragged on a long road trip. To get him accustomed to spending the night away from Andreas, Peter had kept him overnight a few times, which had worked out very well.

"You know lots of people need to leave their pets with friends or in a vacation kennel when they go on a trip," Emilia said. "And it's good to get him used to being without you once in a while."

"I know, and with Peter he's in good hands." Andreas took a deep breath. "He'll be fine."

They took the road to the San Bernardino Pass. Normally, they would have driven over the mountain, which was a beautiful, scenic drive, but since they had a long road ahead of them, they took the faster route through the tunnel. The drive to the San Bernardino Pass was still a pretty trip past meadows carpeted with yellow flowers. After they exited the south end of the tunnel, they drove along fields with shrubs and past pine forests. Emilia rolled down the window a crack and Andreas inhaled the fragrant mountain air and the scent of pines.

They bypassed Bellinzona with its three famous castles and were soon on the highway toward the Italian border and onward toward the metropolitan city of Milano. The drive from Como to Milano led past cities and industrial parks. The closer they got to Milano, the heavier the traffic became. The freeways and tolls always confused Andreas. He was grateful once again to be able to live in a mountain village like Andeer rather than in large cities.

In Milano, they were going to pick up Tonio and Mario. Many years before, Andreas had gone through a difficult time when he learned that his son was gay. In time, however, he came to accept the fact. He liked Mario, who was a few years older than Tonio. He knew the two loved each other, and he felt that Mario was a good influence on his son. He was responsible and a good businessman. The two seemed happy together and that, in the end, was the most important thing.

Andreas had packed the love letter to Bella, hoping to be able to do some investigating in Italy on the whereabouts of Joshua's family. He had the name of a town and a number that looked like a post office box as well as a date.

Tonio and Mario rented an apartment near the center of the city, close to their boutique. To save Andreas and Emilia from having to find a parking spot—almost impossible in this crowded city with its crazy traffic—Tonio and Mario were waiting outside a restaurant that had a large parking lot. After the two had stowed their suitcase in the car, Tonio took over the driving to the relief of Andreas, who hated having to drive through the city.

"Any news about the letter you found?" Tonio asked. Andreas, who was sitting next to him in the passenger seat, gave him a quick overview of the research they had done back in Switzerland.

"Do you really think you can find out something during the time we're there?" Tonio glanced at him.

"I doubt it," Andreas said. "Perhaps I can make some inquiries and then go back at a later date."

"I hope you're not going to run all over Italy. This is a vacation," Emilia said in a stern voice.

Andreas turned around and smiled at her. "Don't worry. This is *your* vacation, and we'll do whatever you want to do."

"That means enjoying the vineyards, eating delicious Tuscan food, and drinking wine," Mario said. He and Emilia gave each other high fives.

"Exactly. Emilia shook a finger at her father. "And you are to relax and have fun."

The drive south took them through the countryside of northern Italy. The ever-present poplar and cypress trees took turns with fields of vines and farmhouses. They talked about visiting Florence on their way but decided to bypass the city since it would take too long.

"Perhaps we can take an extra day on our way back to visit," Tonio suggested. "We've been there many times before, but I always enjoy looking at all the art."

"And the fashion," Mario added.

Instead of Florence, they stopped for a break in Siena, one of the beautiful hill towns of Tuscany. After a brief walk around town, they had a light lunch of sandwiches, water, and cups of espresso on the patio of one of the coffee bars, then continued their drive.

Further south, they came to a crossing. Tonio pointed at a street sign with the name Podere Francesco Ginori. "Let's go to the estate first and then come back to take a look around the town of Vignaverde."

Next to the road, vineyards with neat, parallel lines of vines stretched along the hills. In the distance, Andreas spotted a cluster of small and medium-sized houses as well as larger buildings that looked like barns or storage sheds. The buildings were flanked by pines and cypress trees. Andreas admired the estate and the countryside. He spotted a field of poppies in bloom next to the vineyards.

They parked their car in front of what looked to be the main house, a building in the typical Tuscan style with green shutters and ocher walls. They got out of the car and stretched after the long drive when the door opened, and a young woman stepped outside. She glanced at them, and her eyes widened in surprise.

"Tonio," she called. "What are you doing here? Oh, you must be the guests Mamma told me about. I didn't check the names."

"Julietta?" Tonio called back. He rushed toward her and the two embraced. "My most beautiful woman." Tonio winked at her.

As Andreas noticed, Julietta was indeed very pretty. She was tall with an attractive figure and shoulder-length auburn hair. The most striking feature, however, were her bluish-purple eyes that sparkled in the sunshine.

"You know each other?" Emilia asked.

"Yes. A few years ago, Mario and I were on vacation in Italy. We took a tour visiting some of the vineyards in Tuscany. We really liked Podere Francesco Ginori and decided to spend some time here. That's when we met Julietta, the daughter of the owner. She was a very cute girl, who developed into a beautiful woman, as you can see."

Julietta blushed. "Still the charming flatterer."

"Well, it's true." Mario hugged her as well.

Tonio introduced Andreas and Emilia.

"Let's go inside," Julietta said. "My mother will be back soon. She went to do some shopping. I'll check you in. You're going to stay in my sister's house." Julietta pointed at the smaller home behind the main building. It was built in the same typical Tuscan style as the main house.

"You have a sister?" Tonio asked. "I didn't know. From what I remember from last time we were here, you had only a brother."

"Yes, when I saw you last, I hadn't met her yet." Julietta opened the gate to the garden of the guest house.

"She was born later? So, she's younger than you?"

"No, she's ten years older and lives in the United States, in California."

Tonio scrunched his forehead. "Oh?"

"Yes, it's somewhat complicated," Julietta said. "My father was American. My mother and he were together when he was here, but he also had a wife and daughter in California."

"Whoa, I see. Well, I don't, really." Tonio looked puzzled. "He was leading a double-life?"

"I know." Julietta gave an embarrassed laugh. "A little shocking, isn't it? But it turned out all right in the end."

The house they were staying in was charming with walls of natural stones in gray and ocher tones. The front door was solid oak topped by a stone arch. At the side of the house, the roof extended over a patio that was surrounded by a garden with sunflowers, a patch of dark-blue freesia, red and yellow snapdragons, and a magnolia bush with white and pink blossoms.

"How beautiful," Emilia exclaimed.

They stepped into a small hallway with a wardrobe and a door leading into a living room with a fireplace, a coffee table, easy chairs with brown and orange cushions, and a couch. Julietta opened a glass door and the shutter in front of it that led onto the patio. The sun shining into the room gave it a cheery feeling. An open doorway connected the living room with a modern kitchen. Next to the vaulted doorway was a dining table with a few high-back wicker chairs. Julietta led them upstairs where there was a hallway, three bedrooms, and two baths.

"Very nice and comfortable," Tonio said.

"Good, if you need anything, just let us know," Julietta said. "I'll be waiting in the main house right next door. Come over once you're unpacked and settled in. We have refreshments, and you can meet my mother. You're the only guests for the next few days. You can have dinner with us or, if you prefer, there are a few nice restaurants in town."

"I wouldn't mind having dinner here tonight," Tonio said. "I'm kind of pooped from the long drive. We can explore Vignaverde tomorrow, if that's all right with everybody."

Andreas, Emilia, and Mario nodded their agreement.

"Great," Julietta said. "I'll tell Mamma and we can have a relaxing evening. It's really nice out now. I can show you around the vineyard later."

Once Julietta left, Andreas cleared his throat. "Can you call Peter to find out how Pietro is doing?" he asked Emilia.

Emilia laughed. "Stop worrying about the puppy. Peter is in love with him. You may not get him back once we return. Besides, you have his number. Call him yourself."

Andreas groaned. "I feel embarrassed to call. I don't want to give him the impression I don't trust him."

"Oh, come on, Papa, don't be silly. Let me call him." Emilia pressed the speed button on her phone. "Hi Peter, how are you? Papa wants to know how your namesake is doing."

"It's okay. I'm just being ridiculous," Andreas called.

Emilia grinned and handed the phone to Andreas. "Hey, Peter. Sorry, I already miss him."

Peter laughed, then called Pietro, who gave a happy bark. "He is doing well. He did miss you at first. He sniffed every corner, looking for you, but he gets a lot of hugs from me. Don't worry and enjoy your vacation. How is everything?"

"Thanks, Peter. I know I'm getting a little sentimental in my old age. We're having a good time."

Chapter 11

After unpacking his clothes in one of the upstairs bedrooms, Andreas put on a fresh T-shirt and stood by the window. In the back of the house, he spotted a vegetable garden next to a huge bougainvillea that climbed along the wall of what looked like a garden shed. Behind the yard, vineyards extended all the way to the hills in the background. He took a deep breath, enjoying the view of the colorful landscape. He thought of Karla who would have loved to paint here, but the memory wasn't as painful as it used to be. He smiled as he heard his children stomp down the staircase.

"Papa, let's go," Emilia called him.

Andreas grabbed his sunglasses and joined them. They walked over to the main house. The late afternoon sun was bearing down, and Andreas wiped his forehead. Through the open front door, he heard voices of women chatting and laughing. Julietta came out to meet them and waved them inside.

The house was cool with thick stone walls keeping out the heat. They entered a large living room with a big fireplace. There was a brown leather sofa, some easy chairs with leather backs, and two beautifully carved closets. Andreas admired a few paintings, one of them a poster of a work by Botticelli called *La Primavera*. He walked over to the fireplace and touched the granite mantelpiece.

"Beautiful work," he said. As usual, he had an eye for unique pieces of stonework and the mantelpiece showed some delicate carvings.

"*Buongiorno* and welcome to Vignaverde," a melodious voice said. "I'm Luisa."

Andreas turned around. In the doorway stood an attractive woman. She resembled Julietta, and Andreas assumed she was the mother. She had the same well-proportioned figure, although she was somewhat slimmer than her daughter, and the same facial features—strong chin, small nose. Her shoulder-length auburn hair showed a few streaks of gray. He took her to be in her fifties.

She stepped into the room and smiled at Tonio and Mario, whom she seemed to recognize from their earlier vacation. "Welcome back," she said to them, then focused her gaze with her dark, expressive eyes on Andreas. They shook hands and he introduced Emilia to her. She invited them all to sit.

Andreas realized with a shock that it was the first time since Karla's death that he had paid more than casual attention to another woman.

When they were seated, Julietta and a young woman, whom Julietta introduced as her cousin Diana, brought in jugs of lemonade and a plate with cantucci, a type of Italian cookies made with almonds.

"Tonio told me when he made the reservations that you are celebrating his sister's graduation." She glanced at Emilia and smiled.

"That's right," Tonio said, picking up a cookie.

"As Julietta probably told you, you are free to have dinner with us," Luisa continued. "Only if you wish, though. You may also want to try some of the restaurants in town. There are some good ones. Whatever you chose, just let me know if you want to eat here or go out."

"My mother is an excellent cook," Julietta said.

"I can attest to that. I remember that from last time we were here," Tonio added.

"Sounds delicious. And thank you for the invitation," Andreas said. "We appreciate it."

After they enjoyed the refreshments, Julietta gave them a quick tour of the estate. They walked along the fields of the vineyards with their different varieties of grapes. On the way, Julietta told Emilia that she'd developed a crush on Tonio when he visited the first time. "I was quite disappointed when I realized he liked men."

"Yes, you're not the only girl he disappointed with his preference for men," Emilia said.

Juliette smiled. "He's so darn handsome."

"I know; he's a real heartbreaker," Emilia agreed.

Andreas who was listening to the exchange smiled to himself as he remembered his own ambivalent feelings about his son's sexual orientation. "Well, at least, he picked a very nice man." He patted Mario on the back, who grinned.

"Yeah, he's not too bad," Tonio quipped.

As they walked on, Julietta turned to Emilia. "My mother told me that you are now a veterinarian."

"Yes." Emilia smiled. "I finished my studies and got my first job."

"That's so great."

"I love animals, always have." Emilia hesitated. "I just wish my mother was still alive, so she could celebrate with me."

Julietta gently touched her arm. "I know. When I finished my studies, I would've loved to have had my father here."

They were silent for a while, then Julietta continued. "A friend of ours is a veterinarian here. He treats horses and all kinds of large animals. This seems to be a hard job," Julietta said.

78

"I specialize mainly in pets, you know cats, dogs, rabbits, and so on. My partner, the veterinarian I work with, treats the large animals. We help each other out though."

During their walk through the estate, Julietta pointed out the different grape varieties and facilities, such as the storage sheds to them. "I'll give you a more extensive tour tomorrow and show you the wine cellar," she promised.

After their short tour of the estate, Julietta returned to the main house while the others walked back to the guest house to relax for a while.

Andreas stretched out on the bed in his room to take a short nap. His mind was once again on the mystery of the letter in the cave. When a knock on the door and Emilia's voice woke him, he realized he had fallen asleep. He got up, splashed some cold water on his face in the bathroom, then grabbed a light jacket and went downstairs where his children were waiting. They walked again to the main house to join their hosts for dinner.

The temperature was still balmy and perfect for sitting outside. A rustic granite table on the patio underneath a pergola, covered with vines, was set with colorful place mats. Plates with antipasti—salami, prosciutto, cheese, olives, artichoke hearts—stood next to jugs of lemonade and bottles of red and white wine.

"Wow, what a spread," Mario exclaimed.

Tonio laughed and put his arm around Mario's shoulder. He winked at Julietta, who set a bowl of salad on the table. "Good food, one of his favorite pastimes."

"It sure is," Mario said. He touched his slightly bulging belly. "I have to watch it, but hey, we're on vacation."

"Absolutely," Tonio grabbed him by the waist. "Besides I like your love handles."

"Okay, boys, behave." Emilia gave them a pretend stern look.

Luisa stepped outside. She was dressed in a flowing white summer skirt and a green and white short-sleeved top that accentuated her auburn hair and dark eyes. She measured the display of food with a quick firm look, then called for Julietta to bring another bottle of mineral water.

Andreas had the feeling that underneath her sparkling personality was a fierce spirit. Once again, he caught himself admiring this attractive woman.

"Let's start with the antipasti," Luisa motioned to the table. She smiled at Andreas who smiled back, then averted his eyes, trying hard not to stare. *I'm behaving like a teenager.*

They all sat down and began to eat the appetizers. A little later, Luisa and Julietta went back into the house and brought plates filled with risotto con funghi, fish, and seafood. Luisa poured them more wine.

The mild summer weather, the excellent food, the wine, all contributed to a joyful evening. Andreas took a sip of wine as he admired the meadows and fields of vines that stretched out in front of them. The scent of flowers nearby mixed pleasantly with the smell of food.

He took a deep breath. "This is wonderful. Now, I'm glad I came along. You were right." He put his arm around Emilia, then turned to Luisa and raised his glass of wine. "And this is the best dinner I've had in a long time. Compliments to the chef."

Luisa acknowledged his praise with a smile. "I didn't do it alone; I had help." She put her hand on Julietta's shoulder.

"Well, then, congratulations to the chefs." Tonio raised his glass as well.

Dinner was followed by ice cream for dessert. Then as they sipped espresso and an assortment of after-dinner liquors, they watched the sun setting behind the rows of grapevines and listened to the sound of crickets, the scrambling of other creatures in the fields, and the lonely tune of an owl.

Andreas' thoughts turned to his new project, trying to find Bella and her family, to Pietro, his new companion, to the new sculpture he had begun to work on. A sense of gratitude filled him as he glanced at his children. He remembered Karla but this time without the acute pain he had felt about her loss for the past three years. Something important had changed, he wasn't sure what, but he enjoyed that renewed feeling of peace and excitement. Life was worth living again.

Chapter 12

Julietta had taken a few days off from helping her husband with his architectural project in Rome and was able to show the O'Reilly family around the town. Vignaverde, one of the many hill towns in Tuscany, was surrounded by Etruscan walls. As they drove up the hill, Julietta pointed out a large fortress above a pine-wooded hill. After she parked the car, they entered the town through an arched stone gate.

Julietta led them to the Piazza San Francesco, the center of town, and explained the meaning of the buildings surrounding the piazza. They represented the traditional Christian cycle of life—the baptistery or birth, followed by the cathedral, symbol of daily life. The hospital and cemetery that marked the end of life were no longer part of the piazza. They were moved outside the city in modern times.

"Interesting," Andreas said. "You're an excellent travel guide."

Julietta smiled. "You can actually find the information in any of the tourist guides. Since I grew up here, I should know about it."

They went on to browse through some of the stores and boutiques that sold pottery and small artworks made of alabaster, for which Vignaverde was famous. For lunch, Julietta took them to a trattoria, where they ordered antipasti and wine.

"That's where I met my sister Sofia for the first time." Julietta motioned to the piazza in front of them. She was quiet for a while, thinking back to that crucial moment in her life.

"It was a little awkward at first. Our father had died unexpectedly of a heart attack, and Sofia had just discovered that she had a sister here and had inherited part of a vineyard."

"That must have been a shock," Andreas said.

"It was, and it took a while for her to absorb it."

"Did you know about your sister?" Emilia asked.

"Yes, and the last time my father was here he told my mother and me that he was going to finally tell his daughter in California about us. But then he died before he was able to do so."

"How did Sofia find out?" Emilia asked.

"Dad's lawyer told her."

"Incredible." Tonio's eyes widened. "Can you imagine suddenly finding out your father had another family?"

"How do you feel about your dad now?" Emilia asked.

"We've both forgiven him for keeping this secret for so long. It was more difficult for Sofia since she didn't know anything about his life here with us. She felt betrayed." Julietta hesitated. "I often felt sad when my father left again, but I didn't feel betrayed. I would've liked to meet Sofia earlier. But in hindsight, I understand what made my father keep our relationship hidden. The circumstances with his American wife were very difficult. All I know is that he was a wonderful father to me … and to Sofia. And he did plan to come clean." Julietta took a sip of her lemonade. "And the best outcome was that I was able to stay with my sister and study architecture in California where I met my husband, Adam."

Andreas put his hand lightly on Julietta's shoulder. "In the end, you both loved and forgave your father. He may not have deserved your forgiveness, but we all make mistakes in our lives, hurt each other, and we all need people to forgive us." He gave a wistful smile. "That's part of any relationship, whether between parents and children or husband and wife."

Andreas lapsed into silence, then continued. "I speak from experience. There were times when people in my life had to forgive me for doing stupid things." His brows knitted. "I had to forgive my own father; it took me a long time to be able to do it. But in the end, it was the only way I could keep my soul intact." He paused. "My father was an alcoholic and sometimes violent. He beat my mother and me."

"That's awful," Julietta said. "What made you forgive him?"

"He repented. He went through a lot to track us down. My parents had been divorced for many years, and I had no contact with him. I was so angry at him that it took a lot of courage on his part to come back and confront me. Anyway, I couldn't hold on to my hatred and anger anymore, and so we got back together again. Shortly thereafter he died."

Tonio put his hand on Andreas' shoulder. "I remember Grandpa. He seemed so kind. I couldn't imagine him being violent."

"He'd changed," Andreas said. "See, I found out that he had been abused as a boy himself. It made me understand him better."

Julietta quietly observed Andreas. She liked this serious and kind man.

In the afternoon, Julietta gave them a more extensive tour of the estate and showed them the winery with the assortments of wine-making equipment. At the entrance to the wine cellar, a man came outside and greeted them with a nod.

"This is my uncle Edoardo," Julietta introduced him. "He is my mother's brother. They own the estate together."

"*Buongiorno*." Edoardo, a tall man with salt-and-pepper hair and a short, black beard, said and gave a quick smile. His piercing dark eyes reminded Andreas of Luisa, but this man seemed more reserved and not as vivacious as his sister.

"Can you show them the cellar?" Julietta asked. "I want to go back and help Mamma."

"*Certo*," Edoardo said.

"See you later," Julietta said as she walked back to the main house.

"Follow me." Edoardo opened the heavy door to the cellar. "Let me show you our wine."

Inside, it was pleasantly cool. Edoardo led them around the large cellar with the many rows of wine barrels and bottles. He showed them the different varietals or types of wine. In the middle of the cellar, there was a bar counter with bottles of wine.

"Would you like to taste some of our wine?" He motioned them to take a seat.

"That would be great," Tonio said.

Edoardo proceeded to pour them small glasses of wine and they spent some time tasting the Sangiovese and Merlot, the flagship wines of the estate.

As Edoardo became more animated, explaining enthusiastically how the wine was produced and blended, Andreas began to recognize the similarities in temperament with Luisa.

In the evening, Julietta's husband Adam, who had also taken a break from work in Rome, arrived and joined the guests. He invited the O'Reillys to a party with friends. With his bleached-blond hair, trim body, tanned arms and face, he reminded Andreas of one of the surfers on a TV series about California he had watched a few times. Adam, however, was an architect with a degree from a prestigious university in California.

Andreas wanted to stay back and relax. "I'm not as young as you. Your old dad needs a little time to recuperate. You go and have fun."

Andreas did have an ulterior motif for staying back. He planned to tell Luisa about his discovery in the cave. Perhaps she could give him some advice on how to find out more about Bella's family and possibly locate them. Besides, he was curious about Luisa herself. He wanted to spend more time with her.

Chapter 13

While the younger people were at the party with their friends, Luisa invited Andreas to have dinner with her and her brother, Edoardo, whose wife and children were out of town. They had a light supper of salami and prosciutto, cheese as well as vegetables and salad. Edoardo brought a bottle of a new varietal, a Syrah.

Luisa smelled and swirled the wine, then took a sip. "Very good. It turned out well."

"Yes, it's excellent," Andreas said. "The perfect accompaniment to the delicious food. I could get used to being spoiled like this."

After they finished eating, Edoardo got up. "Time for my walk around the estate." He gave a quick smile. "See you later. Have a nice evening."

Luisa nodded a goodbye, then took another sip of wine. She and Andreas continued to sit outside, enjoying the warm evening.

There was a delicate scent of lemon in the air. Luisa noticed it was Andreas' cologne or aftershave and it triggered a memory of Henry, Luisa's former lover and father of Julietta. Andreas must use a similar brand.

Luisa hadn't thought of Henry much in the past few years. She remembered him with love, that tall, lumbering man with longish wild hair and a booming voice. He had studied chemistry and microbiology, but his love had been wine, the growing of grapes and the making of wine. He had been coming to Vignaverde for several years before he and Luisa became lovers. Henry had bought part of their vineyard when Luisa's stepfather had been in financial trouble and had almost lost the estate. Henry had practically saved the family from ruin.

Luisa and Henry had fallen in love, but the affair wasn't meant to last. Luisa had known that he had a wife and child back in California. Then she discovered she was pregnant. It had been a passionate but turbulent time for both of them.

Luisa gave a quick shake of her head, pushing the memories away. She got up and poured Andreas and herself another glass of Syrah.

Andreas took a sip and raised the glass. "Excellent wine."

"Yes, it's a new addition to our estate," Luisa said. "I like it too."

It was quiet for a while and in the silence, Luisa listened to the chirping of crickets and the cawing of a bird.

"My wife, Karla, would've loved it here. She would've sketched every part of your estate." Andreas paused; Luisa glanced at him.

"She was an artist, a painter," he explained.

"You still miss her a lot, don't you?" Luisa said, then raised her hand. "You don't have to talk about it if it's too painful."

"That's okay. Yes, I still miss her, but I feel I'm finally coming out of that depressive slump, that lack of energy. I feel more alive again." He gazed at the fields and trees in front of them. "She was an amazing woman." He hesitated. "That doesn't mean our relationship was without problems. We had our fights and disagreements; we almost broke up a couple of times." He scratched the dark stubble on his chin.

Luisa wondered if he wanted to grow a beard during his vacation.

"But we never stopped loving each other," he continued. "Even if we didn't always like each other."

Luisa was intrigued by this serious, sometimes gloomy but kind man. Every once in a while, his verdigris green eyes lit up with a humorous glint.

"That's the sign of a good relationship," Luisa said. "I wish I could say the same of my marriage."

Andreas looked at her, his kind eyes encouraged her to continue. "My marriage was a disaster and ended in a bitter divorce. My ex-husband was abusive and a crook. What made the whole thing worse, he poisoned my son with his lies and bad character."

"Oh? I didn't know you had a son. Somehow, I got the impression it was only Julietta." Andreas looked at her surprised.

"Yes, Guido is my son from my first husband, well my only husband, I guess. Julietta's father and I weren't married." She gave a dismissive wave with her hand. "Anyway, after the divorce, my ex moved to Rome and Guido spent time with him. Every time he came back, his behavior had changed for the worse. He was lazy, did poorly in school. We fought a lot. He told me he could make a lot more money working with his dad, knowing the right people. So, one day, he up and left. Unfortunately, by then he was old enough to be on his own, so I couldn't do anything about it."

"That's sad," Andreas said. "What happened to him? Are you still in touch at least?"

"Yes, but it took years for us to reconnect somewhat. My ex ended up in jail. Fortunately, Guido was spared. He now works a regular job in Rome, I think." Luisa nibbled at her bottom lip. "So far at least he hasn't ended up in jail."

"I'm sorry to hear this," Andreas said. "Being estranged from your children is hard. But at least Julietta seems to bring you a lot of joy."

89

Luisa laughed. "Yes, she does. And Adam is a wonderful son-in-law. He's actually more like a son."

They were quiet for a while. Andreas took another sip of wine. "So, you only tried marriage once, I take it?"

"Yes, once was enough, although …." She hesitated. "I did have a good relationship for a few years with a very wonderful man, an American. You know, Julietta's father. The only problem was he was married." She glanced at him to see if he judged her. He continued to watch her with his kind eyes.

"His marriage was in trouble. His wife had severe mental problems which affected their relationship. He wanted to leave her, but he felt he couldn't abandon her when she was so vulnerable. Then she died of an overdose. He believed she committed suicide, and he felt very guilty." A long sigh. "So eventually our relationship cooled, then came to an end. He continued to visit, and he was a very loving father to Julietta. Then he unexpectedly died of a heart attack."

"Julietta told me a little about this," Andreas said. "She has a sister, well half-sister, in California."

"That's right. Her name is Sofia. She visited us a few years ago. She and Julietta became very close. Because of this, Julietta was able to study in California where she met Adam. At first, I wasn't very happy about it. Destiny seemed to repeat itself. My daughter too fell in love with an American, and I was afraid she'd be stuck in a long-distance relationship. Fortunately, it didn't turn out that way. The two are married, they live together, and at least their relationship has a future. After Adam's project is over here, they are planning to return to California. I'll miss my daughter." Luisa lifted her hand in a resigned gesture. "But I went to see her once when she studied there, and we'll be visiting as much as possible. I'm just glad she's happy." Luisa watched as the last rays of the sun sank beneath the pine-covered hills in the distance.

"It's so beautiful here," Andreas said in a dreamy voice.

"It is," Luisa said. "We take it for granted most of the time. It's only when our visitors admire the view that I appreciate it anew."

Andreas brushed his hand through his hair. "By the way, I wonder if you could help me with something. Well, I just need some advice."

"Of course." Luisa glanced at him.

"I found this during a hike in the Swiss mountains near the border to Italy." He pulled out a plastic folder from his backpack and handed her a piece of paper. "This is a copy of a letter to a young woman in Italy during the Second World War." He raised a hand, then let it drop on his thigh. "I would love to find the woman this was addressed to if she or her family is still alive. It sounds crazy I know, but I want to try."

Chapter 14

"*Dio santo.*" Luisa looked up from the letter and stared at Andreas. "What happened to ..." She glanced at the letter again. "To Joshua? Why did the letter end up in a cave? He wrote this over seventy years ago."

"After finding it, I did some research together with a friend of mine who happens to be the local chief of police," Andreas said. "He found a note in their archives about a body that was found at the bottom of an abyss near the cave right at that time. There was no identification on him. It only mentioned the body belonged to a male of around twenty to twenty-five years old."

"And you found the letter by chance in a cave where you waited out a rainstorm?"

"Yes, together with an old backpack with some essential stuff, a passport, a photo, some old lira, and other items."

"But what could have happened to him?" Luisa asked in a thoughtful voice. "Did he fall ... or was he pushed?" She brushed a strand of hair out of her face and looked at Andreas, puzzled.

"We don't think it was foul play. The weather was very bad at that time. That's what the letter and the short notice in the police archive said. There was also a brief article in the local newspaper. They suspected he slipped and fell. Most likely, he arrived too late to be picked up by the Swiss helper." Andreas pointed at the place in the letter where Joshua described his trip. "He was waiting there overnight and perhaps he wanted to walk down by himself or just look around. We'll never know. There was a passport in his belongings with a different name, an Italian name. It was probably a fake name to hide his identity."

"I read somewhere that refugees often had fake passports to hide the fact that they were Jewish," Luisa said, then sighed. "You know the sad thing is that we have another refugee situation today. People fleeing the violence in the Middle East, in Syria, and other countries. This is over seventy years after the Second World War."

"True," Andreas said. "And we in the West don't treat them with the compassion and respect they deserve. Many of us in the West seem to have forgotten that our parents or grandparents were refugees."

"Yes, that's true of us Italians as well. Unfortunately, the European Union totally mismanaged the situation. Italy gets overwhelmed by the refugees that come from the East and Africa, and Bruxelles doesn't help us at all, or at least not enough. If all countries in the European Union would contribute and take their fair share of refugees, it would be easier for everyone. Instead, some countries have an undue burden and people begin to resent the influx of so many people."

"We're not in the European Union," Andreas said. "But there is the same resistance to taking in people from countries with different customs from our own. Resentment is growing."

Andreas was gazing into the distance where the sun had sunk, leaving a band of silver light on the horizon. "But about Joshua," he said, looking back at Luisa. "I have this crazy idea of trying to find the woman the letter was addressed to. I know it's nuts. All I have is a name, a town with a post office box. I don't think it's her real address. He tried to hide her identity, to protect her in case the letter fell into the wrong hands. Besides, she may not be alive anymore. But she was pregnant and perhaps her child or family is still around. Can you imagine never knowing what happened to your husband ... or your father? They most likely don't know what happened to him."

"I don't think it's crazy," Luisa mused as if talking to herself, then livelier, "you know, Edoardo and I have an uncle who lives in Milano. From what I remember Uncle Giancarlo is a historian and his special field is the Second World War. Edoardo knows him even better than I do. He spent a lot of vacations with him and his wife as a youngster. I'll have to ask him. I think we should contact Giancarlo."

"We? ... I couldn't possibly get you involved in my harebrained plan," Andreas said, although, this was exactly what he secretly wished for.

"Why not?" There was a gleam of excitement in her eyes. "You got me all interested. If you don't mind, I'd like to help."

"Okay, wonderful." Andreas drew in a long breath. "I can't do much while we're on vacation. I promised my kids not to get sidetracked. But later, perhaps, I could stay on. If you have time, perhaps we could visit your uncle. But only if you want to. No pressure. Please."

"Sounds like a plan ... and an adventure."

Andreas felt his excitement rise. In fact, he hadn't felt so alive in a long time.

"Here is Edoardo, back from his daily evening walk around the estate. Let's ask him." Luisa waved at her brother who walked toward them.

Edoardo gave a nod in greeting and measured them with his usual earnest expression.

"Any damage from the storm?" Luisa asked. The past night there had been one of the wild Tuscan storms with rain, thunder, and lightning.

"Nothing major," Edoardo said.

Luisa motioned him to sit on one of the garden chairs. "Want some more wine?" She lifted the bottle, but he shook his head. She put the bottle down and handed him the letter. "Andreas found this in a cave on one of his hikes in the Swiss mountains near the Italian border. It was written by a refugee from Italy who still may have family here. He wants to find his wife or the family this letter was addressed to."

Edoardo read the letter, then stared at them. "How … did you find this?"

Andreas gave him an abbreviated version of his hiking adventure.

"We think Uncle Giancarlo may be able to help Andreas. Isn't his specialty the Second World War?"

Edoardo's serious expression gave way to a quick smile. "Yes, that's true, but trying to find a person after such a long time with so little information? I don't know."

"It's worth a try. We could visit Uncle Giancarlo. It's been too long anyway. I haven't seen Aunt Sonia in ages. Always too busy around here."

"Why not?" Edoardo said. "It may not lead to anything, but you can take a little vacation." He turned to Andreas. "I've fond memories of my vacation time there when I was a kid." He handed the letter back to Luisa. "Make sure you bring them some bottles of wine." He got up. "I'll have to finish my round. Let me know what you plan to do."

Andreas looked after him as he walked away. "He is such a serious man."

"Yes, that's true," Luisa acknowledged. "He gives people the idea he is grouchy a lot, but he's really kind and has a good heart."

"Oh, I think so. He gets very lively and excited when he talks about grapes and wine. He seems passionate about it."

"Yes, thank God," Luisa said. "You know we're co-owners, but he and his family are really the ones working the estate. When Julietta decided being a vintner wasn't for her, I was happy to leave the work of the winemaking to Edoardo and his family. When we decided to have guests on the estate, I took over that part."

"Well, it's a beautiful estate and a great vacation spot," Andreas said. "We really enjoy it."

Luisa took the last sip of her wine. "Yes, we wanted to keep it small and sustainable. No noisy crowds. Most of the people who come here know us. They are usually a somewhat older crowd and are looking for a relaxing, peaceful vacation."

Andreas and Luisa sat quietly for a while, enjoying the last minutes of dusk. After the rain and thunderstorm of the previous night, the air was soft and balmy. Andreas inhaled the sweet scent of a patch of roses in the garden nearby. His thoughts turned to Joshua and Bella and his upcoming adventure to try to find the family. He was even more excited now that Luisa had decided to join him.

Chapter 15

"You and Andreas seem to spend a lot of time together. You like him, don't you?" Julietta didn't mean to sound accusing. She gave her mother a quizzical look. She and Luisa were preparing dinner in a kitchen that smelled of garlic and herbs.

Luisa glanced at her surprised. "Yes, he seems to be a very nice man."

"Only nice?"

"Well, okay, more than nice. I find him interesting, deep, kind." Luisa hesitated, her knife hovering over the zucchini she was slicing. "A little sad. There's a hidden darkness in him, probably because he still mourns his wife." She turned to Julietta. "Why the sudden interest?"

Julietta continued to stir the risotto and didn't say anything.

"You look troubled. What's the matter?" Luisa continued cutting the zucchini, then dropped them into a pot with heated olive oil.

Julietta lifted a shoulder. "I like him too, but I don't want him to hurt you."

Luisa wrinkled her forehead. "Why would he hurt me?"

"Well, you know, you fall in love and then he leaves again … just like Papa."

"Oh, Julietta." Luisa sounded exasperated. "First of all, I'm not in love with Andreas. I just like him as a friend. And I can assure you I don't have the slightest interest in a romantic relationship. I had my share of disappointments, thank you very much. A miserable marriage and a tragic love relationship. So don't you worry."

"Uncle Edoardo told me you were going to Great Uncle Giancarlo with him. What's that all about?"

"I told you about the letter Andreas found. Giancarlo is an expert on the history of the Second World War. He may be able to give him some advice on how to find the woman the letter is addressed to. That's all."

"That's all?" Julietta felt her mother was giving her only half the story.

Luisa laughed. "Julietta, you worry in vain. I simply want to help him. And to be honest, it sounds like a great adventure, trying to find a family after all this time." She began to stir the zucchini.

"I think he has a crush on you," Julietta mused as if talking to herself. "I can tell by the way he looks at you."

"You're dreaming. We enjoy each other's company. We're not youngsters anymore; we don't just fall in love like teenagers."

"Well, if you did fall in love, have you ever considered this would be another long-distance relationship?" Julietta stared at her mother.

Luisa continued sauteing the zucchini. "You're the right one to talk. You're married to a foreigner, an American."

"Yes, but we're together. We live in the same place."

"True. But when you first dated, you didn't know that."

"I did worry about it," Julietta admitted.

"Well, so did I," Luisa said. "I mean I worried about you moving to the United States for good, losing you. Or for you to be unhappy in a long-distance relationship like mine. But it turned out all right, didn't it? You're happy with a wonderful man. That's the most important thing."

"I want you to be happy too," Julietta said. "But I don't want to lose you. I want you to be here when Adam and I come back to visit." She gave an embarrassed chuckle. "That's pretty selfish, I know."

"I understand. But you really don't have to worry about me and Andreas. As I said, this is a purely platonic friendship. All right?"

Julietta sighed. "All right, Mamma, I won't worry."

"Well, you better worry about the risotto, so it doesn't get burned or dry out." Luisa motioned at the pot with the simmering *risotto con funghi*.

"I have it under control," Julietta said. "Is Andreas going to eat with us?"

"Something smells good in here," a deep voice said.

Luisa turned around. "Andreas, just in time."

"Thanks for inviting me again," Andreas said. He turned to Julietta. "My children are out shopping. They're going to eat in town somewhere."

Julietta flashed a smirk and lifted the pot with the risotto. "That's done. Do you need me to do anything else?"

"No. Why don't you sit down?" Luisa poured the sauteed vegetables onto a plate. "Actually," she said to Julietta. "Could you bring the chicken?"

"Adam and I won't be here for dinner," Julietta said. "We're going out."

"We're going out?" Adam stepped into the kitchen after Andreas.

"Well, I wish you'd told me earlier. I cooked for everyone." Luisa gave an irritated sigh.

Adam peered at Julietta. "I thought we were going to eat here tonight."

Julietta exhaled loudly. "I just thought maybe Mamma and Andreas want to be alone."

"Stop this nonsense!" Luisa said.

Andreas looked from Luisa to Julietta and back again. "Am I missing something?"

"No, it's okay." Luisa turned to Julietta. "Make up your mind."

"Sorry, a misunderstanding." Julietta gave a quick smile, trying to talk herself out of her increasingly bad mood. "We'll eat here."

"All right." Luisa motioned at the stove. "The chicken please."

Julietta grabbed the plate, pressing her lips together.

Outside, they sat at the granite table. It was quiet for a while with everybody eating.

"Delicious food, as always." Andreas gave an appreciative nod.

Julietta ate quietly, trying to be as pleasant as possible. She couldn't explain to herself why she felt irritated. Andreas was a nice man and her mother looked very happy. What was wrong with her?

After dinner, Adam and Julietta drove back to Rome since they had to work the following day. After driving for a while Adam glanced at Julietta. "What's wrong with you? You've been acting strange all evening."

Julietta lifted a shoulder, then sighed. "I don't know really. I'm worried about my mother. She and Andreas seem to get along really well ... too well, I think."

"Why? That's not a bad thing, is it? Andreas seems like a nice guy."

"He lives in Switzerland. How would they be able to be together? I just don't want her to get into another long-distance relationship. She was hurt badly when my father broke it off." Julietta's voice cracked. "I was hurt too, and then he just went and died on us. Also, Andreas is much older than Mamma. So, they fall in love and then he dies on her again." She groaned. "I know it sounds dumb and selfish."

"I'm sorry, Julietta." Adam touched her cheek. "I can understand why you worry. But Switzerland isn't that far away. It's not America. I'm sure they could manage to see each other if they wanted to. They are old enough to make it work. And him being somewhat older, well, he seems to be healthy and in good shape. I wouldn't worry so much."

"You're right. I don't know what's wrong with me." Julietta glanced out the window. After a while, her mood improved. She was usually not a moody person, so why now? Something in the back of her mind niggled at her. She remembered having felt a little ill in the mornings, thinking it may have been something she ate. She thought back and realized her period was late. She gasped.

"What's the matter?" Adam looked at her perplexed.

"That would explain my mood," Julietta mused.

"What?"

"Adam, I might be pregnant."

"Are you sure?"

"Not one hundred percent, but it could be." She stared at him.

He wrinkled his forehead, then his face lit up. "That would be fantastic."

"You really think so? It's somewhat early, isn't it?" Julietta felt a twinge of fear, followed by joy.

"It's perfect, honey." Adam hit the steering wheel and whooped. The car jerked a little to the side.

"Hey, watch it," Julietta exclaimed. "You don't want to get us killed, do you?" She grinned. "Particularly now when there may be three of us."

Adam laughed. "Don't worry. I have it all under control." He whooped again but kept the car driving straight.

Chapter 16

"What do you think of Papa and his new companion?" Tonio glanced at Emilia.

Tonio, Mario, and Emilia were driving home from their vacation whereas Andreas and Luisa were going to try to find Bella.

"Do you think they may become more than just friends?" Mario asked.

"Papa is still pining for Mama," Emilia said. "I don't think he's ready for a new relationship. That would be strange. Well, they seem to be spending a lot of time together. He hardly ever went out with us in the evenings. I know he's not into partying, but his excuses of being too tired after our daily outings seemed at least somewhat suspicious. Whenever we came back late from our evenings out, they were still sitting outside, having animated discussions or taking walks across the estate. He didn't seem tired at all."

"Well, I haven't seen him in such a good mood in a long time," Tonio said.

"Come on, it would be great if Andreas found love again." Mario, who sat in the back seat, put his hand on Emilia's shoulder.

"I don't know …" Emilia hesitated. "I can't imagine Papa being with another woman."

"Wouldn't you want him to be happy again?" Tonio glanced at her.

Emilia gave a quick sigh. "I guess, yes. It would just be a little strange. I mean … for us."

Tonio chuckled. "Let's just wait and see. Leave it up to them. I'm just glad Papa seemed to have snapped out of his permanent gloom and has energy again. He's really into trying to play detective and find that woman or her family."

"I agree." Emilia laughed. "We may have to spend quite a lot more time in Italy in the future."

"Fine with me," Mario said. "I love Vignaverde, the vineyards, and the excellent wine."

"Here they are," Emilia called out as a car next to theirs honked. She waved at her father and Luisa, who had left Vignaverde at the same time and headed toward Milano, though to a different destination in the city. Soon the two cars would go their own ways. Emilia, Tonio, and Mario were driving to Mario and Tonio's apartment. Emilia planned to spend the night at their place and drive Andreas' car back to Andeer the following day. Andreas and Luisa were on their way to visit Giancarlo, Luisa's uncle, who used to teach at the university but was retired now.

Andreas and Luisa had picked the early afternoon to avoid the rush hours in the city. Andreas enjoyed being a passenger and not having to drive himself through some of the crazy traffic on Italian freeways. Luisa was driving fast, Italian style, Andreas thought, but she was an experienced driver and he felt safe. The drive from Tuscany to Milano was fairly relaxing. It had rained the night before and the grass in the fields was still wet. Sun rays turned the meadows into a shimmering carpet of grasses and shrubs.

After visiting Luisa's uncle, they were planning to drive to the town of Quercia, mentioned on the letter's envelope. It was a small town next to Lake Como in the Lombardy region, not too far from Milano. The address looked like a mailbox rather than a residential home, which was probably planned so the authorities wouldn't have been able to track down the addressee's home that easily if the letter had ended up in the wrong hands.

They made good time and arrived at Luisa's uncle and aunt's place in the late afternoon. Giancarlo and his wife lived in a large home, a renovated old villa at the outskirts of Milano on a hill with a view of the valley. "When the smog permits it," Giancarlo said with a wink. He was a tall, wiry man in his eighties. His clear gray eyes pointed to a sharp mind. Sonia, his wife, was a little plumper and looked like the quintessential Italian mother. She welcomed them enthusiastically. They both hugged Luisa like a long-lost child and shook hands with Andreas. He felt right at home in their company.

Sonia ushered them into the living room that still showed signs of an old villa with just enough modern convenience like a large kitchen attached to the living and dining room, a kitchen island with a marble top as well as modern appliances. They sat down next to the window. Sonia served them coffee and *amaretti*, a popular Italian type of cookies.

They spent some time giving each other the latest news. Giancarlo wanted to know about the grape harvest at Luisa's estate. He told his guests about his new project, a study of the role the Lombardy region played in Italian history. Sonia invited them for dinner and insisted they spend the night in their house. Andreas and Luisa had planned to sleep in a motel, but their hosts didn't accept any rejection. "We have a big house and plenty of guest rooms, so you aren't any trouble at all," Sonia said. "And we hardly ever get to see our niece, so I really enjoy your visit."

Luisa sighed. "I know we should get together more. It's not that great of a distance either. It's just that we're so busy at the estate with the grapes and the guests and all."

"I understand," Giancarlo said. "Sonia and I should visit you once again and enjoy some of your excellent wine. After all, we're retired; we have more free time than you do. I haven't seen Edoardo in a while."

"He still talks about the fun vacations he had with you," Luisa said.

Giancarlo smiled. "I wonder if he didn't get tired of all the historical sites I took him to."

"Oh, no. He appreciated it," Luisa laughed. "And he definitely remembers Sonia's great desserts."

After an excellent dinner of fettuccine with seafood, salad, followed by a homemade tiramisu for dessert, Luisa, Andreas, and Giancarlo sat in Giancarlo's office, drinking espresso and nipping on a cognac. Giancarlo had spread out a large map on the table and opened a folder with papers. Luisa had told him ahead of their visit about Andreas' letter.

"I did a lot of research about the refugees fleeing north from Italy. Not that much is known about it. Most of the focus was on the situation at the borders between Switzerland and Germany or Austria. But there were people in Italy as well who risked their lives during the Nazi occupation and undertook an arduous and very dangerous journey, smuggling refugees, many of them Jewish, into Switzerland. So, Joshua could easily have been one of those refugees."

He pointed at the date on the letter to Bella. "Winter of 1943 was a very dangerous and difficult time for the Jewish people in Italy … and for other Italians as well, of course. Until the invasion by the Germans, Jewish people were subject to a new racial law with restrictions on where they could work or live and what they could do, but when the Nazis invaded, the round-up and deportation to concentration camps in Germany and Eastern Europe began in earnest." He sighed.

"You know, after the so-called Jewish emancipation in 1848 and the elimination of the ghetto in Rome in 1870, Jewish people had very little to fear in Italy. They were considered Italians first, Jewish second. Many of them were very prosperous, had important government positions, good private businesses. They were patriotic and supported even Mussolini's fascist politics.

"But things changed as *Il Duce* aligned himself more and more with Hitler. At first, he ridiculed and condemned Hitler's racist policies. But after the debacle of the Ethiopian War and Mussolini's increasing expansionist tendencies, he became more and more dependent on Hitler and his army against the Allied forces.

"I'm sorry, I'm bombarding you with historical facts. You're not here for a lecture on Italian history or politics. I tend to get carried away. This era was my specialty when teaching at the university, and now it continues to be my interest."

"But it *is* interesting," Andreas assured him. "And it's something I know very little about. All I remember from my history lessons in school about that time was what happened in Germany and how it affected Switzerland."

"As an Italian," Luisa said, "I should know our history, but to be honest, I know very little about that time as well."

"Well, it's not something we generally dwell on," Giancarlo said. "It's a rather inglorious time in Italian history and politics, and I have to add, one of the many rather shameful political periods." He waved his hand in a dismissive gesture.

"But let's get back to our refugee. As I said, December 1943 was a time of great danger for Jewish people. So, it's no surprise that Joshua had to flee. The sad part is that he seemed to have made it into Switzerland and then had that tragic accident."

He moved his finger over the map and pointed at an area northeast of Milano that bordered Switzerland. "That's the general area where some of the refugees were led across the mountains," he said. "It was a treacherous climb, above all in winter, with the danger of avalanches and unsafe paths."

"That's just south of the area I hike in." Andreas pointed at the map. "It's not too far from where I live. Here is the border between Switzerland and Italy, and here is where I found Joshua's things. From there, I can see Italy."

Giancarlo checked the address on the envelope Andreas gave him, then pointed at the name Quercia on the map. "That's the town. Now the question is, where would the family be today?" He scratched his short beard. "As you mentioned, the address is a post office box, so Bella … is that the woman's name? Yes, so Bella would've picked up the letter there. She could've lived in the town or nearby."

Andreas' heart began to beat faster. "I just wonder if we can find out if there are any family members or relatives left."

"All you can do is drive to Quercia and try to find the post office," Giancarlo suggested. "Perhaps ask around. It's worth a try."

Luisa and Andreas looked at each other. "What are we waiting for?" Luisa said.

"What an adventure." Sonia had come into the room with more espresso and sweets. "I wish I could join you, but I'm too old for chasing all over Italy."

Luisa laughed. "We'll keep you informed."

"Yes, definitely," Andreas said. "And thanks for your help and hospitality. I'm getting really excited."

A few minutes later, Giancarlo collected the map and papers and put them on his desk. Luisa and Andreas helped Sonia carry the coffee cups, glasses, and the rest of the dishes into the kitchen. Luisa wanted to help Sonia clean up in the kitchen, but Sonia waved her away. "Not necessary. I have a dishwasher." She put the dishes into the dishwasher, added soap, and turned it on. "See? All done." She smiled. "We live in an old villa, but I insisted on a modern kitchen."

Luisa smiled, then suppressed a yawn. "Tired?" Sonia asked.

"A little," Luisa admitted. "Tomorrow will be an action-packed day, right?" She smiled at Andreas.

He checked his watch. "Yes, we should turn in soon, I think. If that's all right with you?" He turned to Sonia.

"Oh, yes, we're at an age where we go to bed early," Sonia said. "The days of staying up past midnight are long gone for us. But please help yourself to anything you need during the night."

In one of the guest rooms, Andreas unpacked a few items from his suitcase. He put his shaving utensils, and toothpaste and brush into his private bath. Sitting on the bed, he tapped the speed dial number for Emilia on his phone.

"Hi, Papa." Andreas heard laughter in the background.

"Did you have a good drive?" he asked.

"Yes, as you know, I'm spending the night with Tonio and Mario. Tonio said he was going to drive with me to Switzerland tomorrow. He'll take the train back to Milano."

"Oh, good, I'm glad you don't have to drive by yourself." Andreas hesitated. "Have you heard anything from Peter … about Pietro?" He felt guilty for leaving him for so long, and he missed him.

Emilia laughed. "He is very happy. From what I heard Peter is spoiling him rotten. You may have to train him all over again."

Andreas smiled. "That's okay as long as he's happy."

"So how are you doing?" Emilia asked.

"We're fine. We're staying at Luisa's uncle's tonight. He and his wife are very helpful. They're wonderful people. Tomorrow, we're going to check out a town called Quercia on Lake Como. That's the town with the post office box the letter was addressed to."

Andreas heard Emilia clear her throat. "How is Luisa?"

"She's fine, very excited to find out more about the mystery letter."

"Okay, well good luck with it. Keep me informed."

"I will. I'll let you know as soon as we find something. Sleep well, and tell Tonio to drive carefully tomorrow."

Chapter 17

The following morning, Andreas joined his hosts for a breakfast of papaya, fresh rolls, butter, cheese, and jam. He poured himself a cup of coffee as Luisa walked into the room. She wore a sunny smile and her eyes sparkled.

"Good morning." Her voice vibrated with excitement. "I have news."

"Good ones, I hope?" Sonia said.

"Yes, surprising but good. In about seven months, I'm going to be a nonna. Julietta is pregnant."

"Wow. That is great news," Giancarlo said.

"Yes, I was a little concerned about her," Luisa said. "She's been in a strange mood the past few days. I was worried that she and Adam had disagreements. Julietta is normally not a moody person. Now, we know it's hormones." She sat and reached for a roll.

Andreas smiled at her. "That's wonderful. You said they were going to stay in Italy a few more months until Adam's project is finished. So, you think she might have the baby here?"

"They don't know yet," Luisa said. "I guess the whole thing is a surprise for them. Of course, I'd love for Julietta to have the baby here. But I'll have to leave it up to them."

"Well, this calls for a sip of Prosecco." Giancarlo got up and went into the kitchen.

"You know we have to drive," Andreas called after him.

Giancarlo came back with a bottle. "Just a little sip. It won't hurt you. We must celebrate the new baby." He poured them each a small glass of the bubbly wine. They all lifted their glasses. "To the new baby and to Mamma, Papa, and Nonna," Giancarlo said.

A little later, Andreas and Luisa said goodbye to their hosts before beginning their drive to Quercia. Luisa promised to come back soon for another visit, and Giancarlo insisted on them telling him if they found anything.

"And if you have questions, you know I'm more than happy to help if I can," he said to Andreas.

"Give our love to Julietta and Adam," Sonia said as she waved goodbye. "And let us know if it's going to be a boy or a girl."

"We will," Luisa called, as she and Andreas drove away.

Leaving the busy streets of Milano, they drove through more peaceful and pleasant countryside. Andreas took a deep breath. "I don't know how people manage to drive in this crazy traffic."

Luisa lifted a shoulder. "You get used to it. Though I have to admit I prefer the smaller towns of Tuscany, but I do love the countryside of the Lombardy region. You know Lake Como, right?"

"Yes, I've been there on vacation once," Andreas said. "It's a beautiful area."

"Well, from what I know, Quercia is on the southeast side of the lake," Luisa explained. "Have you ever been to Bergamo?"

"Once, but I was just driving through. I didn't have time to look around," Andreas said. "But from the little I saw, it's a beautiful city."

"We could check it out," Luisa suggested. "It's a detour, but we have time. I think it would be worth it."

"Sounds good," Andreas said.

When they arrived in Bergamo an hour later, they drove to the old part of the city, the *citta alta*, which was on a hill overlooking the rest of the town, the valley, and the mountains in the background. After Luisa parked the car at the side of the road, they took a walk along the narrow cobblestone streets through town. At one of the piazzas, they sat down on the patio of a cafeteria and ordered coffee and lemonade. They relaxed for a while, enjoying the view of the castle and of the town below with its rustic reddish-brown stone houses, the window ledges with baskets of flowers, and the ever-present churches and cathedrals.

"It's a beautiful town and countryside," Andreas said. "It must have been so difficult for Joshua and the other refugees to leave all this behind."

"Yes," Luisa agreed. "And not knowing if they could ever come back again. Not knowing where they would end up." She hesitated, then checked her watch. "But we better leave. Perhaps we can have a closer look at Bergamo on our way back."

After another hour's drive on highways and country roads, they saw the sign to Quercia. They decided to stop at the post office first and then look for a hotel.

Quercia was a small town right on a hill above Lake Como. Unlike its larger neighbor, Lecco, it didn't give the feeling of a tourist place. A small building at the town square housed the post office. It was almost empty. The only other person at the counter was an old woman, dressed in a black top and skirt with a black scarf covering her hair. She was in the process of leaving and glanced at them with an inquisitive look, probably wondering who these strangers were.

They went up to the counter where a skinny, middle-aged man sat, shuffling through some papers.

"Scusi, signore," Luisa addressed him. "We hope you can help us locate a person who seemed to have had a post office box here a long time ago … during World War II. This letter was addressed to someone here." She put the copy of the letter and envelope on the counter and pointed at the address on the envelope. "This looks like a post office box. The letter was never sent because we believe the man who wrote it died before he was able to mail it."

The skinny man stared at them with his watery gray eyes, as though he had two lunatics in front of them. He looked sideways as if searching for someone else who could defend him against two obviously crazy intruders. "World War II?" he exclaimed, then stared at the envelope and the piece of paper in front of him. He looked at the letter without touching it as if he was afraid it would bite him.

"This was more than seventy years ago," he croaked. "How would I know now? I'm sure we don't have any documents about mailboxes from that time." He moved the letter toward Luisa.

She pushed it right back. "Read the letter. This is a letter written by a young refugee who fled to Switzerland. He wrote it to his young and pregnant wife who must have lived somewhere around here. The young man was never able to mail the letter."

Luisa fixed the man with an imploring look. "Don't you think the woman it was addressed to or her family, the ones who are still alive, deserve to know the truth, that their father or grandfather loved them, that the reason they didn't hear from him was because something terrible happened to him? Imagine you were the child and had no idea who your father really was. Wouldn't you want to know?"

Andreas suppressed a smile. Luisa sure knew how to appeal to the man's emotions.

The man hesitated, scratched his balding head, and measured them quietly with a thoughtful look, then lowered his eyes. "I don't know who my father is, either." It was quiet for a while, then he sighed. "Okay, let me do some research. Come back tomorrow. I can't promise anything though. He wrote down the address, the names, and the date.

"Thank you so much. I'm sorry to hear about your father," Luisa said. He gave a quick sad smile.

Once outside, Andreas chuckled. "You can be very persuasive."

Luisa smiled. "Well, you know, Italians respond to love stories, in particular to tragic ones."

"Something might come of it," Andreas said.

"It's a good first step." Luisa glanced at the lake at the bottom of the hill. "Wouldn't it have been easier to flee across Lago di Como and then escape that way to Switzerland?" she wondered.

"I'm sure the refugees considered it, Andreas said. "Don't forget though, by that time the border into Switzerland was most likely closed. So they had to find more hidden roads."

Luisa nodded. They got into the car and drove to one of the few hotels in town. They found an old but clean and comfortable pension. It was located in one of the back streets away from traffic and fairly quiet. The hotel looked as if it had once been a private home. Their rooms had a connecting door and were on the ground floor facing a small plot of grass and a narrow road. They had a view of a pine forest and the mountains in the distance.

They checked in, left their luggage in the rooms, then went out for something to eat. It was a little after lunchtime and there was a trattoria-style restaurant and a bar nearby. They chose the restaurant.

It was fairly dark inside. Only a group of older men occupied one table. They turned around as Andreas and Luisa entered and measured them with intense looks.

"They don't seem to be too happy having strangers here," Andreas said in a low voice.

Luisa smiled. "They'll get used to us."

Andreas locked eyes with one of the men, who frowned, then averted his eyes. After they sat at a table near the small window where it was a little lighter, the men began to talk in low voices in what Andreas assumed was a local dialect.

The waitress, a roundish woman with bleached-blond hair asked them in a gruff voice what they wanted. Luisa gave her a friendly smile and asked for the menus. There weren't any. Instead, the waitress listed the one meal they served, a pasta dish to start, then beef or fish with vegetables. They both opted for fish.

"What to drink?" the waitress asked, a little more friendly now, thinking perhaps of her tip.

"Let's have some wine," Andreas suggested. They were in Italy after all, one of the wine countries of Europe.

"House wine okay?" Luisa asked him. "It's usually the best choice."

"Sounds good." Andreas said.

"A bottle of your red house wine," Luisa said to the waitress, who now seemed to have softened and gave them a smile. "*Certo, signora.*"

The food was good, a simple family-style meal, flavorful with herbs and spices. The wine too wasn't anything fancy, but it was smooth and complemented the dish.

After the meal, they ordered an espresso and a glass of grappa. Andreas took a sip of the strong liquor and leaned back in his chair. "This feels like another vacation."

"It does; you're right," Luisa said.

"Well, you deserve one, you work hard at the vineyard and as hostess. We really had a great time at Vignaverde." Andreas finished his espresso.

"It's hard work during the growing season, but Edoardo and his family do most of the heavy-duty work. I'm the hostess and I enjoy it. The guests we have are nice people like you." She smiled and lifted her glass of grappa. "You know, people interested in agriculture, winemaking, and ecotourism."

Andreas admired Luisa's handsome face, her bronze cheeks a little flushed from the wine.

Chapter 18

In the evening, Andreas and Luisa decided to take a walk through town. They strolled along one of the cobblestone roads down to the lake. Sitting on one of the benches along the boardwalk, they watched the sun set, leaving a band of purple on the horizon. Andreas took a deep breath, inhaling the fresh air floating up from the water. Once the sun had disappeared behind the mountains on the other side of the lake, the water reflected the lights of the boats on the lake and the streetlamps along the border.

"Beautiful," Luisa said. As she turned her face toward him, her eyes sparkled in the fading light of the evening.

Warmth spread through Andreas' chest. He smiled at her. "Yes," he said and didn't mean just the landscape.

As it got darker, they rose and walked up the hill to the main piazza of the town, which was flanked by old houses, a building that looked like the city hall, the obligatory church, and a bar. The patio in front of the bar was shaded by two large old-looking oak trees which may have given the town its name. A few men were drinking beer and liquor.

Andreas was used to their measuring and stern looks by now. He raised his hand. "*Buona sera.*" They kept staring, but one of them, an older guy with curly white hair and a white beard, lifted his hand in greeting.

"What about an espresso?" Andreas asked Luisa.

"Sounds good," Luisa said. They sat at a table on the patio. A waiter came out and they placed their order. After the waiter brought their coffee, they sat quietly, enjoying the pleasantly cool evening after a hot day. Andreas felt relaxed and was getting sleepy. He glanced at Luisa and smiled when he saw her suppressing a yawn.

"You must be tired after the long drive," he said.

"A little yes," she admitted. "We should turn in early. I hope we'll find some information from the man at the post office tomorrow."

"Yes, so do I." Andreas took the last sip of his coffee. He waved the waiter over and paid.

It took Andreas a while to fall asleep. He was thinking back to the exciting time he'd had with Luisa since they had left Vignaverde and realized that he had hardly thought of Karla. It shocked him; he felt guilty as if he were betraying her. Usually, she was on his mind at least once a day, normally when he woke up and before falling asleep. Although thinking of her wasn't as painful as it had been the past three years, she was still a vivid presence in his life. He knew he would never forget her, but he had to admit, having Luisa as a companion made his heart feel light and even joyful. He felt increasingly attracted to her. Would she return his feelings? He doubted it.

Though she was warm and friendly, he didn't feel she was interested in a romantic relationship. No wonder, with her bad luck with men, her failed marriage, and unhappy love affair with her American boyfriend. He'd better curb his emerging passion, or he would end up with a broken heart again. *I'm a fool. I'm finally getting over my grief for Karla. Why would I throw myself into another situation that would just add more pain? Better just settle for friendship.*

The next thing he was conscious of was a sun ray that had landed on his face. He looked at his watch. It was still early, but the sun was just rising. He realized he had fallen asleep thinking about two women. It seemed kind of humorous in

119

hindsight. He got up, took a quick shower, and shaved, then listened at the connecting door to Luisa's room. When he heard footsteps, he gently tapped the door with his knuckle. Luisa, still in her bathrobe, opened it and smiled at him.

"I'm going downstairs to get some coffee," he said. "Want me to bring you some?"

"Give me a few minutes," she said. "We can go to a coffee shop or coffee bar; coffee is usually better there than in the hotel."

"Okay, good. I'll wait outside."

In front of the hotel, Andreas looked across the street at the forest and mountains. It was a pleasant morning, cool, even a little nippy. Soon Luisa joined him, and after a quick breakfast of fruit, rolls, and coffee at the coffee bar nearby, they went back to the post office, only to realize that it wasn't open yet.

"What was I thinking?" Luisa slapped her forehead. "This is Italy after all. Well, let's do another quick sightseeing. Let's check out the church. Perhaps, there's something to see there."

Andreas agreed, and they walked across the piazza to the small church. It had a simple interior with only a few small statues of saints and paintings on the walls. Two older women were praying in the pews. Andreas and Luisa walked to the altar, looked around, then sat on one of the benches. It was peaceful, only the hushed murmuring of the women praying broke the silence. After about fifteen minutes, Luisa got up and Andreas followed her outside.

In the meantime, the post office had opened. It was still empty, and fortunately the man they had talked to was there. His name was Emilio, as he'd told them during their first visit.

"I don't have much." He put a slip of paper with a name and address on the counter. "I haven't been able to find any name associated with that box yet. No wonder, it was too long ago. But this man, Lorenzo, is in his eighties and he was one of the few people who lived here at about that time. He may be able to give you more information. He may know something. In the meantime, I'll continue to see if I can find anything about the mailbox."

"Thank you for your help," Luisa said.

Outside, they looked at the slip of paper with the name and address. There was a phone number as well, but Luisa felt it would be better to go there in person. They walked uphill along a small cobblestone path to the address on the note. The house they found was small but surrounded by a lush garden. Some of the shutters were closed. "It looks as if nobody is home." Andreas felt disappointed.

They knocked on the door and waited, but nothing happened. They stepped back a little and looked up at the windows. Andreas felt he saw a curtain move a little but wasn't sure. "Let's try again." He went back to knock on the door, but again in vain. As he glanced across the street, he saw someone step out of the house on the other side. The woman looked at them, then turned and went back inside.

Just as they were about to leave, the door did open, and an elderly woman stood on the threshold. She didn't step outside. Luisa showed her the slip of paper.

"We are looking for Lorenzo."

The woman stared at them, then glanced at the paper. "Who gave you this name?" She seemed suspicious.

Luisa explained that they received it from the post office and that they had a few questions about a family who lived here during the Second World War. "Emilio at the post office told us that Lorenzo had been around at this time."

It must have been the wrong thing to say. "He isn't home," the woman said in a gruff voice and all but slammed the door in their face.

"When will he be home?" Luisa called through the closed door. No answer.

Luisa and Andreas looked at each other. "Of all the places and people I've encountered in Italy, the citizens of this town are the most unfriendly I've ever met," Andreas muttered.

"I agree," Luisa said. "Very strange. I think we should talk to Emilio again. Perhaps he could introduce us personally."

They walked back to the post office. Fortunately, Emilio was still there. When they explained what happened, he lifted a shoulder. "People here are very hesitant to talk about the war."

"But why?" Andreas asked.

Emilio lifted a shoulder. "Perhaps they feel guilty. Don't forget, some of the people collaborated with the Nazis, and some were part of the resistance."

"But that was so long ago," Andreas said.

Another shrug. "Well, I'll give Lorenzo a call. Come back in about an hour."

"Thanks for your help," Luisa said.

"Now what?" Andreas said as they stepped outside. He looked around. "Not much to see. Let's walk down to the lake again."

They strolled down the hill to the boardwalk. Andreas pointed at a cafeteria next to the lake. "What about another cup of coffee?"

They sat down and ordered an espresso. The waiter brought it with a slice of lemon rind and sugar. "Espresso in Italy is the best," Andreas said as he sipped the fragrant liquid.

They relaxed in the now warm sun, admiring Lake Como and the picturesque towns along its border. The surface of the lake shimmered like diamonds in the sun. Andreas pointed across the lake. "Switzerland is not far from here." He glanced at Luisa. "Have you ever been there?"

"No, I've always wanted to, though. I really haven't been outside of Italy, except visiting Julietta in California."

"Well, perhaps you can visit me and my family one of these days," Andreas suggested. "It's not far, really."

"Yes, perhaps," Luisa said in a matter-of-fact voice. "But now we better go back to the post office."

They paid and walked back up the hill. When they approached Emilio again, he waved at them from behind the counter. "Go back. He's waiting for you."

When they walked up the steps to the patio of the house, an old but fit-looking man was waiting for them outside. He looked familiar, and Andreas tried to remember where he had seen him. Lorenzo measured them with piercing eyes. "You want to know about the Second World War? Are you journalists?"

"No, not at all." Andreas now remembered why he looked familiar. He was one of the men sitting on the patio of the bar they had visited the night before, the one who had raised his hand in greeting. Andreas pulled out the letter and explained how he found it in a cave in Switzerland. "We just want to find the woman or her family it was addressed to. So, they know what happened."

Lorenzo read the letter. His eyes widened. "My God," he said, then invited them inside.

Chapter 19

When Andreas and Luisa entered the living room of Lorenzo's home, Andreas looked around surprised. The room was modestly but tastefully furnished with simple but sturdy wooden bookcases filled with books, a coffee table covered with colorful tiles next to a few easy chairs. What attracted his attention, though, were paintings on the walls in a modern style which reminded him of Karla's work. He walked up to one to look at it more closely. Lorenzo joined him.

"These are beautiful," Andreas said.

Lorenzo smiled. "Our granddaughter is an artist."

"My wife was a painter." Andreas brushed through his hair and continued to admire the art. "These pictures remind me of her paintings. They are different, but she painted in a similar style."

"You talk of your wife in the past," Lorenzo said.

Andreas gave a quick nod. "She died three years ago."

"Sorry to hear that." Lorenzo's eyes expressed warmth.

Luisa joined them. She pointed at the coffee table with the mosaic top. "Did your granddaughter make this as well?"

"Yes," Lorenzo stated with a proud smile.

"Gorgeous," Luisa said.

"Thank you." He invited them to sit. "Would you like something to drink? Espresso or tea?"

"Espresso sounds great," Luisa said, and Andreas nodded.

He wondered about the whereabouts of the unfriendly woman who had slammed the door in their face. Was she Lorenzo's wife?

Lorenzo opened the door to what looked like a kitchen and said something to someone, then came back in. He sat in one of the easy chairs. "My wife will be right with us. She wants to know about the letter too," he said.

At that moment, a woman carrying a tray with cups of espresso, a jug of milk or cream, and a plate with cookies came inside. Lorenzo got up and helped her put the tray down and handed them cups of coffee. Andreas was relieved to see that it wasn't the rude woman from earlier. This one, called Maria, gave them a friendly smile.

At Lorenzo's prompting, Andreas told them how he found the letter during a hike in the Swiss mountains, how with the help of friends at the police station and the library, he was able to find out that Joshua, the writer of the letter, had fallen to his death before being able to mail it.

Lorenzo and Maria looked at each other. "That's so sad," Maria said.

"Do you know the family, the person the letter was addressed to?" Luisa asked. "As you can see from the envelope, it was addressed to a Bella Goldman."

"I didn't live here at the time." Lorenzo pointed to the date. "I was a kid; my parents and I moved here shortly after the war. But I heard of the family. Nobody really talked about what happened to them. The only thing I heard as a boy was that a Jewish man from the village had fled, and that the Nazis punished the family for harboring him."

"Does that mean this Bella, the wife of Joshua, was hurt or even killed?" Andreas asked with a sinking heart.

"This I don't know for sure, but I think she was able to flee as well."

"Would Aurelio know?" Maria asked her husband. "He is in his eighties, and he was here during the war."

"Yes, that's possible. You're right. I didn't even think about him. You should ask him. Now there is a man with a reputation." Lorenzo sounded excited. "He was a youngster during the war, but from what I heard, he worked for the resistance. He told me some amazing stories about how he was delivering messages to people in the resistance. It was an extremely dangerous thing to do, and he could easily have been killed." Lorenzo smoothed his beard. "The soldiers didn't just punish the resistance fighters if they caught them. They took it out on their families. Men, women, and children were mowed down in the cruelest ways to show the citizens what would happen to them if they betrayed the Nazis." He gave a long sigh. "It must have been horrible."

They were quiet for a while, then Andreas faced Lorenzo. "When we came here earlier, a woman answered the door. She wasn't very friendly and seemed upset with us for asking about Joshua's family."

Lorenzo chuckled. "That was Elena. She is a distrustful woman. She cleans for us occasionally." Then he became serious. "Actually, come to think of it, her family was around during the war. She was a child then, like me, but her family had quite a reputation from what I remember. The rumor was they cozied up to the invaders, the Nazis."

"Could it be that this was the reason she was so cold and hostile?" Luisa asked.

Maria and Lorenzo glanced at each other. "Possibly," Lorenzo said. "People don't like to talk about that time, in particular those who have something to hide. There were people who denounced the Jews to the Nazis, people who sold their fellow citizens for money. There was a bounty on the heads of Jewish people." Lorenzo's brows knitted.

"But at the same time, there were many Italians who hid Jewish people, who risked their lives to help them. And those who smuggled them to and across the border into Switzerland.

"Then there were those who were terrified, who simply tried to survive." Lorenzo rubbed his forehead. "I'm grateful I wasn't old enough to have to make such a terrible decision, to either hide and conform or risk my life and the life of my family." He gave a short bitter laugh.

"In hindsight, it's easy to judge what was right or wrong. At the time, it wasn't that easy."

Andreas nodded. "You're right. I, too, am glad, I never had to make such a fateful choice." He hesitated. "Well, we're very grateful for your help. May we tell Aurelio that you sent us? Perhaps, he would trust us more that way."

"He's a good man, but yes, tell him I sent you," Lorenzo said. He picked up a pen and a small notebook, ripped out a piece of paper, and wrote down an address which he handed to Andreas. "In fact, I'll let him know to expect you."

After finishing their coffee, they thanked Lorenzo and Maria for their help, then walked back to the hotel.

"See, not all the villagers are rude," Luisa said.

"You're right. I shouldn't judge them too early." Andreas' forehead furrowed. "Now I really hope Bella survived."

"So do I," Luisa said. "I can barely wait to talk to this Aurelio." She glanced at her watch. "But I think we should wait until tomorrow."

"Yes, that way Lorenzo has time to prepare him for our visit." Andreas rubbed his chin. "You know I'm learning a whole lot about the history of World War II, at least some of what was going on in Italy."

"So am I," Luisa said. "People don't really want to deal with it anymore, so we don't talk about it."

"How was your family affected by it?" Andreas asked.

"Well, I was born quite a while after the war," Luisa said. "My parents were children or youngsters. Every once in a while, my mother would remind me how much better I have it, how much harder life was. You know, when I complained about something, or I wanted something I couldn't have she'd say, 'When I was your age, we were happy to have one meal a day, no ice cream.' Of course, I don't know how much of that was true."

Andreas chortled. "Well, I guess that's something parents tell their children all over the world. That reminds me, I promised to call Emilia with an update on 'our quest' as she called it. Let's go and have lunch somewhere."

Luisa motioned at the trattoria where they had eaten before. They sat at a table outside and ordered their lunch menu—chicken marsala, risotto, and salad—and a bottle of the house wine.

While waiting for their food, Andreas pulled out his phone and tapped the speed dial button for Emilia. When she answered, Andreas heard Pietro bark in the background. "Hi sweetie, what's the matter with Pietro?"

Emilia laughed. "He's ready for his walk, trying to pull down the leash hanging by the door."

"Okay, give him a kiss from me. I just wanted to let you know what's going on with our search." He told her about their visit with Lorenzo and his wife and what they had learned.

"God, this sounds more and more fascinating," Emilia said. "Now I wish I was there."

"I'll keep you informed as soon as we hear something new," Andreas said. They talked for a while, and when Andreas asked her about work, Emilia seemed to hesitate.

"Everything is okay," she said, sounding somewhat subdued.

"How is Peter?" Andreas wanted to know.

Silence, then, "He's okay." A matter-of-fact statement.

Andreas felt she wanted to say more, but since she didn't elaborate, he let it go. "All right, take care of yourself. I'll call you again soon."

"Okay, Papa, say hello to Luisa."

Andreas' forehead furrowed. He slipped his phone into his pocket. "I think my daughter is in love with her fellow veterinarian, but he may not return her feelings."

"Unrequited love?" Luisa asked.

"Not sure, but it's a little hard to talk about it over the phone. I don't want to sound like the worried father. I'm sure she'll share when she's ready."

Chapter 20

Yes, we'll go for a walk." Emilia rubbed Pietro's ears. She had just finished feeding him and had enjoyed a light dinner herself—homemade soup, salad, and a piece of focaccia with olives and tomatoes.

"Let's go, Pietro." Emilia grabbed the dog's leash. Whereas Pietro expressed his excitement by turning in circles and pulling his mistress toward to door, Emilia was more subdued. She was thinking of Peter, musing about their relationship. They were friends, but Emilia wanted to take it beyond friendship. She was in love with him and sensed he had feelings for her as well. They often went out after work for a drink or coffee and talked about the clinic and Peter's plan to add a rescue operation to the business. He wanted Emilia to be in charge of it. They had animated discussions about all kinds of things. Peter often looked at her with a loving expression in his eyes. There were sparks between them, weren't there? Or was it only Emilia who felt this attraction? Was she kidding herself? She didn't have a lot of experience with boyfriends. The past few years, she had been so busy studying veterinary medicine and preparing for her exams that her social life had taken a backseat.

At first, she had been reluctant to admit her feelings for Peter, thinking that a romantic relationship with her working partner was a risk. She didn't want to jeopardize her job if it didn't work out. But the longer she was around him, the more she was attracted to him, but his behavior toward her confused her. It seemed to her that whenever there was a moment to get closer, he withdrew as if taking a step back emotionally.

Peter was a good-looking man with reddish brown hair and deep blue eyes. He was tall, trim, and always full of energy. Once in a while though, she caught him looking sad. One thing that puzzled her was his reluctance to speak about his family. Emilia had told him about her father and siblings. Peter was a good listener, but whenever she asked him about his family, in particular about his father, he hesitated. He talked lovingly about his mother. He had also told her how lucky she was to have such a close relationship with her father. He mentioned that he and his father didn't get along, but again, he didn't elaborate, and Emilia didn't want to pressure him.

Pietro's barking at a squirrel that raced up a tree pulled Emilia out of her musing. *I just have to let it go.* She felt she had given Peter enough clues that she really liked him. It was now up to him to react. Perhaps it was better for their working relationship if they remained just friends.

She checked her watch. "Come on, Pietro. Perhaps Marianne will join us for a walk." Pietro's tail wagged enthusiastically. As Emilia was about to pass the inn where she and Peter had eaten lunch, she saw him. He came out of the grocery store, and Emilia was just about to call him when a young woman with long blond hair walked toward him. He smiled at her, put his arm around her, and pulled her close. They kept walking the other way, seemingly engaged in a lively discussion. Emilia's heart skipped a beat. She stopped Pietro and waited. She didn't recognize the woman, since she only saw her from behind, but it was obvious that the two loved each other. Just before the couple turned the corner toward Peter's apartment, he kissed the young woman. It was a kiss on the cheek, but Emilia felt as if someone had punched her in the stomach.

Now, she understood. Peter had a girlfriend. "Why did I never think of this?" she murmured. Pietro gave her a questioning look and pulled on the leash. And why did he never mention anything? She knew he didn't talk much about his family, but a girlfriend? He must have been aware of at least some of her feelings for him. She turned around and walked in the opposite direction trying to stem the flood of tears that threatened to escape. She took deep breaths. "I'm so stupid," she muttered. "Let's go, Pietro. We'll go on a hike up the mountain."

She walked through town as if in a daze, barely aware of people around her. When someone called her, she waved a quick hello and continued past her house and up the hill toward Via Spluga. She remembered that this was the road her father usually took on his hikes. She stopped as Pietro eagerly sniffed the many smells at the side of the road. Looking around at the fields, the pine woods, and the mountains in the distance, she could understand the attraction of a hike in nature when depressed or worried. She wasn't depressed, just sad and angry at herself for overlooking the obvious, namely that Peter wasn't interested in her as a girlfriend. She was also angry at him for being so secretive about his relationships. They were friends after all; why didn't he ever mention a girlfriend?

Emilia's mind was in turmoil. Her canine friend, however, had the time of his life running around, exploring holes in the field along the road. A dark cloud blocked out the sun, its shadow racing across the grass. Emilia checked the sky and noticed that the weather was changing. Looking around, she realized she had hiked quite far, forgetting about the time. It was eight o'clock in the evening and with the sunlight gone, the sky darkened fast. A wind kicked up.

Letter from a Cave

Emilia called Pietro who was digging a hole in the field. She walked toward him, trying to get his attention. A stone caught her foot; she tumbled and fell in an awkward way, twisting her ankle.

"Darn it." She tried to stand up, but her leg hurt too much, so she sat in the grass. Pietro came rushing to her. He looked at her worried and licked her hand while she was rubbing her foot and leg. She hugged him. "It's not your fault, I'm just clumsy ... or preoccupied. But what am I going to do now?" Fortunately, her phone had a connection. She tried to think of people she could call. Peter was the first one she thought of, but she certainly didn't want to call him. He was probably busy with his girlfriend. She gave a bitter laugh. "Yes, I'm jealous." She decided to try Marianne, but her call went to voice mail and she didn't want to leave a message. It was getting late, and her friend was probably out. She tried a couple of more people but to no avail. "Oh, Pietro, I feel so alone. I wish Papa was here." But he was traveling through Italy with an attractive woman, trying to find Bella. Emilia sighed.

More licks from Pietro. Finally, she gave in and called Peter. A woman answered his phone. Emilia almost hung up. This was getting worse and worse. "Hello?" the woman asked a second time.

"Hi, this is Emilia ... is Peter there?"

"Yes, he is, just a moment." The voice was friendly.

"Emilia?" Peter asked. "What's happening?"

"I'm so sorry for interrupting your evening." *Actually, I'm not sorry at all. Serves you right.* "I feel so stupid. I went for a walk with Pietro up Via Spluga. I fell and twisted my ankle. I tried to call some friends, but I couldn't get a hold of anyone. It's late and there is nobody around who could help me. I'm so sorry."

"Oh, Emilia, are you badly hurt?" At least he sounded concerned.

"I hope it's just a twisted ankle, not broken, but I can't really walk that far."

"Let me know where you are. I'll be right there."

Emilia described her location. Peter called something to someone in the background, probably his girlfriend.

"We're leaving right now. Don't worry, we'll be right there."

"Thanks, Peter." *We? Is he bringing his girlfriend along*?

"Okay, Pietro. The knight in shining armor will arrive shortly … with his maiden." Emilia snorted. "Yes, I'm being ridiculous."

Pietro, however, didn't mind. He continued to lick Emilia's hands, and it felt comforting. "At least I still have you." She put her arm around him and held him close.

Chapter 21

Twenty minutes later, Peter and the young woman Emilia had seen him with earlier arrived. By then, it was almost dark. Pietro recognized Peter and raced toward him, wagging his tail.

"How come you're in the middle of the field?" Peter asked as he was walking toward Emilia.

"I rushed after Pietro, who was digging a hole in the grass, and then I slipped."

"So, Pietro is the culprit." Peter knelt down and rubbed the dog behind the ear. The young woman came closer and bent down to check out Emilia's ankle. She gently touched it. "Does that hurt?"

Emilia nodded. "A little."

"I don't think it's broken," the woman said to Peter, "but it's probably a good idea to get an x-ray."

Who is this woman? A doctor? Emilia felt irritated again.

As if Peter guessed her thoughts, he put his hand on the young woman's shoulder. "By the way, I don't think you two have met. This is my sister, Anna. She lives in Lindau and is here for a visit. She's a doctor."

"Oh ... I see." Emilia was glad they couldn't see her probably bright red face in the gathering darkness. She'd never felt more embarrassed and stupid. Of course, Peter had mentioned a sister once who lived on the German side of Lake Constance. *What a complete fool I am.*

135

"Pleased to meet you." Emilia hoped her facial color was back to normal again. "Peter mentioned you, but I didn't realize you were a doctor." *And not his girlfriend.*

"Well, let's get you home, Emilia," Peter said. He and Anna helped her up and supported her as she hopped on one leg toward the road. "You know I think it's easier if I just carry you."

"I might be too heavy. Are you sure?" Emilia blushed again.

"Heavy?" Peter laughed. "You're light as a feather. It's just a short distance. We can drive you home."

"Why don't you drop me off at your apartment?" Anna said to Peter. "I think I have something for the pain that I can give Emilia. By tomorrow, we should know more, and then she can get an X-ray just to be sure it's not broken."

"Thank you so much. You're so kind, and I ruined your evening." Emilia felt more than a little guilty.

"No, you didn't. We had no special plans." Peter lifted her up and carried her to the car. "Come on, Pietro." The dog, all excited from all the attention, stayed close to Emilia.

"Why don't I keep Pietro with me for the night, so you don't have to worry about him?" Peter suggested.

"That would be great. Thanks, Peter. I hate to cause all this trouble."

"No trouble at all. You know I love to have my little namesake, and he's used to me," Peter said.

On the way to Emilia's house, Peter stopped to drop Anna off at his apartment above the veterinary practice.

"Why don't you bring my crutches along as well," Peter said to Anna. "You know the ones I used years ago when I broke my leg. I think they're still in my hall closet."

"Great idea," Anna said.

"I feel so stupid." Emilia meant it in more than one way.

"Well, this can happen to anybody," Peter said. "I just wonder what you were doing up at Via Spluga so late."

You don't want to know. "I just needed a nice long walk ... to clear my head," she said. "It's the place from where my father always starts his hikes." She snickered. "Wait til he hears about this. I've always given him hell for going on these long hikes and spending the night outside. At least he always made it home without help, while I ..." She laughed. "I'm so sorry."

"Hey, don't beat yourself up. I'm glad you called me." Peter gently touched her arm and gave it a reassuring squeeze, which sent a spike of energy through her body.

At that moment, Anna came back with a bottle of painkillers and Peter's crutches. She handed Emilia the bottle. "These are pretty strong; they should help you sleep."

"You know I should check on our newest patient," Peter said to Emilia.

"You mean Flick?" Emilia said. "You're right. I almost forgot about him. I meant to check on him before going home, but then I got sidetracked by my adventurous hike."

"I'll do that and have Anna drive you home if that's all right. Anna, can you help Emilia into the house?"

"No problem," Anna said. She scooted into the driver's seat after Peter got out of the car.

"Come on, Pietro. You're going to have a little vacation at my place tonight." Peter lifted Pietro out of the car.

"Thanks, Peter. I hope I can make it to work tomorrow," Emilia said.

"Don't even think about it. You should see the doctor first, get an X-ray and find out what's wrong with your foot. I can manage on my own for a while."

Emilia moved her foot around. "It actually feels a little better already. I bet you it'll be okay tomorrow."

"You should take it easy anyway," Anna suggested. "A twisted ankle, even if it's not broken, can take a while to heal. One of us can pick you up and take you to the doctor."

"Thank you. Let's see how I feel tomorrow. Fortunately, it's my left foot, so I can drive okay."

Anna drove Emilia home. After they got out of the car, Anna handed Emilia the crutches. After a few attempts, Emilia was able to walk on one leg. Her foot was still painful, but she was able to put a little pressure on it. Emilia handed Anna the key to the house, and Anna opened the door.

"I just want to make sure you have everything," Anna said.

"Sit down." Emilia pointed at the sofa. "Would you like something to drink or to eat. I hope I didn't interrupt your dinner."

"No, we were done," Anna said. "What about you? Have you eaten? Can I make you something?"

"You're so kind, but I'm fine. I had a light meal before going on my adventurous hike." Emilia rolled her eyes. "What about a glass of wine?" All of a sudden, she didn't feel like being alone.

"Hmm." Anna put her finger on her chin. "It's tempting, but I don't think you should have any alcohol if you're taking one of those pills." Anna put the bottle on the coffee table. "I'll take a rain check, though. Let's have a glass together once you don't need the pills anymore."

"Okay, sounds like a deal. What about some tea or water?" Emilia tried again.

"Tea would be nice, but let me make it," Anna said.

"Well, I'm not an invalid but, okay. The tea bags are in the kitchen cabinet above the sink and the mugs right next to them. There's a kettle on the stove."

Anna went into the kitchen and started the kettle. She came back and sat down. "Tea like in England. I went there on vacation last year. Have you been there?"

"Yes, once. My nephew and nieces, the children of my older sister, are there for a while, so I went to London to visit."

The kettle whistled, and Anna got up and brought back two mugs with steaming tea. "Thanks," Emilia said. While sipping their tea and talking, Emilia was able to observe Anna more closely. Now she saw the resemblance to her brother. Anna's hair was blond with a reddish shine, and she also had Peter's deep blue eyes.

"Peter really likes you," Anna said all of a sudden. She took a sip of tea. "He talks a lot about you."

Emilia felt she was blushing again and averted her eyes. "Really?" She took a deep breath. "I like him too … a lot." She felt Anna's eyes on her. Emilia glanced at her, wondering. Was it true? Was Peter really interested in her?

"He's very shy. It's a little hard for him to open up. He's had a somewhat turbulent childhood, lots of fights with Dad."

"He doesn't talk much about his family," Emilia said. "But he did say that he and his father didn't get along."

Anna put her cup down. "Yes, he's close to our mom and to our younger brother, Harry, and me. We get along really well. Dad … he isn't a bad man, not at all, but he comes across as cold sometimes, and he's stubborn." She narrowed her eyes. "And Peter, being the older son, well, Dad was harder on him than on his younger siblings. For a long time, Peter tried to please him, but when our father insisted he take over the farm, Peter fortunately resisted and decided to go his own way. Dad has never forgiven him."

"That's sad," Emilia said.

"Yeah, I know. I hope he comes around one day. I hate the tension in the family. At least, I don't have to deal with it. I live far enough away."

They were quiet for a while, then Anna got up. "I think I should go so you can get some rest. How is the foot?"

Emilia moved it. "Not bad. I'll take one of those pills, before going to bed."

"Sounds good. You have Peter's phone number. Please don't hesitate to call, okay? I'll be here for a few more days." Anna carried the cups into the kitchen and rinsed them out.

"Thank you so much for your help. I'm really happy to have met you." Emilia felt herself blush again, thinking about how she'd misjudged the situation with Peter and Anna.

"I'm happy too," Anna said. "I'll call you tomorrow. Don't forget to call the doctor about the X-ray."

"I will, and we'll have that glass of wine." Emilia tried to get up."

Anna wrinkled her brow. "Can you make it to bed? Shall I help you?"

"Oh, no, I'm fine, really." Just to prove it, Emilia stood and grabbed the crutches. "This was a great idea. I can hardly feel my foot." She accompanied Anna to the door, favoring her good foot and supporting herself with the crutches.

The two women hugged, and Emilia waved a goodbye, then went inside. She sat on the sofa and exhaled deeply. *What a day. I can't believe how wrong I was. Not only is Anna not Peter's girlfriend but a really nice person.* She thought they would become good friends. "You're such a dummy, Emilia," she said to herself. She grabbed the bottle with the painkillers, took one of the pills, washed it down with water, and went to bed.

Lying in bed, she thought about Anna's remark that Peter really liked her, but that he was shy. Perhaps he needed some encouragement? She grinned, feeling the pain medicine take effect, pulling her into a relaxed state of mind and body. "Wait until I tell Papa about falling down on one of his hiking paths. He's going to tease me, I won't hear the end of it," she mumbled as she was slowly falling asleep.

Chapter 22

The morning after their visit to Lorenzo and Maria, Andreas opened the door of his room. As he stepped outside, something rustled under his foot. He looked down at a piece of paper lying on the ground. It must have been put there during the night or in the early morning. He picked it up; something was written on it. As he read the crude handwriting, his jaw clenched.

Stop digging up old stuff. Go away and leave us alone.

He turned the paper over, but aside from the message, there was nothing else. Just as he was about to knock on Luisa's door, she opened it and came outside. He stretched out his hand with the note in it.

"What's this?" she asked.

They both read it again, then looked at each other. "Somebody sure doesn't want us here. What are they afraid of?" Luisa said.

They went to the receptionist and showed him the paper. "Any idea who left this outside my door?" Andreas asked.

The receptionist, a thin man with a balding head, wrinkled his forehead as he read the note. "What's this?" he barked.

"That's what we want to know too," Luisa said.

"No idea." The man looked at them. "Must be a crazy person. What did you do to upset him ... or her?"

"We didn't do anything. We're looking for someone who used to live here a long time ago. Obviously, some people in this village are afraid of what we may find." Andreas picked up the note again.

"We should show this to the police," Luisa said. "That may reflect poorly on your establishment." She gave the receptionist a piercing look.

"I'll ask around if one of the staff had seen anyone or anything suspicious. I'm sure it's just a bad joke, but I'll look into it." The man was clearly getting worried about the reputation of the hotel.

"*Grazie.*" Luisa gave a quick nod.

They stepped outside and decided to have breakfast at the same coffee shop as the day before. It had rained during the night; the air was fresh but pleasantly warm. The fragrance of flowers in the pots on the patio mingled with the scent of coffee as the waiter brought their cappuccinos and an assortment of rolls and fresh fruit.

Andreas took a sip of coffee, then narrowed his eyes, watching a few pedestrians walk by. "I sure wonder what we did to anger some of the people here."

"Good question," Luisa said. "Perhaps we'll find out more from Aurelio."

After breakfast, they went back to their rooms to get ready for their visit to Lorenzo and Maria's friend. Aurelio lived a short distance away, so they decided to walk to his place. Climbing up a cobblestone path past a few small stores, a church, and a children's playground, they arrived at a hill, from where they had a beautiful view of Lake Como. The calm surface of the water shimmered like a myriad of pearls in the sun.

"Nice part of the city," Andreas said.

"Yes, this definitely looks like the more expensive area," Luisa agreed.

"If Aurelio lives here, he must be doing well," Andreas said. "He deserves it, I guess, having been a hero during the war."

"True," Luisa said. "Although from what I heard, some people in the resistance were quite cruel as well. But I'd like to think that this man was a good sort."

Andreas checked the address on the piece of paper Lorenzo had given them.

"This must be it." He motioned with his head at a house with yellow walls and green shutters and a front yard full of flowers. Andreas inhaled the scent of lavender. He opened the garden gate, and they walked through the yard. When he knocked on the door, an old man opened it.

Aurelio must have been in his eighties, but his short, wiry body belied his age. His sharp gray eyes studied them for a quick moment, then he smiled and motioned them into the house before they were able to introduce themselves. Obviously, Lorenzo had announced their visit, and perhaps Aurelio had heard through the grapevine that a strange couple was snooping around the village, asking questions. He led them to a sparsely furnished but cozy living room and pointed at a sofa asking them to take a seat.

"Would you like some coffee? I'm sorry I'm not the best host. My wife used to do that kind of stuff. But I do have an espresso machine." He proudly pointed at an espresso maker in the kitchen adjacent to the living room.

"Don't worry about it," Luisa said. "You don't have to serve us."

"Oh, it's no problem. I'm ready for a cup myself. Besides, these modern things are so easy to use." He walked into the kitchen and pulled out some cups and saucers from the kitchen cabinet, then pressed a button and the espresso maker began to grind the beans."

"That's a fancy machine you got there," Andreas said.

"*Si,* Aurelio said. "My kids got it for me this past Christmas. My wife used to make coffee the old-fashioned way in a Bialetti pot. It tasted as good if not better than this one." He motioned at the cups that were filled with deliciously smelling coffee. "But it sure is faster and it does make good coffee," he said with a chuckle.

"Your wife ...?" Luisa began.

"She died two years ago," Aurelio said. "Still miss her like crazy. Not that we didn't fight occasionally. Brenda was a strongheaded woman."

"I'm sorry to hear that," Andreas said. "I lost my wife three years ago as well." He took a deep breath. "I still miss her and yes, we did fight occasionally as well. So, I can relate."

Both men locked eyes, then gave a quick chortle. Andreas and Luisa helped Aurelio carry the cups, a jug of milk, and a bowl of sugar to the table.

Andreas, who drank his coffee black, confirmed. "It *is* good coffee."

After taking a sip, Aurelio looked at them. "Lorenzo told me you were looking for the family of Bella and Joshua?"

"Yes," Andreas said. "And there are people who seem to feel threatened by our search." He told him about the note he found outside his hotel room.

Aurelio nodded. "Bad things happened during the war. People don't want to have anybody dig up the past."

"We're not here to make accusations. We just want to find the person or her family this letter was addressed to." Andreas pulled the copy of the letter out of his backpack and gave it to Aurelio. "I found this in a cave in the Swiss mountains close to the Italian border." He told Aurelio the story of his research that had brought him and Luisa here.

145

Aurelio read the letter, then covered his eyes with his hand. "God, this is so sad. He made it to Switzerland after all and then died?"

"It looks that way. Did you know him and Bella?" Andreas wanted to know.

Aurelio sighed, still staring at the letter, then looked up. "I was a youngster then ... but I knew the family. It's a sad story." He hesitated.

"What happened?" Andreas asked.

Aurelio brushed a hand over his forehead, then looked at them with a painful expression in his eyes. "It was war, of course. At first, our village didn't feel much of it. We heard some of what was going on, rumors of German soldiers occupying people's homes, of certain people being arrested, disappearing. By that time, the war wasn't going well for Germany and, of course, Italy wasn't in good shape either. Although on paper the Germans were allies, but in reality, we hated them. They took everything: our food, our animals, our harvest. They took over houses for the soldiers and left the owners to fend for themselves." Aurelio's voice grew tense as he seemed to remember those times. "Anyway, that's all over." He took a sip of coffee.

"Bella's family," he continued, "lived a quiet life until that time. The parents were fairly well-to-do. The father had his own business, something to do with textiles. The mother helped out in the business, doing paperwork, I guess. I don't remember too much about the parents. One thing we all knew is that Bella, the daughter ... there was also a brother ... went out with a friend of her father's and that he was Jewish. At first, there wasn't much talk about that. But in the course of the war that became increasingly an issue as the Nazis began jailing some of the Jews and moved them to so-called labor camps.

Then we heard that Bella and Joshua were married. That's when all the trouble started."

"Why?" Andreas asked.

"There was a new law that forbade marriage of Italian citizens to Jewish people. If the soldiers, both Italian and Nazis, heard of a person of Jewish background the likelihood that they were eventually jailed and deported was very high." Aurelio paused and looked down at his hands. "Bella wasn't directly in danger since she was not Jewish, but the situation for Joshua became dire. One day, he disappeared. Rumors had it that he fled north. Almost the next day, the Nazis came looking for him. There was a very strong suspicion that someone in the village betrayed them."

"That's terrible. Betraying their own people?" Luisa said.

Aurelio gave a heavy sigh. "Yes, but so much happened during the war. People changed. They were trying to survive. By denouncing someone they might have saved their own lives. When you're hungry and cold, this might be an incentive. But of course, that's no justification."

"Lorenzo told us you worked for the resistance as a youngster," Luisa said. "That was dangerous work."

Aurelio smiled. "I was crazy. When you're young, you don't see the danger. You feel invincible. I wasn't involved in any killings or bomb attacks. Although I was very young, I had one advantage. My grandmother was born in Germany. She didn't speak Italian very well and since I spent quite a lot of time with her, I learned fairly good German. One of the German soldiers heard about it and often used me as an interpreter. That way I was sometimes able to overhear information about some of their plans and activities and pass it on to my friends at the resistance. No idea if it helped them a lot, but I felt like a spy." Aurelio chuckled. "It was only much later that I realized how I put myself and my family in grave danger. Fortunately, we were lucky, and I wasn't caught."

"I think you were a hero," Andreas said.

Aurelio waved his hand dismissively. "Crazy, probably, but a hero? I don't know."

"Do you know what happened to Bella and the family?" Andreas asked.

"Bella was gone as well when the Nazis came," Aurelio said. "From what I heard later she left to stay with a relative in a different town. She was pregnant and the family was afraid she would be questioned about her husband, jailed, or worse."

"She survived?" Andreas was holding his breath.

"Yes, she survived," Aurelio went on. "Unfortunately, her parents didn't. We heard that the Nazis shot her father when he didn't want to give away Joshua's whereabouts. The mother was taken away and never heard from again."

"Just horrible," Luisa said. "I heard of the many atrocities and betrayals that happened in Italy during that time, but I never knew anybody who was directly affected. I was born after the war, but my parents told me about the hunger and hardship."

"I too grew up right after the war in Switzerland," Andreas said. "And so, my family and I were spared the horrors of war." He pointed at the letter. "But that means that the family, Bella's present family, or she herself may still be alive today. She was young at the time of the letter writing, so she must be, well, in her nineties now, if she is still alive."

"Possibly," Aurelio said. "I met her once after the war when she came back to visit her brother who still lived here. She came with her young boy."

"She was pregnant with a boy then?" Andreas said.

"Yes, a cute little guy." Aurelio smiled, then his smile faded. "Bella desperately tried to find out what happened to

Joshua. As she told me, she never heard from him again and suspected he had been killed while fleeing. Some people thought that he had made it and disappeared, looking for a better life. There were some ugly rumors like 'you know how those Jews are. Always out for money. He probably didn't want to be stuck with a woman and a child.' Bella, however, never doubted Joshua."

"Is there any way we could find out where she lives today?" Luisa asked.

Aurelio looked out the window into the distance as if reeling in memories. Then he faced them with a quick smile. "I remember Bella telling me that she lived in Bellano. But don't forget that was, well, over sixty years ago. She may have moved several times since then."

"Still, it's something." Andreas felt elated. This was another clue.

"I know where Bellano is," Luisa said. "It's north of here, also next to Lake Como."

"Great," Andreas said. "Perhaps some people there will remember her or her family." He paused then scratched his head. "I assume she went by her married name at that time?"

"Yes, her name was Bella Goldman." Aurelio hesitated. "Wait, I heard that she got married again quite a few years later. What was her married name?" Aurelio tapped his forehead as if to juggle his memory. "I think it was Bar ... no Borgia, that's it. Bella Borgia."

"Oh, good to know," Luisa said. "We would've have searched for someone by the name of Bella Goldman."

"Wonderful." Andreas checked his watch. "Could we still make it today? No, we should wait until tomorrow. It's getting late and we wouldn't have enough time to search for the family."

Luisa agreed. "Besides, it's past checkout time at the hotel, so we might as well stay another night."

Luisa and Andreas got up and thanked Aurelio for the information and the help. He accompanied them to the door. "Good luck to you. Would you let me know what you find out, if you have time?"

"Yes," Luisa said. "Give us your phone number. We'll let you know." She punched his number into her phone.

They left and walked back to the hotel.

Chapter 23

Later that evening, Andreas and Luisa got ready to go out for dinner. Andreas picked up his backpack and a jacket, then knocked lightly on the connecting door.

"Come in." Luisa had changed into a green-and-orange-patterned dress that flattered her auburn hair and dark eyes. Andreas marveled again at how beautiful she was. She grabbed her purse, and they had just started toward the door when a rock shattered the window, spraying the room with shards of glass.

"Get down," Andreas shouted, grabbing Luisa. As they both fell to the floor, a second rock came flying through the broken window and hit the wall. There was a moment of shocked silence. Andreas slowly raised himself to his knees and put his hand on Luisa's back. "Are you all right?"

She nodded and sat up slowly, brushing her hair out of her face. "What was that?" She stared at Andreas with frightened eyes.

Andreas got up, scanning the shattered window. The rock that had broken the glass was lying by the window; the second one had hit the wall and was dropped next to the bed. When his heartbeat slowed down, anger flooded him. He looked through the window but didn't see anybody, then opened the door.

"Be careful," Luisa called.

He stepped outside, looking around. He recognized Irina, the manager, rushing toward him. "What happened?" she asked. "I heard a crash."

"Somebody threw rocks through our window," Andreas shouted. "This is getting ridiculous. First the threatening note and now this. I want to report this to the police."

Irina nodded. "I'll call them right away," she said. "Is anybody hurt?"

"No, fortunately not." Luisa joined them outside. "But either we change hotels, or we want rooms upstairs."

"Certainly," Irina said. "Why don't you come with me to the lobby? You should be safe there."

Andreas and Luisa gathered their luggage and followed Irina to the lobby.

An officer of the local police arrived half an hour later. He was bald but looked young and, as Andreas suspected, tried to hide his obvious inexperience behind a swagger and a rough demeanor. He asked them a few questions, checked out the broken window. "You're not hurt?" He eyed them up and down.

"No, but it was pure luck. If the rocks had hit my friend, she would be seriously hurt or worse." Andreas' heart clenched at the thought. He stared at the officer, disliking him for his cavalier attitude. "And yesterday I found this note outside my door." Andreas searched through his pocket and pulled out the note.

The officer read it, wrinkling his brow, then glared at them. "What did you do to make them want you to leave?"

A flash of irritation surged through Andreas. "That's the wrong question," he yelled at him. "We didn't do anything to warrant such an action. We were looking for someone who lived here a long time ago, during the Second World War. Emilio at the post office gave us the name of some people who lived here during the war and may have known the person we are looking for. There is nothing suspicious about this. The right question would be, what have these people done to make them feel so guilty?"

The officer gave them a defiant look. "We'll station someone around here for a while. I still think this is a one-time occurrence, a fluke."

"A fluke?" Luisa glared at him, then motioned him inside the room and pointed at the rocks that had shattered the window. "I think that's a little more than a fluke. I pay taxes in this country, and I expect you to do your job."

"*Calma.*" The officer raised his hands. "We'll look into it. Don't tell me how to do my job." He stormed off, pulling out his phone and talking in a rapid voice.

"He's getting someone to come here and watch," Luisa grumbled.

Irina apologized again for the disturbance. She showed them two rooms upstairs. "I suspect these were kids. We've had a few incidences with drunken teenagers around here. You should be safe on the second floor though. I told our handyman to watch for anybody that doesn't belong here." Andreas and Luisa thanked her and stowed their luggage in the new rooms.

"I don't believe these were teenagers," Andreas said as he stepped into Luisa's room through the connecting door. "I bet you this has something to do with what happened during the war and with our snooping around." He sighed. "I shouldn't have dragged you into this. You could've been hurt or worse."

Luisa glared at him. "You didn't drag me into this. It was my decision, and I don't regret it at all. On the contrary, I'm hooked, and I really want to find out what happened to Bella as well. It's become my mission too. I'm not a maiden in distress, so stop apologizing." Her voice was fierce.

153

Andreas lifted his arms in surrender. "I don't doubt you're fully capable of taking care of yourself." He sighed. "But I can't help being worried. I mean if the rocks had hit you …."

Luisa waved his argument aside. "They could've hit you too."

"You're right." Andreas brushed through his hair.

Luisa's face softened; she smiled at him, which warmed his heart.

They stepped onto the balcony of Luisa's room. Andreas spotted a man in uniform walking by the hotel. "Must be our protection," he said. "Do you think it's safe to go out for dinner?"

"Let's go to that trattoria at the corner," Luisa suggested. "The food there was decent, and it's close. It's still light, and we shouldn't be out in the dark."

They walked to the restaurant and sat on the patio. Andreas exhaled deeply after they ordered pizza and salad. "I sure didn't realize that this would turn into such a dangerous adventure."

There were a few other guests on the patio, but everything was peaceful. Nevertheless, Andreas kept looking around, seeing suspicious shadows everywhere. After a couple of glasses of wine, he felt more relaxed again.

Back at the hotel, they locked the doors to their rooms carefully, leaving the connecting door open for the night.

"That way, we can keep an eye on each other and know what's going on," Andreas said.

They both got ready for the night. After taking a hot shower and brushing his teeth, Andreas went to bed. He listened to Luisa pulling back the comforter on the bed and heard her click the light off.

"Sleep well and sweet dreams," he called.

She laughed. "More like nightmares."

"You're scared?" he asked.
"No, not really."
"Don't worry, I have a gun," he said with a chuckle.
"What?"
"I'm sorry, just kidding."
She groaned. "Stop it."

It took Andreas a while to be able to fall asleep. The tumultuous occurrences of the past few days kept swirling through his mind — the hostile behavior of the woman whom they had met initially when visiting Lorenzo's house, the threatening note, the rocks that could've seriously hurt or even killed Luisa. His fear and concern for her safety showed him how much he cared for her. He realized with a guilty shock that Karla hadn't been his prime focus anymore. He knew it was the natural order of things. "Time heals," his children and friends had tried to convince him. He'd never forget the love of his life, but the oppressive gloom that had hovered over him for the past few years, coloring his moods and everything he did, had lifted.

Now, however, there was a new friend in his life he felt worried about. Love and pain, so closely related. He shouldn't count on anything, he told himself. Luisa still hadn't given him the feeling she saw him as someone who was more than a friend. Better not get too involved. Another heartbreak was the last thing he needed.

Chapter 24

The following morning, Luisa got up and opened the window of her room. The air was muggy and oppressive. She narrowed her eyes, scanning the sky. There was a layer of mist on the horizon but no rain clouds to be seen. It smelled of dried grass. The comforting hum of a lawn mower nearby was spoiled by the aggressive roar of a motorcycle with a seemingly wide-open throttle. Luisa closed the window. *Crazy kids.* As she left the room, Andreas opened his door and stepped outside.

"Good morning." He gave her one of his warm smiles. "Sleep well?"

"Yes, how about you?"

"Okay." He scrunched his forehead as the roar of the motorcycle increased again. "What the heck? Well, let's get out of here. I'll get us checked out."

While Andreas settled the bill, Luisa went outside. She put her luggage into the trunk and was about to give the car a quick once-over when she saw it. "*Porca miseria,*" she shouted. "Damn it."

"What's wrong?" Andreas stepped outside. "Oh, no." All four tires of Luisa's car were flat.

"This doesn't make sense," Andreas said. "Obviously people here don't like us. But why prevent us from leaving?"

"I don't know." Luisa was shaking her head. "Well, we won't be going anywhere soon. The tires are slashed."

They went back inside and told Irina what happened.

"This is just ridiculous," Irina said. Her facial color darkened, and her lips formed a thin line. "We've never had anything like this happen here." She gave them a reproachful look as if she blamed them for creating this situation but then caught herself. "I'm so sorry you had such a terrible time here. I'll call the police."

"Get over here right away," Irina shouted into the phone, then slammed the receiver down. "The police here are incompetent." She seemed to have found a different target for her anger.

About fifteen minutes later, Carlo, the police officer, arrived in his cruiser. He was the same one who had taken the report when someone threw rocks through Luisa's window. He got out of the car and glanced at the slashed tires. "This looks like the work of disgruntled teenagers."

Andreas glared at him. "Throwing stones through the window and slashing our tires? This doesn't seem the work of teenagers. Someone obviously doesn't like us asking questions. There are people here who seem to feel guilty about their role in the past."

"Then how come the same thing happened to one of the citizens of the town? His tires were cut as well," Carlos said.

"Who was it?" Luisa asked.

"Aurelio Boschetti," Carlo said.

"There you have it." Luisa pointed an accusing finger at him. "He was the man we asked about the person we're looking for. He helped us. So obviously they wanted to punish him as well."

"Why don't you tell me what you want to know that makes people here so angry?" Carlo asked.

Luisa told Carlo about their search for Bella and her family. Once again, Andreas pulled out Joshua's love letter and handed it to Carlo, who read it, his forehead full of wrinkles. When he looked up, his expression was thoughtful, almost kind.

"We suspect that a few people here feel guilty about their role during the Second World War," Luisa said. "They don't want us to dig up the past."

Carlo nodded and rubbed his bald head. He handed the letter back. "But that's so long ago."

"There was a woman," Andreas said, "who opened the door when we went to visit Lorenzo Russo and his wife. Her name is Elena. She was very hostile when we asked to talk to Lorenzo. Lorenzo told us that she belonged to a family who was rumored to having collaborated with the Nazis." Andreas shrugged. "She may have thought we were out to expose her family. Perhaps she has something to do with trying to discourage us from asking questions."

"I see." Carlo squinted his eyes. "That is indeed interesting. Her grandson belongs to the group of teenagers who have been causing problems around here."

"There may be a connection," Luisa suggested.

"Let me look into this," Carlo said. "Could you stay around for a few more hours?"

Luisa pointed at her car. "We can't leave anyway until we have new tires."

"We'll stay as long as we don't get assassinated." Andreas gave a quick snort.

Carlo's somber face showed the slightest sign of a smile. "Don't worry; we'll take care of the slashed tires for you."

"Well, we might as well have some breakfast while we wait for them to fix the tires," Andreas said. Luisa nodded and they walked to their usual trattoria. They ordered coffee, rolls, and some fruit, then sat on the patio, enjoying the sun. The muggy air and the mist had lifted.

"I can't believe this search for Bella turned into a thriller. I hate having pulled you ...." Andreas stopped and gave Luisa a guilty look.

"Stop this. I told you I'm not some helpless woman who needs protection. Get that out of your mind, once and for all." Luisa paused. "Unless you'd rather be on your own."

"No, of course not," Andreas said. "I very much enjoy having you along."

Luisa gave a light toss of her head. "Okay, that's settled."

They both lapsed into silence. Luisa resented Andreas' exaggerated protectiveness. Then again, she appreciated his concern. She just wasn't used to it. She had been on her own for so long, lived an independent life, and the last thing she needed was getting involved with some knight in shining armor, some man who wanted to protect … and control her.

Half an hour later, Carlo called Luisa's phone and asked them to come to the police station nearby. It was housed in an old building with ugly gray walls. Plaster was crumbling in a few places. Inside, it was spartan: empty walls, no pictures, nothing personal. Luisa sniffed the smell of stale coffee, old human sweat, and … was it fear? *I must be watching too many detective shows*." She gave a chuckle. Andreas looked at her puzzled.

A young man in police uniform welcomed them and pointed to an open door halfway down a corridor. "He's waiting for you."

They walked to the open door. Carlo waved them inside. To Luisa's surprise, Elena, the hostile woman from earlier was there, sitting on a chair opposite Carlo, her hands clasped together. She gave them a guilty look. Her lined face seemed even more wrinkled than it had been when they had first encountered her. She was dressed in a black skirt and top, her hair tied in a tight knot.

"Gino isn't a bad boy," she said, her voice trembling.

Carlo motioned Andreas and Luisa to sit. "Her grandson was one of the teenagers who wrote the threatening note,

159

threw the rocks through the window, and slashed the tires." He glared at the woman.

"It's my fault," she said, her voice trembling. "I didn't like them snooping around. They asked questions about … Bella and Joshua. Gino heard me complain. He wanted to prevent us from being hurt." She faced Andreas and Luisa, then averted her eyes again. "I … my uncle had something to do with telling the Germans about Joshua. Not sure who did it actually. But I didn't want this old stuff to be dragged out again. The resistance killed my uncle and other members of my family. The war is over. We want to forget it, move on."

"Signora, we are not here to blame anybody," Andreas said. "We just want to find Bella or her family. Her husband fled to Switzerland and died there. He was never able to let his young wife know what happened. He left a letter. We want to give her or her children the letter."

"What your family did during the war is not our business," Luisa added.

"It was war. We were hungry, afraid, and those rich Jews …." Elena stopped and lowered her eyes. "I'm sorry."

"Well, so we know now who had caused the uproar. I'm sorry, Elena, but Gino will have to take responsibility for his actions."

Elena nodded and wiped a tear off her face.

"We'll talk about it later. You can go now, Elena," Carlo said.

Looking after the old woman who shuffled to the door, Luisa turned to Carlo. "What's going to happen to the kid?"

Carlo gave a snort. "He's a minor, so it's probably going to be a few hours of community work. A lot of good it will do." He sighed. "Anyway, I'm sorry you didn't have a more pleasant stay here." His phone rang. He answered it, then nodded and put it on his desk. "Your car is all fixed again."

160

"Thank you," Luisa said.

Carlo nodded. "I hope you find the woman you're looking for."

"We hope so too. Thanks for your help," Andreas said.

When they got back to the hotel, a couple of mechanics had just finished putting four new tires on Luisa's car.

"Carlo sent us," one of the workers said.

"Thank you very much." Luisa nodded at them. "How much do we owe you?"

The men waved them off. "Courtesy of the police," one of them said. "Well, actually, courtesy of Carlo," he added and grinned.

"Thank you, we appreciate it," Luisa said.

They watched as the mechanics got into their truck, waved, and drove off. "Well, Carlo turned out to be much nicer than I took him for," Andreas said.

Chapter 25

Luisa tossed her jacket on the backseat of her car. "We'll try that town Aurelio told us about."

"Are you still up for it?" Andreas asked.

"Oh, yes. We've come this far. We can't stop now."

"Should we wait until tomorrow and spend another night here?" Andreas looked at his watch. "If we leave now, we'll hit rush hour traffic. It's after five o'clock."

Luisa hesitated. "I checked the GPS yesterday. There is a mountain road up on the hill that takes us to Bellano in about two to three hours, depending on how fast we drive. That way we can avoid the freeways. I really feel like leaving this town behind."

"Okay," Andreas said. "But let me drive this time. I'm familiar with mountain roads." He started the car and rolled down the window. When a breeze tussled his hair, he scrutinized the sky, but there was no sign of bad weather.

"There's a forecast for rain," Luisa said. "But it doesn't look like it. The weatherman must be wrong. Wouldn't be the first time."

While driving up the curvy road for about half an hour, Andreas felt the wind pick up. The steering wheel shook occasionally, and small tree branches were blown across the street.

"Oh, no," Luisa groaned. "All of a sudden, it doesn't look that promising. There are dark clouds in the west. Perhaps I've been too impatient. We should have waited after all."

"Don't worry," Andreas said. "The road seems to be in good condition. We should be okay even if it starts to rain." He gripped the steering wheel harder, hoping the wind wouldn't develop into a full-blown storm. The dark shadows from the clouds swept across the meadows. When they arrived at the highest point, Andreas gave a sigh of relief and stopped at the side of the road. They got out of the car.

"That must be Bellano." Andreas pointed to the town at the bottom of the hill. The wind had gained in strength, howling through the trees, bending the bushes and grasses.

"Yes, looks like it." Luisa's hair was blowing in the wind, and she tried in vain to brush it out of her face. "We better hurry," she said. "With those clouds and the wind, it will get dark fast."

They got back into the car. When Andreas turned the key in the ignition to continue their journey, the car wouldn't start. There was a weak coughing sound and then nothing. They glanced at each other. Luisa looked as concerned as he felt.

She exhaled loudly. "What's happening?"

They got out of the car again. Andreas opened the hood. He checked the obvious places, water, oil, cables. Everything looked all right. He tried to start the car again, but after a brief coughing sound, nothing happened. "We may have a dead battery. You know how old it is?"

"At least five years. Let me check." Luisa took a manual out of the glove compartment and paged through it, checking the maintenance table.

"Wow, you actually keep track of your maintenance work," Andreas said. "I'm impressed. I'm not as diligent about it as you are."

"A lot of good it does." Luisa sighed. "Yes, here it is. Six years actually."

"Okay, that's possible then," Andreas said. "It's about the time batteries begin to give out." He checked his phone and breathed a sigh of relief that it showed bars. They still had a connection to the outside world.

"What are we going to do?" Luisa looked around, then pointed at the sky. Dark clouds rushed overhead chased by the wind.

"Well, our best hope is for a car with jumper cables to drive by and help us start the car." He knitted his brow. "But that's unlikely since we haven't seen anybody else driving here. Most people probably use the road along the coast of the lake. The other possibility is calling a repair shop. Do you have something like Touring Club, you know, an organization that you're a member of that comes to rescue you when you're stranded?"

With a moan, Luisa covered her face with her hands. "I used to, but I let it lapse. I'm so sorry. It's my fault we're stranded here. I shouldn't have suggested using a mountain road to nowhere."

"Don't blame yourself," Andreas said. "It was a good idea to avoid traffic. This is just an unlucky coincidence. We can always call a repair shop and have someone come to give us a jump start. We'll pay for it."

"At this hour?" Luisa checked her watch. "We can try, but I'm afraid they're closed." She began to search for repair shops on her smart phone. After calling a couple of numbers with no answer, she stopped.

Andreas rubbed his forehead. "I have an idea," he said. "What if I push the car a couple of meters until we reach the downhill part? Then we can drive down in neutral. It should work at least until we reach an uphill part again. Then we'll wait. We may have to spend the night in the car, but it's not cold. If no car shows up by tomorrow, we'll just have to walk to the village. It wouldn't take more than about two hours. We could walk now, but with a storm raging and it getting dark, that may be too dangerous." He glanced at the sky where more ominous clouds towered. "I think it's better to wait until it's light again."

Luisa hesitated then nodded. "You're right."

Andreas looked at Luisa's shoes. They seemed comfortable enough for hiking down. "Okay, let's try. Do you have a screwdriver?"

Luisa opened the trunk and searched through a toolbox. She pulled out a flat-head screwdriver.

"Perfect," Andreas said. "We have to get the car out of park to be able to put it in neutral." He took the screwdriver and inserted it into a small slot next to the gears. He carefully lifted the small cover, then put his finger into the hole and pressed the button there. He moved the gear from park into neutral. "There we go."

"You're a genius," Luisa said.

"Hardly, it's just that I watched a friend of mine who is a mechanic do it once. That is the extent of my mechanical expertise."

"Well, I'm impressed," Luisa said.

"Okay, now. Why don't you drive, and I'll push? When the car starts to roll downhill, hit the brake, and I'll jump in."

Luisa slid into the driver's seat, loosened the hand brake, and Andreas began to push. It took him a while to get the car moving. When the car reached the downhill part and began to roll, Luisa stopped. Andreas opened the passenger door and jumped inside. He was out of breath from the exertion. "I'm getting too old for this."

Luisa let the car roll down the road. It went well for a couple of kilometers, then they hit a flat part followed by a slight incline in the road. It was too long a stretch for Andreas to push.

"I think that's all we can do," Andreas said. "Let's park the car on the side here." He pointed to a small rest area. "At least we'll be off the road in case someone comes by during the night."

Andreas pushed again while Luisa maneuvered the car over to the side.

"We really have to spend the night here?" Luisa muttered with a long, slow sigh, as they got out of the car.

"Well, I would have preferred a more romantic place to spend the night with you too, but hey, we'll make it as comfortable as possible." Andreas noticed Luisa was blushing, but her facial expression was serious. "Let's see what we have." He searched his backpack for something to eat and pulled out a few granola bars. They each had a bottle of water and Luisa had packed apples, rolls, and a bar of chocolate."

"Wonderful," Andreas said. "A feast."

Luisa laughed. "There is a blanket on the back seat, and I have another one in the trunk."

"We're all set then," Andreas said.

"Problem is. I need a restroom," she said.

Andreas pointed at some bushes next to a tree at the side of the road. "Nobody is here. We have enough privacy. You need tissues?"

"No, I have some." Luisa pulled some Kleenex out of her bag and went behind the bushes. Andreas watched the sky with a sinking heart. He felt less optimistic than he let on, but he wanted to be upbeat for Luisa. Then again, she'd made it clear she wasn't the kind of woman who needed pampering. As soon as she came back, it began to rain hard. They rushed to the car and jumped inside. The wind raged; leaves and small branches tumbled across the fields and the road. The wind rattled the windows, and for a moment Andreas felt the car shake. He exhaled deeply, scanned the hill next to the road, and hoped they wouldn't be hit by a falling rock or tree.

They talked for a while, then as soon as there was a break in the rain, Andreas went outside again to relieve himself in the bushes. He scanned the landscape around him, but it was too dark to see much except a few lonely lights of the village at the bottom of the mountain.

Back in the car, they tried to get comfortable. They lowered their seats back as far back as possible.

"Feels like sleeping on a plane," Andreas said.

"Yes," Luisa murmured with a yawn.

Andreas put his hand on hers and gave it a reassuring pat. She took his hand and squeezed it. Encouraged by her response, he took deep breaths and tried to relax. Thoughts of Emilia and Pietro flashed through his mind. He had called Emilia before they left Quercia. His daughter had assured him that Pietro was a happy camper and keeping her busy. He was his usual energetic self. At work, Emilia and Peter took turns walking him. Andreas smiled at the thought, then his mind turned to Karla for a brief moment. He felt content thinking about her and was sure she would approve of his adventure in Italy. Would she approve of his interest in Luisa? He knew she would want him to be happy, but with another woman? *You'll always be first, my love*, he assured her in his mind.

He thought back to the adventures he had had with Luisa. It amazed him how comfortable it felt being with her. He enjoyed her company and, he had to admit, there was also a physical attraction that got stronger the longer they were together. He had tried not to think about it. They lived far away from each other, and he didn't think she was the kind of woman ready for a simple fling. Neither was he, really. He glanced at her; she had her eyes closed and her breathing was regular. Perhaps she had already fallen asleep.

After a while, the rain stopped. He relaxed and let his eyes wander over the racing clouds above. Finally, his eyelids began to droop, and exhaustion got the better of him.

Chapter 26

Andreas kept waking up, shifting his body from one uncomfortable position to another. He finally got out of the car to stretch his legs and aching back. The storm had stopped, and there was a thin sliver of the moon visible in the sky. The hooting of an owl and the rustling of tall grass in the meadow next to the road were the only sounds. He took a deep breath, inhaling the musty smell of wet leaves. After a while, he opened the car door softly so as not to wake Luisa. He sat back down and closed his eyes, not expecting to sleep.

The next thing he heard was the noise of a car engine. He checked his watch. It was a little after six in the morning, so he must have slept after all.

Luisa stirred next to him. "What's this?" she murmured.

Andreas got out of the car. A white van with a *poste italiane* sign drove around the curve. Andreas stepped into the road and waved him down. The van stopped and the driver, a young man, eyed him suspiciously. Luisa got out as well and came over.

"*Signore*," she said, "our car broke down. It may be a dead battery. Do you happen to have any jumper cables?"

The young man gave a hesitant nod. He still seemed suspicious, probably wondering what a man with unruly hair and a woman with still sleep-filled eyes, both of them in crumpled clothes, were doing in the middle of nowhere in the early morning.

Luisa went on to explain that they were coming from Quercia and got stranded when the battery of her car died, and the storm hit and it got dark. "We spent the night here. That's why we look a little ... well, disheveled." She brushed her hand through her wavy dark hair and gave him a kind smile.

The young man smiled as well and got out of the van. Danilo was the name stitched on his uniform shirt. He was in his twenties or early thirties, muscular and athletic. When he opened the back door of the van, he reached beyond a bunch of boxes filled with mail and dug out a pair of jumper cables.

Andreas gave a sigh of relief. "You're our lifesaver."

"Let's hope that it is in fact the battery," Danilo said.

Andreas opened the hood of Luisa's car. Danilo told Luisa what to do and fastened the cables. He started his van, and soon Luisa's car started as well. "Just let it run," he told her. "Don't turn off the engine. You need to drive to the nearest car repair shop. There are a few in Bellano."

"Thank God," Luisa said. *"Grazie mille.* Do you have the address of a good one?"

Danilo pulled out his phone and scrolled through the entries to find an address.

Luisa entered it into her phone. "Thanks again," she said.

Danilo snapped his phone closed. "It's not open yet. You'll have to wait until nine o'clock. You can park the car there though." He gave a quick smile. "I guess you're lucky I was early. I need to deliver the mail to Quercia."

"That's where we came from," Andreas said. "Do you live in Bellano?"

"Yes," Danilo said.

"We're looking for a family by the name of Borgia. We're looking for a Bella Borgia. Do you happen to know them?"

Danilo, surprised, scrutinized them. "I do know them. Francesco Borgia is a friend of mine."

"Oh, my God," Andreas exclaimed. "We've been searching all over Northern Italy for them."

"Why?" Danilo cocked his head. His suspicious expression was back.

"It's a long story," Andreas said. "I found something in Switzerland from a long time ago that I want to give them. I know it sounds crazy, but if you're friends with the family, I'm sure you'll find out about it. It's an amazing story."

"Now, you've made me very curious. I'll definitely talk to Francesco once I'm back." He glanced at his phone. "I'd better hurry though; it's already late."

"Sorry for holding you up," Luisa said. "We're very grateful for your help. Can you give us the current address of the family? We have an old one, but they may have moved in the meantime."

Danilo hesitated for a moment. "I guess that would be okay." He pulled out his phone once more and gave Luisa an address.

"Thank you so much," she said.

Danilo nodded, then got back into the van, waved at them, and drove off. As his vehicle disappeared behind a curve, the noise of the engine faded, and it was quiet again, except for the humming of the engine of Luisa's car.

"Look at that." Luisa pointed at the horizon in the east. The sun was about to rise and painted the mountains a fiery red. In the west, far down the hill, the surface of Lake Como shimmered in the early morning light.

Andreas nodded, put his hand on Luisa's shoulder, and pulled her a little closer. "Gorgeous." He was happy she didn't resist his hug.

They quietly admired the colorful display of nature for a moment, then Luisa motioned at the car. "Well, we better leave."

They got into the car, and Andreas drove the curvy road downhill, hoping the car would hold up until they reached the town.

Bellano was a small and pleasant-looking town at the edge of Lake Como. It was still early in the morning, and the town was just waking up. As they drove along the main road, they saw a few restaurants and coffee shops. Shop owners were hosing down or sweeping the sidewalk, and in front of the cafeterias, waiters were arranging tables and chairs on the patios in preparation for the guests. A few tourists with backpacks were strolling down the road.

Luisa had entered the address of the repair shop into the GPS of her phone and was guiding Andreas through town. As expected, it was still closed, so they parked the car next to the repair shop.

Andreas grabbed his backpack as Luisa took her purse, and they walked toward one of the cafeterias they had seen. It was still a little nippy from the rainstorm the night before; there was a refreshing breeze from the lake.

They sat outside on the patio of the cafeteria. A young waiter with disheveled hair, suppressing a yawn, walked up to them. They ordered coffee, rolls, and fresh fruit. When the waiter came back with their order, he spilled some of Andreas' coffee. He apologized, cleaned up the spill, and rushed inside to get him a fresh cup. The welcome smell and taste of coffee revived Andreas.

After the waiter went back inside, Luisa sniggered. "I wonder if he spent the night in a car as well. He looks as crumpled as we do."

Andreas laughed. "Or he was partying all night."

"That sounds more like it," Luisa said. "Well, I'm going to find a restroom and try to make myself a little more presentable."

"You look fine, Luisa, very natural."

"You mean like a bum?"

Andreas grinned. "No, that's not what I meant."

Luisa walked inside and, in the meantime, Andreas paid. When Luisa returned, he used the restroom as well. He brushed through his hair, trying to tame his naturally messy mane somewhat. Fortunately, he'd shaved the day before. He rinsed his mouth and splashed cold water on his face.

Since it was still too early for the repair shop, they walked through the town and took a stroll along the lake. Sun rays refracting from the water turned it into a surface of shimmering lights. The boardwalk was still mainly empty with the exception of a few joggers in their workout outfits. A couple of ferries crossed the lake.

"It's beautiful here," Andreas said, then checked his watch. "Should we try the repair shop?"

Luisa agreed, and they walked up the cobblestone path to the main road of the town. The repair shop had opened in the meantime. Two men in overalls were there, one working on a car engine and the other one in the small office. Luckily, they had a new battery and installed it right away. While the mechanic was working, Luisa asked the man in the office about the address of the Borgia family they had received from the postman. The man told them it was about five minutes by car, at the outskirts of town.

Once the car was fixed, Luisa took over the driving again, and it didn't take them long to find the house. On the way, Andreas' phone pinged. He pulled it out of his backpack and glanced at it with a smile. It was a picture of Emilia and Peter with Pietro in Emilia's arm. The caption said, "Getting ready for an outing." Peter had his arm around Emilia.

Andreas texted back: "Getting ready to visit Bella's family in Bellano."

Another ping: "Cool! Can't wait for news."

He showed the photo to Luisa. "As I mentioned before, my daughter is in love with her partner. For a while, it was uncertain if he reciprocated her feelings. Now, it looks like they've become quite close."

Luisa glanced at the picture and smiled. "Ah, young love."

Chapter 27

Emilia grabbed the leash and her overnight bag, then opened the front door of her house and stepped outside. She waved at Peter as he got out of his car. Pietro rushed toward him, wagging his tail with abandon. While Peter greeted him with cuddles, Emilia put her baggage into the trunk of the car.

"Ready?" Peter asked. He was wearing a pair of tan cargo shorts and a light-green T-shirt. Emilia couldn't help but admire his firm body and deep-blue eyes.

"Yes," she said, "but wait, let's take a picture to send to Papa." She activated the selfie feature of her phone, lifted Pietro up and took him into her arms. She stood next to Peter, enjoying the warmth of his body as he put his arm around her.

"Cheese," Emilia said and tapped the camera button, then checked the photo. "Not bad for a selfie." She sent it to Andreas' phone with a brief text.

"Okay, ready." Emilia climbed into the passenger seat, and Peter started his car.

A couple of days ago, they had lunch together at their favorite inn. They talked about Emilia's former home in the southern part of Switzerland. When Peter told her that he loved the Ticino but hadn't been there in years, Emilia offered to take him and show him around her old neighborhood in the Maggia Valley. Peter had jumped at the idea, and so here they were on a beautiful summer day, driving south.

Emilia was looking forward to spending some private time with her partner. Their relationship hadn't gone beyond friendship, but Emilia increasingly got the feeling that Peter liked her more than just as a friend. Ever since his sister Anna had told her that she knew he liked Emilia but was in fact a shy person when it came to women, she had felt encouraged that they may be closer in the future. A trip to the romantic south of Switzerland sounded like a perfect opportunity. She tried not to expect too much. Just being together for a weekend might be the beginning of something more permanent.

They drove from their village to the town of Splügen and decided to drive across the San Bernardino Pass rather than through the tunnel. The weather was perfect; the scenic mountain drive and the landscape were beautiful at this time of the year. The green and rust-colored fields with patches of yellow, white, and purple flowers interspersed with gray granite rocks and mountain streams next to dark-green pine trees were a feast for the eyes. On top of the mountain pass, they drove by a deep-blue lake.

When they arrived in Bellinzona, they stopped for coffee and a bathroom break for them as well as for Pietro. Afterward, they continued their drive past the three castles of Bellinzona onward to Locarno and the Maggia Valley.

They would spend the night with Lena, a close friend of Emilia's mother. Lena had cultivated and sold roses while her husband, Luigi, had owned and bred sheep and goats. Now, they were in their eighties and retired.

As they parked the car in the driveway of Lena's house, Lena, a somewhat plump but lively woman with curly gray hair came outside and welcomed them with an enthusiastic waving of her hands.

"Look at you." She hugged Emilia tightly. "It's been a while. You look splendid."

"You look great yourself, Lena," Emilia said, then took Peter by the arm. "This is Peter, my friend and partner I told you about."

"Welcome," Lena said. "I've heard a lot about you."

"Oh?" Peter gave a quick smile. "Good things, I hope."

"Of course." Lena laughed and winked at Emilia, then bent down to pet Pietro, who as usual enjoyed all the attention.

Emilia felt herself blushing. When she had called to announce their visit, she had confessed her crush on Peter and hoped Lena, who was an outspoken woman, wouldn't let on that they had talked about it. Fortunately, Lena was discreet.

"Let's sit on the patio; it's such a pleasant day, although it's going to get hot in the afternoon." They stepped into the yard where there was a patio with a long granite table underneath a trellis of grapevines. Pietro sniffed at every corner of the yard, then lay down on the lawn in the shade.

"Where is Luigi?" Emilia asked.

"He went to the store to get a bottle of wine. He'll be back in a minute. Are you thirsty? I made some lemonade. We'll have brunch once Luigi is here."

"I love your homemade lemonade," Emilia said.

Peter nodded. "Sounds perfect."

"I still remember we always came down to drink your lemonade," Emilia said. "Mama's lemonade wasn't sweet enough."

Lena laughed. "But probably healthier than mine." She went inside and Emilia followed her. They brought out glasses and a pitcher of lemonade and set it down on the granite table.

"Well, well, look who is here, the lady veterinarian," a deep voice said. Luigi, a short, stout man, opened the gate to the yard. His warm brown eyes glittered mischievously. "So, Dr. O'Reilly, you haven't forgotten us after all." He handed the bottle of wine to Lena and put his arms around Emilia, hugging her, then petted Pietro who welcomed him with his usual enthusiasm. The dog lay down on his back and let Luigi rub his belly.

177

"I know it's been a long time," Emilia said. "I would never forget you, though. It's just that we have a lot of work. But I want to come down more often. I miss you and this village. I have such fond memories growing up here." She introduced Peter. "This is my partner in crime."

"Very pleased to meet you," Luigi said.

"Since we're all here, let's have something to eat," Lena suggested. "You must be hungry."

"Let me help you," Emilia offered, then turned to Peter. "You two can talk shop in the meantime. Luigi used to have all kinds of animals—sheep and goats, from what I remember."

Lena and Emilia went into the kitchen where an assortment of cold, smoked meat—salami and prosciutto—as well as cheese, hard-boiled eggs, a plate of cold vegetables, and slices of dark bread, was laid out on the kitchen table.

"Boy, Lena, you went all out. What a feast," Emilia said.

Lena gave her a quick hug. "It's not every day that I have the pleasure of your company." The two women brought the plates outside.

"That calls for a glass of wine," Luigi said. "Are you up for it? You're not planning to drive anywhere today?"

"That sounds good to me," Emilia said. "But just one glass. We want to go swimming in the Maggia later."

"Bring some mineral water too," Lena called after Luigi.

When everybody was settled and began to eat the delicious antipasti, Luigi raised his glass. "Good health to everyone."

"How is Andreas?" Lena asked. "Still going for long, crazy hikes in the mountains?"

"Oh, you don't even know the latest," Emilia said. "Papa seems to be much better. You know we were on vacation in Tuscany?"

"I heard about it, yes," Luigi said.

"And do you know about the letter he found on one of his hikes?"

Lena gave her a puzzled look. "No, what's going on?"

Emilia filled them in on Andreas' find and his attempt to find the woman the letter was addressed to. "And now," Emilia continued, "he's chasing all over Italy with Luisa, the owner of the vineyard we stayed at, to find the family of this Bella. I just got a text from him, saying that they found the family."

"Oh, my God, how exciting," Lena exclaimed. "There is a woman with him? What's that all about?"

"Well, yes, that's what we are all wondering too," Emilia said. "They seemed to get very cozy with each other. No telling what's really going on. He's very evasive right now."

Luigi laughed. "I'm happy to hear that Andreas is having an adventure like that. Who knows, this Luisa may just heal him of his depression. I don't think he ever got over the loss of Karla."

"Yes, it would be great," Lena agreed. "I just hope that this doesn't bring on another heartbreak."

"Yes, that's what I'm worried about too. But she seems like a really nice person," Emilia said. "At least, he is in a much better mood and sounds very upbeat when we talk."

"That's great," Luigi said. "He deserves some happiness again."

After they finished their meal, they had an espresso and homemade blueberry pie with whipped cream.

"Ah, heaven," Emilia said as she savored the sweet delicacy.

"It sure is," Peter agreed, licking the last bit of cream from his spoon. "Now, we better walk and swim off some of the calories we just consumed."

179

"Oh, you're both so skinny," Lena said. "I, on the other hand …." She put her hand on her belly.

"That's okay, *cara.*" Luigi grinned. "These are love handles."

They all laughed. Emilia realized how much she enjoyed being with her old friends. She would make more of an effort to visit them regularly. She had so many precious memories of living next to them as a child.

They continued to chat and give each other the latest news. After about an hour, Luigi and Lena decided it was time for a nap, and Emilia and Peter got ready to go swimming.

Chapter 28

After putting on her bathing suit, Emilia stepped outside. Peter was waiting for her, and Pietro, who had been resting in the shade, got up and wagged his tail expectantly. On the way to the river, they stopped at the cemetery to put some of Lena's roses on Karla's grave. She was buried in the town where the family had lived for many years.

At Karla's grave, Emilia gently touched the gravestone. "This is the last tombstone Papa ever carved," she said, her voice trembling. "He would sit in front of it, holding his chisel, tears streaming down his face. It was so heartbreaking."

Peter put his arm around her and held her close. He pointed at the stone. "Beautiful carving."

Emilia nodded. "It's from one of her last unfinished pictures, just the outline of a sketch. He said that perhaps she could finish it wherever she was now."

"Why not?" Peter said. "We don't know what's going to happen after we die, so perhaps? Who knows? It's a comforting thought."

Emilia gave a quick smile, then put the vase with the roses on the plot. "Well, let's go swimming. It's getting rather hot." She wiped drops of sweat from her brow and brushed a strand of hair out of her face.

They walked down the narrow path to the river while Pietro explored the new environment.

"Does he love to swim?" Peter asked.

"He's not crazy about water, it seems," Emilia said. "He likes to cool off in a shallow pond or pool but he's not like some dogs who jump into a river and swim. He's a little bit of a sissy about that, aren't you, Pietro?"

The dog gave her a quick and, as it seemed to Emilia, irritated look. "I don't mean to offend you, Pietro." She laughed. "I'm actually glad he is not that eager to jump in. The Maggia is a mountain river and can be quite wild at certain places."

Down at the river, a few people were collecting stones or splashing in the water. Emilia searched for a somewhat secluded area and picked a place in the shade underneath an oak tree. They put down their towels and stripped off their shorts and T-shirts. "Stay," Emilia said to Pietro. "We'll be right back." Pietro watched them eagerly at first, then searched for a shady spot and lay down.

Emilia tested the water with her toes. "Not bad. Usually, the water is freezing, but this isn't too cold."

"What?" Peter who had dipped his foot in the water, stepped back quickly. "Not too cold?"

"Come on, be brave." Emilia walked into the water, testing the ground with her feet. The stones were slippery, and she held on to a boulder with one hand. She turned around and waved at Peter who was still standing on firm ground. "Come on," she called again. "You won't feel the cold after a while." She heard him grumble something. He took a step into the water, gave a painful groan, then dove in, splashing and yelling, "That's freezing, darn it." He began to crawl toward her, and she realized he was a good swimmer. Splashing each other, they giggled like kids.

When Peter continued to swim farther down the river where it was deeper, she warned him to be careful. "There are some powerful currents down there." Not sure he had heard her, she began to swim after him. Just when she wanted to warn him again that they were too close to the rapids, she felt the strong current herself. She knew she should stop but was aware that Peter didn't realize how close they were to a dangerous whirlpool where a few people had actually drowned in the past. "Stop," she called. Peter turned around and looked at her. "The rapids," she cried again, then waved toward the bank, "Let's get over there." Then, she felt a powerful pull toward the middle of the river and the rapids. She desperately tried to change course. Her leg slammed into a rock, and the next thing she knew, Peter was beside her.

"Hold on." He stretched out his arm toward her, but she couldn't reach him. With all her strength, she crawled toward the shore. It was slow going, and she was losing strength. Then she saw a tree with overhanging branches and steered toward it. Peter seemed to realize what she was trying to do. He reached for one of the thinner branches, broke it off, and held it out to her. She got a hold of it with one hand, and Peter pulled her toward him. He grabbed her around the waist and together they made it to the riverbank. They latched on to some brush, then Peter hoisted himself up and pulled Emilia up as well.

"That was close." Peter exhaled loudly. "Are you okay?"

Emilia was still trying to catch her breath. "Afraid you were going down the rapids. Tried to warn you … about the current." She brushed her wet hair out of her face, then gave a quick laugh. "Instead of saving you, I almost got swept down myself."

Peter put his arm on her shoulder. "I'm sorry. It's my fault for not waiting for you. Thanks for trying to save me."

Emilia took another deep breath. "Well, it was you who ended up saving me … oh, no, Pietro," she screamed. The little dog must have followed them, perhaps sensing that they were in trouble. He was paddling and swimming furiously, trying to reach them.

Peter jumped back in and swam toward the dog. He reached him fast with his powerful crawl and while he held him, Emilia was getting ready to slip back into the water, but Peter waved her off. "Stay put. I have him." He swam back, lifted the dog up, and handed him to Emilia.

"Oh, my God, Pietro, what were you trying to do? Rescue us?" She hugged the little dog who licked her all over as if making sure she was all right.

Peter hoisted himself back up. "You're a hero," he said to Pietro, then turned to Emilia and grinned. "You better apologize for calling him a sissy."

"I know." Emilia kissed Pietro. "I'm sorry, I'll never call you a sissy again." Pietro acknowledged the apology with a quick bark, then shook himself and sprayed them with drops of water.

Peter and Emilia sat next to each other, with Pietro snuggling between them. They both took deep breaths. Emilia, after getting her strength back, reached over and picked a leaf from Peter's hair. Peter lifted Pietro up and moved him to the other side of him, then pulled Emilia close and put his arm around her. They locked eyes; she felt his warm breath on her face and closed her eyes. His lips were cold but warmed up quickly; he tasted of river and sun. They kissed slowly, then more passionately.

"Emilia." He pulled back a little. "I've been in love with you for a long time."

It's about time. She hugged him. "I love you too, Peter."

Pietro, not wanting to be left out of the snuggling, jumped over Peter's legs and sat himself smack in the middle between them, licked Emilia's hand, then turned to Peter and did the same to him. They both laughed. "He seems to agree," Peter said.

184

They gathered their things and walked back to the house, holding hands. On the way back, Emilia's heart was beating fast, not just from the exertion in the river but from joy at the turn of events. Peter loved her. She had been right about his feelings, and he had finally found the courage to accept and admit them.

Pietro, having fully recovered from his attempted rescue mission, was running ahead, turning back occasionally to make sure they followed him.

At Luigi and Lena's home, Emilia told their hosts of their adventure at the Maggia. Pietro got the royal treatment, a large piece of sausage and lots of hugs and affection.

"This is quite a dangerous river," Luigi said. "It doesn't look that way on a sunny day, but it can be treacherous."

In the evening, they had dinner at Lena and Luigi's place, where they were going to spend the night. After showering and changing into their clothes, Emilia went into the kitchen to help Lena prepare dinner.

"You look happy," Lena said. "Your face is glowing."

Emilia smiled. She looked back outside to make sure they were alone. "He finally confessed, loving me." She hugged Lena. "I'm really happy."

"Good for you." Lena hugged her back. "He is a very nice man ... and quite good-looking too."

Emilia's phone pinged. "A text from Papa. They're going to visit Bella's family today. They're standing in front of their home. How exciting."

Chapter 29

At the outskirts of Bellano, on a hill above Lake Como, Andreas and Luisa were gazing at an old house. It looked like one of the renovated villas that are common in Italy. The walls were whitewashed in an ocher tone. In a section in the middle of the front wall, the natural stone was left exposed.

Luisa checked the address Danilo had given them on her phone, then motioned at the house. "That must be it."

"Looks like it," Andreas said.

It was a charming home, he thought. There was a large front yard with a colorful flowerbed. Two umbrella pines flanked the property. The view of Lake Como and the mountains in the background was spectacular. From the looks of it, the estate seemed to belong to a well-to-do family.

Andreas wondered what kind of life the inhabitants had led since the Second World War. Were they happy? Was it a peaceful existence? What kind of feelings would the discovery of their long-lost family member stir in them? He had been so eager to track them down, but now he was almost afraid to confront them with what he had found. Would it upset the family? Cause heartache and turmoil?

He took a long breath and glanced at Luisa, who seemed in deep thought as well. "I'm almost afraid to give them the letter," he murmured.

Luisa touched his arm. "So am I. I haven't even considered what this discovery would mean for them. Would they be as unhappy about our digging up old stuff as the people in Quercia were?"

186

"God, I hope not," Andreas said. "But they do need to know the truth, don't they?"

"Yes, of course," Luisa agreed. "Let's get it over with."

They walked up the path through the yard. At the front door, Andreas gave an admiring glance at its lovely wood carvings. He pushed the button to ring the doorbell, which gave a melodious sound. At first nothing happened, then just as he was about to ring again, he heard footsteps. A portly man of medium height, about in his fifties, with curly black hair and a receding hairline opened the door. "*Buon giorno.*"

"*Buon giorno,*" Luisa said. "We are looking for a woman by the name of Bella or members of her family."

The man stared at them perplexed.

"I realize this may come as a shock," Andreas said. "We have information for them from a long time ago. I found a letter from her husband."

"From her husband?" The man's forehead creased. "How is this possible? Her husband died two years ago."

Andreas and Luisa looked at each other. "Not her second husband, the first one," Andreas said.

"What are you talking about?" The man gave them a stunned look. He must think we're crazy, Andreas thought. He pulled out the letter from his backpack.

"This is a letter from what we think was her first husband," Luisa said, pointing at the piece of paper. "Joshua Goldman."

The man paled. "Joshua? But Joshua ..." He sighed. "You better come in." He opened the door all the way and motioned them inside.

"I'm Francesco," he said. "I'm Bella's son from her second marriage."

"Doesn't she have a son from her first marriage?" Andreas asked.

"Yes, that would be Paulo, my older brother, well half-brother … but Joshua? What happened to him? Where is he? How do you know all this?"

"It's a long story, it sounds crazy, but it will make sense once you hear it all," Andreas said. "First of all, from what I learned, Joshua made it to Switzerland but died there right after arriving. He must have slipped and fallen down a gorge in the mountains. It was snowing heavily." Andreas realized how confusing this all must sound after such a long time.

"I don't understand." Francesco ran his hand through his curly black hair. "We thought he was killed somewhere in Italy while fleeing, but we never had any definite confirmation, just what the government told my mother. How come you know? Why did nobody tell my mother?"

"I found his belongings by accident in a cave where he must have spent the night after his arrival on the Swiss side of the border."

Francesco stared at him. "Why in a cave?"

"From what I learned, the cave was a temporary shelter for refugees from Italy. They stayed there if they arrived too late or the weather was bad and the guide on the Swiss side couldn't reach them the same day."

Francesco still looked confused. "Go on." He motioned them to sit on a sofa in the living room.

"A few weeks ago," Andreas continued. "I was hiking in the mountains and got overwhelmed by a storm, so by chance I waited in that very cave until the weather improved. I had my dog with me. He started exploring the cave and found an old backpack that was almost falling apart. It was hidden in the very back of the cave underneath dirt and stones. It must have been there all these years, hidden away. I opened the backpack and found these items in it."

Andreas handed him the passport. "The name in the passport is probably a fake name. I'm friends with the chief of police, and so we did some research in the archive and found this note." Andreas gave him the copy of the short article. "It's in German but it says that the body of a young man was found at the bottom of the abyss underneath the cave. There was no identification. In the news, it said that there was a heavy snowfall and that he must have fallen to his death." Andreas handed Francesco the letter. "I also found this, a letter addressed to Bella Goldman, obviously Joshua's wife." Andreas put his hand on Luisa's shoulder. "We've been trying to find Bella, the woman it was addressed to. It's been quite an experience."

Francesco sat on a chair opposite them and read the letter. He put it down and covered his eyes with his hands. "Oh, my God."

"Is Bella still alive?" Andreas asked, his heart beating fast.

"Yes, she is. She is ninety-five and still in good health. She lives with my sister, her daughter from her second marriage, and off and on with her granddaughter nearby. She also has four great-grandchildren."

"That's wonderful to hear," Andreas said. "We were hoping to still find her alive and to be able to give her the letter."

"We'll have to go about it carefully," Francesco said. "I don't want to give her a heart attack."

"Definitely," Luisa said. "It will come as a terrible shock to find out what happened to her husband."

"Yes, it will be emotional. But also good for her. I know she was happy in her second marriage. She loved my father. But I think she never forgot Joshua."

"There was also a photo of a young woman. It must be Bella." Andreas handed him the photo.

189

"Oh, my God," Francesco exclaimed. "Yes, this is my mother as a young woman." He smiled and handed the photo to Luisa, who nodded. "She was beautiful," she confirmed.

Francesco pointed at the passport photo. "That's definitely Joshua. I've only seen a couple of photos of him, but it's definitely him."

Andreas exhaled relieved. It seemed that at least for Francesco, the surprise was a happy one.

They heard a noise, then the door opened and a slim woman, probably in her fifties, stepped inside. She looked at them surprised, then smiled.

"This is my wife, Sandra," Francesco said. He motioned her to sit down.

"You won't believe this, *cara*," Francesco said. "They brought a letter from Joshua, Mother's first husband, the one who fled during the war and disappeared. Look at the photo."

Sandra opened her mouth, then closed it and stared at them. "What?"

Chapter 30

After Francesco, with the help of Andreas and Luisa, told Sandra the story, she said they had to call some of the family. She invited Luisa and Andreas to stay with them.

"We have guest rooms; it's no problem. This is such an amazing story. Wait until your mother hears this." She hugged Francesco.

"Thank you for inviting us to stay, but we can easily stay at a hotel. We don't want to inconvenience you," Andreas said.

"Nonsense," Sandra protested, then wrinkled her forehead. "Are you a couple or just friends?"

"We're just friends," Luisa said.

Andreas couldn't help feeling a little disappointed by Luisa's matter-of-fact assessment of their relationship. Of course, it was true. What else did he expect?

"Okay. In this case, Luisa can stay in our guest room and Andreas can have Giorgio's room. Giorgio is our oldest son. He lives in Rome. He is a pilot for Alitalia. I hope you don't mind sleeping with model airplanes hanging from the ceiling. He has been crazy about airplanes since childhood."

Andreas chuckled. "That wouldn't bother me at all."

Francesco picked up his phone and called his brother, Paulo, urging him to come by. He didn't tell him the whole story, just mentioned it had to do with his father. "We have some information on Joshua. I have some visitors here who found a letter of his in Switzerland."

The news must have taken Paulo completely by surprise, evidently rendering him speechless since Francesco asked if he was still on the line. "Okay, see you soon." He put down the phone. "He's on his way with Diana."

Sandra brought out cups of espresso. Luisa and Andreas briefly described their journey through Italy to find the family. Francesco and Sandra told them a little about their life. Sandra was a primary school teacher and Francesco was an IT specialist and worked as an independent contractor.

Shortly thereafter, they heard a car door slam and voices outside.

"They're here." Sandra went to open the door.

Paulo and Diana walked inside. Paulo measured Andreas and Luisa with clear, blue eyes. He was a tall man, a little overweight, with a slight paunch, probably in his seventies, about the age of Andreas. Diana seemed a little younger, perhaps in her late fifties, early sixties.

They looked at Sandra and Francesco, then focused again on the visitors. "What is this about … Joshua?" Paulo asked.

Andreas noticed that he didn't refer to Joshua as "father." Most likely, he considered Bella's second husband his true father.

"I found some items of his as well as a letter in a cave in the Swiss mountains," Andreas said.

"*Cosa?*" Paulo stared at him. "What are you talking about?"

"Relax." Francesco put his hand on Paulo's shoulder. "Sit down and listen to his story. This sounds like a mystery novel."

All eyes were on Andreas and Luisa now. Andreas cleared his throat and began to tell the story again. By now, he could've told the events in his sleep, he had told them so many times. He also told them how some people in Quercia had helped them and how a few had threatened them because they didn't want them to find out about their role during the war. Finally, he handed Paulo the letter.

"I heard that my mother's family had been betrayed," Paulo said, holding the letter without reading it. His hand shook lightly as if he was afraid of what he might find out.

"Her parents, my grandparents, were killed by the Nazis because they thought they were harboring a Jew." He shrugged. "Which was of course true. My mother was Catholic, but she was married to a Jewish person. That's why Joshua had to flee."

Then he began to read. It was quiet for a while. They all stared at him expectantly.

"Oh, my God." Paulo lifted his head and looked around, then back at the letter. "This is incredible. I can't believe this." He put the letter down and covered his face with his hands. Then he looked up again and continued with a deep sigh that turned into a sob. He caught himself, then handed the letter to his wife.

"My mother waited for many years, still hoping to hear something about my father. She and her brother, my uncle, did everything they could to find out what happened to him. By then, however, the family had lost so much of their money and properties, they couldn't afford a large search. In the end, they had to accept what the authorities told them, that Joshua was killed by the Nazis while fleeing. Of course, the body was never found. It was assumed, he was buried somewhere in a mass grave.

"Eventually, she met my second father," Paulo continued. "They wanted to marry, and so she petitioned to have Joshua declared deceased."

"I still can't believe it." Paulo turned to Andreas. "And you're sure the body they found was Joshua?"

Andreas lifted a shoulder. "Of course, there is no hundred percent proof, but when you compare the date of the letter, the identification in the backpack, the place in the abyss right underneath the cave where the body was found, I don't think we could come to any other conclusion."

Paulo nodded. "Mother never doubted that something terrible happened to him. She never believed what some other people, even the family, suggested, that he left without her, started a new life in America."

"This is such a heartfelt love letter, so full of longing," Diana said. "He was clearly devoted to his wife and was looking forward to his child." She faced Paulo. "You."

Paulo smiled. Francesco handed him the photo of Bella and the passport with Joshua's picture.

"Mamma," Paulo said, looking at the photo. "And this is Joshua, my father." His voice broke and he wiped tears from his face. "Sorry."

Diana hugged him.

"We'll have to tell Mother," Paulo said. "But we have to be careful. She has a pretty strong heart, but still, this will create a lot of upheaval."

"We'll have to prepare her, but yes, we need to tell her," Diana said, and the others agreed. "And the whole family. *Dio mio*, what news. "And thank you, dear Andreas and Luisa, for taking all this time and trouble to find us."

"It was well worth it," Andreas said. "We didn't know if we would succeed, but we just had to try. We're so grateful not just to have found the family but to know that Bella is still alive." He put his hand on Luisa's shoulder.

She looked at him with a warm smile. "Yes, believe us, it was more than worth it."

Chapter 31

On a pleasantly warm August day, with a light breeze floating up from Lake Como, Andreas and Luisa together with Francesco, Paulo, and their wives were walking the short distance to Bella's home. Andreas felt both excited and nervous so close to the meeting with the woman for whom they had searched so long. What kind of a person was Bella? What did she look like? From the old photo, he knew that she had been a beautiful young woman, but that was over seventy years ago, a happy time before the terrible war that had not only killed her parents but her husband as well. Would she be bitter about it? Paulo had told him that Bella was a kind, gentle but also strong woman, and she didn't linger in the past. Andreas hoped the news that they brought her wouldn't tear open old wounds again.

Luisa tapped his shoulder. "A penny for your thoughts."

He gave her a quick hug. "I'm nervous."

She smiled. "So am I."

As her family had told them, Bella lived with her granddaughter from her second marriage in a nice-looking house in the center of town. She was still in good health, but she needed help on a daily basis. Since they didn't want to put her in a retirement home, the family took turns taking care of her. Family was very important for the Borgias, Paulo had told them. Growing up after the war, having lost members of the family, some missing, some dead, made them aware of the meaning of taking care of each other.

Francesco, Paulo with their wives and children had introduced the topic of Joshua carefully, as Paulo had told him. Paulo wasn't sure if Bella had fully understood the whole thing.

"Joshua?" she had first said, then immediately, "I always knew he had died." It was as if she wanted to disperse the ugly rumors that he had abandoned her.

When they had tried to explain that a man in Switzerland had found a letter Joshua had written to her before he died, she gasped and covered her face with her hands.

"I was afraid she was having a heart attack after all," Paulo said. But then she told him she wanted to meet the couple who had brought the letter to them.

When Bella's granddaughter Isabella, a slender, middle-aged woman opened the door, they heard an anxious voice asking, "Is it them?"

"Yes, Nonna, it's Andreas and his friend, Luisa," she said. "They have come all the way to find you."

"Well bring them in. Don't let them stand outside."

Isabella smiled and waved Andreas and Luisa inside. The other members of the family followed. Isabella walked to an old woman who was sitting by the window of a large living room. She motioned Andreas and Luisa to join them.

The minute Bella saw Andreas and Luisa, she got up, supporting herself with a cane and holding on to her granddaughter's arm. Once she was standing, she let go of Isabella and measured Andreas and Luisa with dark, vivid eyes in a wrinkled face.

Bella was tall, slim with carefully coiffed white, curly hair. Even in her nineties, she was still radiant. Her most striking feature was her dark, shiny eyes that measured them with great interest. She didn't seem to need any glasses for vision.

She greeted them with a slightly hoarse voice and a tentative smile.

Andreas held out the clear plastic folder that protected the letter from further damage to her. The edges of the letter had yellowed, and the page was torn in places, but it was still readable. "Signora, we're so happy to have found you and are able to give you this." He stepped back to give her some privacy.

Bella nodded, then sat down again. When she held the sheet of paper, her hand trembled and the expression on her face was one of fear. She took a deep breath, looked around the room as if for help. She seemed to be afraid to read the letter. Finally, she grabbed a pair of reading glasses from the coffee table near her, put them on, and began to read, moving her lips as she did. It was completely silent in the room; everybody seemed to hold their breath. When Bella finally looked up, she took off her glasses, and then the tears began to flow. There was no sound at first, just rivulets of water running down her cheeks. Then she uttered the name "Joshua," followed by a loud sob. "*Amore mio.*"

By then, everybody's eyes glistened with tears. Andreas saw the others through a blur. He pulled out his handkerchief and wiped his face.

When Bella composed herself a little again, she put the letter carefully on the table next to her, then tried to get up. Her granddaughter supported her, and Paulo got up to help, but she managed to stand on her own. She stretched out her arms toward Andreas and Luisa and motioned them to come to her.

"*Grazie mille.* Thank you so much. You can't imagine what this means to me. It's as if Joshua is back. He's home with me."

After they all sat down again, she wanted to hear the whole story. "Don't leave anything out."

Andreas smiled and described how he found Joshua's belongings and the subsequent research they did. Bella hung on his every word.

After he finished, he also handed her the passport and the photo of her as a young woman. She opened the passport and pointed at the picture. "Yes, this is my dear, dear husband. My Joshua. We had someone make a fake passport for him when things became too dangerous for Jewish people." She gave a quick smile when she looked at the photo of herself. "*Dio mio, so long ago.*" She showed the photo to Isabella. "See, your old Nonna was once a beautiful young woman too."

Isabella hugged her. "You still are, Nonna, you're still beautiful."

Everybody else voiced their agreement. Andreas and Luisa smiled at each other.

"How wonderful," Andreas said to himself. "She still cares about her looks. She still has so much life in her."

Bella then smiled through her tears. "We are both at peace now. Joshua and I."

Paulo went up to Andreas and Luisa and hugged them. "We're so grateful for your effort to find us and to bring us this news. I heard that some people in Quercia tried to prevent you from finding us, even attacked you."

Bella looked at them shocked. "What happened?"

Luisa told her about the rocks through the window and the slashed tires. "In the end, everything went all right. Other people helped us, the man at the post office as well as Lorenzo and his wife and Aurelio."

"And Danilo, the mailman," Andreas added.

"And you were brave enough to continue trying to find me?" Bella said. "I'm so grateful." She folded her hands and put them in her lap. "Many people in Quercia helped us back then. Some betrayed us. It was war. People were hungry, afraid. It's over. No need to be bitter about it."

Andreas was amazed how mentally agile and perceptive the old woman still was.

Bella smiled. "You're probably too young to know much about what happened here during that time."

"After I met Andreas and found out about the letter, I talked to my uncle in Milano," Luisa said. "He is a historian, and his specialty is World War II, so he told us about it. But to be honest, not having lived through that time, I really know very little about it."

"Same for me," Andreas said.

"Well ..." Bella was looking out the window as if gathering her memories. Then she faced them with a deep sigh. "I want to tell you more about that time, but I'm a little tired from all of this." She gave a sad smile and pointed at the letter. "Can you come back and visit me again tomorrow? I would love that."

Andreas and Luisa looked at each other. "I'd love to come back," Andreas said.

"Yes, so would I," Luisa confirmed.

Bella hesitated, then touched Joshua's letter tenderly. "And you're sure, it was Joshua? The body that was found, I mean?"

Andreas gave her the same explanation as he had given Paulo, that the time and the dates as well as the article in the newspaper and the report in the police archive seemed to confirm it.

"It's so sad that he made it all the way to Switzerland and then died there." A tear trickled down Bella's face. "At least he wasn't killed by the Nazis or deported and gassed, like so many others."

Andreas took her hand in his. "I saw the abyss. He would've been killed instantly. He wouldn't have suffered."

He knew it was a white lie, since he had no proof that Joshua hadn't suffered, but he felt it was a justified one.

Bella held out her arms, embraced Andreas and Luisa again. "I'm just so grateful to you. It's a great comfort to all of us. Thank you so much. Please come back tomorrow." They assured her they would.

After saying goodbye to Bella and her granddaughter, they walked back with Francesco and Paulo and their wives to Francesco's house, where Andreas and Luisa spent the night. In the evening, they had dinner on the patio. It had cooled down enough from the heat of the summer day that it was pleasant to sit outside. From where they sat, they had a beautiful view of the lake.

Andreas took deep breaths, inhaling the scent of flowers and enjoying the cool breeze that came up from the water. Having accomplished his task of finding Bella, he felt relaxed and content. He was also tired. The meeting with Bella had been emotional and had exhausted him. He noticed that Luisa looked tired as well.

After a light dessert of fruit, cheese, and a cup of espresso, they all decided it was time to get a good night's sleep after all the excitement of the day.

In his room, Andreas thought of calling Emilia, then decided to wait until the second visit with Bella the following day.

Chapter 32

The following day, Andreas and Luisa, accompanied by Paulo, went to see Bella again. Isabella, the granddaughter, led them to a gazebo in the garden, where Bella was waiting for them. It was a sunny and warm day. Bushes and flowers bordered the gazebo, and Andreas inhaled the sweet scent of roses. In the middle of the gazebo was a table with a pitcher of lemonade and a bowl of fruit and pastries. Isabella poured them glasses of lemonade and passed around a plate with pastries.

"Eat, eat," Bella said. "They aren't homemade, but our baker is quite good."

"*Profiterole*," Luisa said. "Cream puffs. I love them. You don't have to tell me twice."

As they were eating and drinking, Bella asked them about their families. Luisa told her about her vineyards in Tuscany. Andreas described his work as a sculptor and talked about his children. He also mentioned the death of his wife.

"I'm sorry to hear that," Bella said, her dark eyes kind and warm.

"I know the pain of losing a loved one," Andreas said. "But I can't imagine what it must have been for you, never knowing what happened to your husband." He put down his glass and tried to decide how to ask Bella about her past without stirring up painful memories.

As if she had read his thoughts, she put her hand on his arm. "I'm sure you have some questions."

"Yes, but I don't want to cause you pain. The war, losing your loved ones must have been so difficult for you."

"Don't worry. I've come to terms with what happened in the past. In spite of everything, I've had a good life. And the news you brought about Joshua now gave me closure."

"Signora, from the letter I gathered that you were planning to join your husband in Switzerland?" Luisa said.

Bella nodded. "But please call me Bella. Yes, that was the plan. You see, well ..." Bella seemed to gather her memories. "We had planned to leave together. We were going to Switzerland and from there to the United States. Joshua had a few relatives there. But then I got pregnant." She smiled at Paulo. "And we were all hoping the war would soon be over. We didn't realize that the worst was still to come before the German and the Italian armies were defeated.

"Times were hard all through the war, that's true. But Quercia was a quiet town. We didn't feel that much of the war at first. Joshua had a teaching job in one of the schools. My father had a clothing business that was prosperous. Joshua and I got married. At first, Jewish people in Italy were not persecuted. But once the Germans invaded the country, things began to change." Bella started coughing.

Paulo poured her another glass of lemonade. "Is this too much for you, Mamma?"

Bella took a sip, then smiled at him. "No, I'm fine. Anyway," she said with deep sigh. "Because of new racial laws, Jewish people were prevented from working in any government jobs or holding government offices. Joshua lost his teaching job. Then my father hired him to take care of the accounting in his firm. Since his was a private business, Joshua was allowed to work there. I worked in my father's office as well." Bella took another sip of lemonade. "By then, it was forbidden for non-Jews to marry Jewish people. It didn't affect us directly since we were already married, but we realized how much worse things were getting for Jewish people.

"In 1943, it got really bad. The Germans started losing battles and the Nazis became increasingly cruel. By then, we were aware of some of the horrors that took place in German and Polish concentration camps. It became more and more dangerous for Jewish people. My father encouraged Joshua to leave, to go to Switzerland. He said he had heard that some people in town were informants for the Nazis and it could get really ugly for Joshua." Bella brushed a hand over her face and looked at Andreas with a sad smile. "And he was right. Instead of arresting me, they killed my father and took my mother away. I lost three of my loved ones within a couple of days." A sob escaped her.

"Mamma." Paulo hugged her, but she caught herself and continued. "Although we originally planned to leave together, we made contingency plans in case Joshua had to leave unexpectedly. We organized a guide who could smuggle him into Switzerland. By then the borders to Switzerland were closed." Another sigh. "Thank God we did prepare. A friend of my father's told us that someone had betrayed us, that the Nazis were looking for Joshua. So that very night, Joshua left. It was the most heartbreaking moment of our lives. I so much wanted to go with him, but I was too far along in my pregnancy. I couldn't have made it. The same day that Joshua left, my father insisted I leave as well and sent me to a relative in a neighboring town. He was afraid I could be arrested.

"Of course, I never saw or heard from Joshua again. We were told by the Italian police that he was killed while fleeing. We never heard from his Italian guide again either. The person who recommended him to us said he was killed by the Nazis, so we assumed this happened to Joshua as well. After the war, we tried to find out more, but to no avail. Eventually, we had to give up and accept the official version. But we never had a definite confirmation. Then again, if he had been killed while fleeing, his body could easily have ended up in a mass grave, like so many others."

Bella gave a deep sigh. "I waited for a long time, hoping for a sign that he was still alive, but finally, I had to face the fact that Joshua was gone forever. I had to go on with my life, take care of my baby. My parents were dead. My brother helped me as much as he could."

It was quiet for a while. Isabella and Paulo hugged Bella. She gave a sad smile.

"Anyway," she continued, "eventually, I met another wonderful man and fell in love again. After the appropriate time, we had Joshua declared deceased. It was a very difficult thing for me to do."

She looked at Andreas and Luisa with sad eyes, then smiled. "Now, knowing the truth, having this wonderful letter from Joshua is such a great relief. I can't thank you enough. May God bless your kindness."

"It was an honor for us to do this," Luisa said.

Andreas felt a knot in his throat. "It brought me much joy. Of course, it also made me sad to have to tell you of his death."

Bella put her hand on his. "I hope you'll come back to visit me again. My family is deeply grateful as well." She put her other hand on Paulo's arm.

"I'd love to visit you in Switzerland and see where my father spent the last moments of his life," Paulo said.

"That would be wonderful. I'd love to take you there," Andreas said.

"Yes, Paulo you should go and say goodbye," Bella said. "He would've been a wonderful father, I know. He was so much looking forward to knowing you. I'm too old to go, so you'll have to do it for me, and for yourself."

That night, Andreas dreamed about Karla, the first time again in weeks. When he woke up, all he remembered was that she had smiled at him as if saying he'd done a good job. In the morning, he called Emilia to ask about Pietro and tell her that they had found Joshua's wife and family. Emilia was elated and assured him that Pietro was doing great but would be happy to see Andreas again.

"He probably forgot about me," Andreas said.

"Dogs don't forget. They adopt to new situations, but they always remember those they love," Emilia said. "Talk about love," she continued. "How is Luisa?"

"Doing fine. We had a wonderful time together and quite some adventures. I'll tell you about them later." He paused. "I do really care for her. I don't know if we'll ever become more than friends. We'll see. I hope though you don't take my feelings the wrong way. I didn't forget your mother. She's still my first love. But I was able to come to terms more with her passing."

"I'm happy for you, Papa," Emilia said. "You don't need to explain."

Andreas and Luisa visited with Bella again during the next couple of days It seemed that a great peace had come over the woman. It made Andreas feel joyous. They spent two more days in Bellano, enjoying the beautiful town. The family invited them to a private memorial service for Joshua at Paulo's home. Paulo who himself was raised Catholic recited "El Malei Rachamim" or "Merciful God," a Jewish prayer for the soul of a person who had died, in honor of Joshua's Jewish faith. It was a simple but moving ceremony.

Before Andreas and Luisa left, Andreas and Paulo made plans for Paulo to come to Switzerland and visit the place where Andreas found the letter. Andreas wanted to stay in touch with the family whose destiny had affected his own life in such an important and meaningful way.

Chapter 33

After Luisa and Andreas returned from their "quest" as Andreas called it, he spent a few days at Vignaverde, recovering from their trip through Italy and enjoying the food and excellent wine. Having dinner one evening on the patio outside, they were watching the sun set.

Andreas tried to find a way to talk about his feelings for Luisa. Ever since finding Bella and her family, Luisa had treated him with more warmth and surprised him even with a spontaneous kiss. It was a kiss on the cheek, but it gave Andreas hope that Luisa had felt a shift in their relationship as well. If anything more than friendship was their destiny, he needed to open up now before his return to Switzerland in a few days. He took a deep breath; he was nervous not just because he hoped not to have misjudged her feelings for him, but also because he didn't know how a long-distance romance would work out. "Come on," he told himself silently. "Stop being a coward."

As the sun was sinking behind the horizon, the crimson and purple sky gave way to the ink-blue shadows of dusk. When Luisa stood up to light the lantern on the table, Andreas got up as well. He put his arm around her. Shadows and light from the lamp danced across her face.

"Luisa ... I love you."

She smiled at him, put her hand on his neck, and brought her face close to his. He inhaled the light scent of her honeysuckle shampoo. They kissed, softly at first, then with increasing passion. Coming up for breath, Andreas stood back a little. He put the palm of his hands on her cheeks. "What are you thinking?"

It was quiet for a few seconds, then Luisa exhaled deeply and smiled. "I'm done thinking, wondering, doubting." Her voice was fierce. "To hell with caution." She grabbed his hand and led him inside to her bedroom.

Surprised at her quick and unexpected reaction, Andreas followed her, his heart racing.

At the beginning of their lovemaking, he thought briefly of Karla, then the memory dissipated, and for the first time since his wife's death, he abandoned himself fully to the love and passion for another woman.

In the morning, he watched the still sleeping Luisa in the faint light of the emerging day, enjoying her beauty—the firm features of her face, her auburn hair with a few streaks of gray, spread out on the pillow. As the first sun rays shone through the window and landed on Luisa's face, she began to stir, her eyelids fluttered. She opened her eyes, then closed them again against the glare of the daylight.

"Good morning," he whispered and kissed her. She wrapped her arms around him.

Later, they ate a breakfast of coffee, rolls, fruit, and cheese in the garden. It was already warm and promised to be another hot summer day. After finishing her coffee, Luisa sat back, glanced at him, and smiled. "Now what?" she said.

"I imagine you're talking about us?" He snickered, then became serious. "Thank you for a wonderful night. I'm in love with you. I want us to be together … somehow."

"I feel the same way," Luisa said. "Let's take it one step at a time. We're not twenty anymore." She brushed a strand of hair out of her face. "Although you did make me feel young again last night." Her sun-tanned skin darkened slightly as she blushed.

Andreas kissed her. "Yes, we'll take it slow ... but not too slow."

"Ah, here you are, you lovebirds," a cheerful voice sounded.

Andreas turned around. Julietta and Adam walked toward them.

"Cara," Luisa exclaimed. "How are you?" She hugged her daughter and gently rubbed her belly. "How is my grandchild in there?"

Adam laughed. "I think the baby is better than the mother."

"What do you mean?" Luisa looked alarmed.

"Oh, nothing serious," Julietta said, "Just awful morning sickness. It really cramps my style. The last few days have been better though." She walked up to Andreas and gave him a quick hug. He was relieved that she seemed to approve of him more. When they last met, she had acted suspicious and unfriendly toward him. He had attributed it to her being concerned about her mother getting involved with a man but realized that it may have been the pregnancy that made her moody.

"I remember my wife's morning sickness all too well," he said.

"So, what's going on with you? I heard you found the woman," Julietta said. "Let me get something to drink first."

"Let me make you some coffee or tea," Luisa said. "What would you like?"

"No, sit down, Luisa, I'll get it," Adam volunteered. "Tea?" He looked at Julietta. She nodded. "What about you?" Adam asked Andreas and Luisa.

"Tea would be fine for me too," Andreas said. "I've had enough coffee already."

"Same here." Luisa smiled at Adam. "Thank you."

"Tea coming right up." Adam sauntered toward the kitchen.

"I'll help him," Julietta said.

They came back carrying a tray with a teapot, a jug of milk, sugar, and cups.

After pouring the tea, Julietta sat. "Now, tell us about your amazing adventure."

Luisa laughed. "Andreas can tell the story in his sleep now."

After Luisa and Andreas filled them in on what happened on their trip, Julietta lifted her cup of tea. "Congratulations. This is awesome that you found Bella and her family and that she is still alive and well."

"It's truly wonderful," Luisa said. "She is a lovely and very strong woman. She made a good life for herself, but she never forgot her first love."

"Was she heartbroken when she found out that her husband had died after arriving in Switzerland?" Adam asked.

"Yes, I think that's what hurt her the most," Andreas affirmed. "He had been so close to freedom, and then died. But she had long ago accepted the fact that he had perished somewhere and knowing where it happened gave her closure."

The four of them spent the rest of Sunday strolling through Vignaverde. Andreas wanted to buy a few presents to take home with him. In the late afternoon, Julietta and Adam left for Rome since they had to work the following day.

Andreas and Luisa spent the evening enjoying the balmy air outside, eating a light dinner of antipasti, salad, and a glass of Prosecco, then retired to the bedroom. Lying next to each other after lovemaking, they tossed around some ideas how they could continue their relationship.

The following morning, they began to make more definite plans for their future. They decided that Luisa should visit Andreas in Switzerland between Christmas and New Year. Before leaving for his vacation in Tuscany, Andreas had found out that he was going to take part in a sculpture exhibition in Rome. Luisa invited him to spend a few months at Vignaverde in the summer and prepare for the art show at the estate. There was enough room for his sculpting work, and it would give them a chance to be together for a longer period of time.

The following day, Luisa drove him to Florence where he took the train back to Switzerland. After they said goodbye and the train pulled out of the station, Andreas took a deep breath. Being by himself, he had time to reflect on all that had happened the past few weeks. He felt a sense of achievement, having completed his search for Bella.

Looking through the window at the disappearing city with its beautiful old buildings, then the less attractive industrial parts, and finally the fields dotted with small farms, rows of cypress trees, and the occasional cows or goats, he smiled. Who would've thought he would fall in love again? "You're just an old fool," he said to himself, but being foolish felt enjoyable. *Why not? I've been moping around long enough.* He sipped the coffee he had bought at the station and took a bite of his prosciutto and tomato panini. His phone beeped. It was a message from Emilia with a selfie of herself and Pietro. She had promised to pick him up in Bellinzona. He was looking forward to seeing his children and his canine friend again.

Chapter 34

"Hi, sweetheart." Peter kissed Emilia and hugged an excited Pietro. They got ready to drive to Bellinzona to meet Andreas, who had taken the train from Florence.

Emilia packed a thermos of coffee and some sandwiches and fruit for the trip. "Ready."

"Actually ..." Peter hesitated. "Before we leave, I have t-t-to..." His occasional stutter always revealed nervousness. He began again, "I want to show you something. Let's go inside for a moment."

"Okay? Is everything all right?" Emilia looked puzzled.

"Yes, everything is fine." Peter put his arm around her as they stepped into the living room. Pietro gave a quick bark as if to say he was ready to leave.

Peter gave him a reassuring tap on his head, then coughed and pulled a small box out of his pants pocket. "I'm not very good at this."

Emilia laughed. "Are you blushing?"

"Would you please be quiet for a moment while I ..." Peter fiddled with the small box.

"Yes?" Emilia smiled.

"Well ... I ..."

"The answer is yes." Emilia giggled.

Peter stared at her and opened his arms. "You don't even know what I'm going to say. Oh, well." He bent down on one knee, then held out the box to her. Pietro who took this as a sign that Peter wanted to play, put his paw on Peter's knee. Emilia's heartbeat quickened. Peter opened the box.

"May I ask for your hand in marriage?" Peter said.

"Yes," Emilia called out again.

He got up; they hugged and kissed. Emilia took out the elegant vintage ring with an aquamarine stone. "This is so beautiful." She held it up and gazed at the stone sparkling in the light from the window.

"It belonged to my grandmother. She gave it to me and said, 'for that special girl.' Well, you are that special girl." He touched her hand. "I hope it fits, but it can be adjusted."

Emilia put it on her finger. "It fits perfectly. I'm honored to have your grandmother's ring. This is very special." She admired the ring, and her heart was full. "So, we're engaged?"

"Yes, indeed." Peter smiled and hugged her again, then looked at his watch. "We better leave though, or we'll be late picking up your father."

As they drove to Bellinzona, Emilia's heart swelled with joy. She had felt for a while that Peter would eventually pop the question but hadn't expected it to happen so soon. She was ready though, looking forward to a life together.

They arrived in Bellinzona just as the train pulled into the station.

The first thing Andreas saw as he got off the train was a black and brown furry something racing toward him. Pietro was so excited that he turned in circles, then leapt at him, barking and whining as if to say, "How could you abandon me for so long?"

After plenty of hugs, kisses, and licks, Andreas stood to welcome Emilia and Peter. His daughter winked at him. "It's okay, Papa, I know Pietro tops the list of most favorite family members."

Andreas hugged and kissed her. "Don't be jealous, you're still my favorite youngest daughter." He grinned, then held up her left hand. "And what is this?"

212

"A surprise," Emilia said. "We're engaged."

Andreas looked from Emilia to Peter. "Wow, that really is a surprise."

"I'm sorry I didn't ask you first if it was all right," Peter said.

Andreas laughed. "I may be old, but I'm not that old-fashioned to expect my future son-in-law to consult with me first. It's wonderful. I'm happy for you both." He hugged Emilia and clapped Peter on the back. "I couldn't wish for a better son-in-law. Have you set a date yet?"

"He just asked me this morning. I'm still digesting all this. I'm just enjoying the feeling of being engaged. But you'll have to tell us all about your adventure in Italy. And how is Luisa?"

"She's fine, thanks." He paused. "I miss her already."

On the way home, Andreas filled them in on everything from the time they separated before Milano after their vacation in Tuscany.

The following evening, Tonio came by to congratulate Emilia on her engagement. "Well done, Emilia. I've only met Peter a couple of times, but I like him a lot."

They sat together, drinking a bottle of wine they had brought with them from their vacation in Tuscany. Tonio lifted his glass and toasted Emilia. "Have you met his family at all?"

"I've met his sister, the one who lives in Germany. We actually became good friends."

"That's the one you thought was his girlfriend?" Andreas said.

Emilia gave an embarrassed chuckle. "Yes."

"What's that all about?" Tonio wanted to know.

Emilia told him about her seeing Peter with a young woman, thinking it was his girlfriend, who turned out to be his sister. She looked at her father imploringly, hoping he wouldn't elaborate on her adventure while hiking angrily up Via Spluga and twisting her ankle. Knowing Tonio's love of teasing, she wouldn't have heard the end of it.

Andreas gave a slight nod, signaling he wouldn't betray her.

"But back to his family," Emilia continued. "His mother once came to the practice. She is very nice. But I've never met his father or his younger brother. His mother invited us for dinner when Peter told her of our engagement. We're going there the day after tomorrow. I know he doesn't have a very good relationship with his father."

"Well, you'll meet him, finally," Andreas said. "That should be interesting."

"Yes, I'm very curious. I hope it'll be okay. I hope he doesn't hate me."

Tonio wrinkled his forehead. "Why would he hate you?"

"Well, from what Peter told me, he seems to be opinionated. He is angry at Peter for refusing to take over the farm and instead pursuing his profession as a veterinarian."

Tonio put his hand on Emilia's shoulder. "Come on, dear sister of mine. He'll love you. You'll melt his frozen heart, you'll see."

Chapter 35

Emilia was busy stocking their medicine cabinet at the practice when Peter came down the stairs from his apartment and entered the office. He hugged and kissed Emilia. "Hi, sweetheart. Any patients?"

"Marianne is bringing in her kitten to be spayed today. That's all for now," Emilia said.

"Ah, yes, Marianne, the punk librarian." Peter laughed.

Emilia grinned. "My father said something similar, but she is an expert librarian too. She got a lot of information about the refugee and his family, helping my father and his ... girlfriend, I guess, you could call her, to track them down."

Peter held up his arms defensibly. "Oh, I know, I didn't mean that in a negative way. I like Marianne, and she disperses any notion that librarians are boring."

"What do you mean, librarians are boring?" Emilia said.

"Oh, you know, maybe not boring, kind of nerdy." Peter put on his veterinary coat. "I better watch my mouth. I'm getting into trouble here."

"Yeah, you better," Emilia quipped, just as the phone rang. "She answered it. It was Peter's mother and she sounded upset. "Is my son there?" she asked. Emilia handed the phone to Peter.

"Hi, Mom, what's the matter?" After a pause. "What?" he snarled. "What about Ambros? I'm not your vet. Dad made that very clear."

Emilia observed Peter as his facial expression changed from concern to anger. "Okay, okay, I'll be right over." He slammed down the phone and exhaled deeply.

"Sorry about that," he said.

"What's the matter?" Emilia asked.

"One of their cows seems to be having a difficult birth and their regular vet as well as Harry, my younger brother, are out of town, and they can't get a hold of the vet on call. Mom is in tears. Hedy is her favorite cow, and Dad, of course, is too proud to ask me for help." Peter began to collect his usual arsenal of medical instruments. "I guess instead of having lunch with them as planned, we'll have to postpone because I'll have to work."

"I'll come with you," Emilia said. "You may need help."

Peter hesitated, then nodded. "Okay, if you don't mind. I'd appreciate it."

Emilia took off her lab coat. "This gives me a chance to learn something. I've only helped with delivering a calf once. But at least, I can give you emotional support."

"Thanks, Emilia. You better put the emergency message on."

"I'll call Marianne to postpone her appointment," Emilia said.

A quick smile lit up Peter's tense face. "Yes, tell her, to keep her darling away from any of the roving males until tomorrow."

After making a quick phone call to Marianne, Emilia followed Peter outside. He stowed his medical bag in the backseat of his SUV, and they drove off.

Emilia had never been to Peter's family farm, though she knew where it was and had driven by the house. A quiet lunch with his parents would have been an ideal way to meet them.

Instead, she would be introduced in a tense situation. Still she was excited to help Peter with the calf delivery. She was also nervous. Would she be able to help him and what would the family, especially his father, think of her?

When they arrived at the farm, Emilia realized that it was much larger than she had imagined. Peter parked in front of the stables when his mother came rushing outside. She was a tall woman with light-brown hair tied in a messy ponytail. She looked harried.

"Thank God, you're here," she said. "It looks like Hedy's calf is not in the right position. Robert is trying to help, but with his arthritis, he's having a hard time. You know how stubborn he is."

Peter got out and grabbed his bag. "Does that mean he doesn't know you called me?" He stared at his mother, his face pinched, a thin line forming between his eyebrows.

"Oh, he knows. He was relieved. Of course, the stubborn mule wouldn't say so, but I can tell." She turned to Emilia. "Hello, and thanks for coming."

When they entered the stable, the first thing Emilia saw was a cow lying on her side on a bed of straw, and an older but sturdy-looking man with Peter's reddish hair, streaked with gray, sitting behind the cow with his arm deep inside the animal. He was groaning with exhaustion. When he heard them, he turned his head and gave a quick nod.

"What's happening, Dad?" Peter asked.

"One of the legs is twisted. I can't hold on to it," he said, his voice tense. Just then, the cow groaned as well.

"Oh, Hedy, it's going to be okay, sweetie," Peter's mother said. She was sitting down next to the cow and gently stroked her head.

Peter's father gave an exhausted sigh. "Oh, Jesus. I'm not strong enough anymore."

"Don't worry, Dad. Let me get close." Peter knelt next to his father, who got up slowly, pulling a face, and holding on to the side of the partition. He nodded a quick hello to Emilia.

After covering one arm with a plastic glove, Peter put it deep into the cow, groping around. "Yes, the leg is twisted. "How long has this been going on?"

"Well, we noticed she was getting ready to deliver this morning," Peter's mother said. "But Robert has been at it for about three hours."

"You should've called me earlier," Peter grumbled. "Don't push, sweetheart," he said. "She's pushing against my arm." Peter breathed heavily. "Work with me, Hedy, not against me." After a few more seconds. "Okay, I got the leg turned around." He brushed his free hand over his forehead, wiping away the sweat pouring down his face. Emilia pulled out a Kleenex from her pocket and wiped his forehead.

"Thanks," he said. "Fortunately, the calf is in the right position. It's not a breech."

Emilia saw one of the legs poking out. "Need the chains?" she asked, pointing at the obstetrical chains in a bucket of water next to the cow.

"No," Peter said. "Hand me the ropes instead." He pointed at his bag. "I prefer the ropes. They don't slip off as easily and they're strong but gentler on the legs."

Emilia opened the bag, pulled out a pair of ropes, and handed it to him.

Peter reached inside again and pulled the second front leg out, then wrapped the ropes around the legs and pulled hard but carefully. After a while, there was another groan from the cow, and the calf slipped out.

Emilia grabbed a handful of straw, rubbed some of the mucus off the calf and massaged it. Peter removed the fluid from its mouth and nose, then tickled and pinched the nose to stimulate the calf to breathe.

"Hello there, little one, welcome," Peter said, his voice gentle and loving. "What were you trying to do? Come into the world with only one leg? You know that wouldn't have worked, would it?"

Peter moved the calf gently toward its mother. Hedy turned her head to the calf and began to lick it.

There was a general sigh of relief. "She accepts the baby. Oh, I'm so happy," Peter's mother said. She wiped tears from her face. They all watched Hedy and her baby getting acquainted.

Peter chuckled. "It's always a magical moment. It never gets old." He put his arm around Emilia. Peter's father looked at them, and Emilia noticed his face had softened. He gave a quick smile. He went up to Peter and touched his shoulder. "Thanks, Son, I owe you."

"You don't owe me anything. It's my job," Peter muttered.

"I didn't mean it that way. I mean … I'm glad you became a vet, after all." He looked embarrassed.

"Well, that's a first," Peter said, surprised. He grinned. "I'm glad you finally came to your senses."

"Okay, boys," Peter's mother said, "it's about time you made up." She raised an eyebrow and smiled at Emilia. "They're both stubborn as mules." She pointed at the house. "But let's go inside and have something to eat. I was too preoccupied to prepare the lunch I planned, but I made a stew yesterday I can warm up. You're not a vegetarian, are you?" She looked at Emilia concerned.

Emilia smiled. "No, and stew sounds wonderful."

"Great. By the way, we haven't been properly introduced. My name is Martha." She gave Emilia a quick hug, then winked at Peter. "And I hear that congratulations are in order."

219

"Oh, yes?" Robert looked stunned. "What do you mean?" The deep fold between his eyebrows was back.

"Peter and Emilia are engaged," Martha said.

Robert looked irritated. "And how come I don't know about this?"

"Peter just told me a couple of days ago, and you were gone out of town," Martha said. "And now with the whole birthing excitement with Hedy, I forgot to mention it."

"Well, okay," Robert looked from Peter to Emilia and back. "I guess that's something to celebrate then."

"It sure is," Martha said. "Let's open a bottle of the good wine."

They went inside. Robert still looked a little irritated, but Emilia hoped he would approve of her.

The Walser family home was a farmhouse typical of the Rhaeto-Romanic region of the canton of Grisons. It had thick walls and small windows to conserve energy and heat during the cold winter months. The outside walls were decorated with drawings, scratched into the plasterwork in the so-called Sgraffito technique. Inside, the rooms were fairly small but cozy with hardwood floors and embroidered curtains. There was a tiled stove as well as an open fireplace. Martha asked them to sit in the living room while she went into the kitchen.

"Can I help with something?" Emilia asked Martha.

"No, just relax. This won't take long." Soon the smell of food wafted in from the kitchen, and Emilia realized she was famished. She had only had a cup of coffee and a piece of toast for breakfast.

They had their lunch in the den adjacent to the kitchen. The beef stew with vegetables was delicious. Martha served it with fresh crusty bread and salad. Peter opened a bottle of red wine and poured each a glass.

"Congratulations on your engagement again," Martha said.

"Yes, congratulations." Peter's father lifted his glass, toasting them. "And please call me Robert." He smiled at Emilia, his facial expression warm albeit a little cautious. But Emilia felt he approved of her. He was obviously not a very expressive man. Peter seemed to have inherited his somewhat withdrawn and quiet demeanor from his father. His mother was more vivacious. Peter, however, was warm and loving. His father seemed more aloof.

After a few glasses of wine, however, Robert lightened up and told them a few stories about the farm.

Half an hour later, Peter and Emilia got ready to drive back to the practice. Before they left, Robert took Peter aside, and they had what seemed an amiable talk. Robert gave Peter a friendly pat on the shoulder.

"Your father was really nice," Emilia said as they were driving back. "He seems to approve of you now."

Peter lifted an eyebrow. "I hope it'll last. I don't trust the old man yet."

"He was grateful that you helped with the birth of the calf. That may have changed his mind about your profession."

"Could be. He asked me to be his vet from now on."

"That's great. He's had a change of heart."

"Maybe," Peter muttered.

Emilia gently poked his arm with her finger. "Your mom called you *both* stubborn mules."

"She's right in a way," Peter admitted. "I'm known for holding grudges sometimes. I should've been a little more forgiving. I always expected him to take the first step."

After driving for a while in silence, Emilia tittered. "Hedy, the cow, was the peacemaker."

Peter laughed. "Good old Hedy, I'm so glad she's all right." He cleared his throat. "Dad really likes you."

"Thank God," Emilia exhaled relieved. "At first I wasn't sure, but he seemed to warm up to me."

At home that evening, Emilia went to her father's workshop to watch him put the finishing touches to a sculpture. After Andreas put the chisel down and pulled off his gloves, Emilia told him about the birthing experience and her introduction to the Walser family.

"I think they liked me," she said.

"Of course, they did." Andreas hugged Emilia. "Who wouldn't like you?"

"We'll have to all get together soon," Emilia said. "And the best thing is, it seems that Robert, Peter's father, and Peter made up. Robert wants us to be his vet now."

"Great, so he changed his mind about his wayward son?"

Chapter 36: December 2018

The day after Christmas, Andreas prepared to drive to the train station in Bellinzona in the south of Switzerland to pick up Luisa. When he stepped outside, he zipped up his warm padded jacket and pulled his woolen cap over his ears. It was a cold but clear day, and the snow-covered trees and meadows shimmered in the sunlight. He took Pietro for a quick walk so the dog could do his business, then put him in his doggy seat in the back of the car. He couldn't remember if Luisa liked dogs. There were a few cats on her Tuscan estate and unlike some of the stray cats in that part of the country, theirs were well kept.

"She'll just have to get used to my canine companion, right Pietro?" Pietro gave a quick bark in agreement.

The drive from Andeer to Bellinzona was easier than he had expected. It had snowed quite heavily the night before, but the roads were well plowed and the traffic moderate. The day after Christmas was a holiday in Switzerland, and Andreas thought there would be more cars on the road. Then again, vacationers tended to take public transportation more during the wintry weather.

The trip took him a little over an hour, and he arrived twenty minutes early. Fortunately, he found a parking space right next to the station. He checked the timetable for the arrival time and the platform of the train from Milano, then got himself a cup of coffee at City Bistro, a coffee shop in the station.

The train arrived on time, and Andreas waited at the end of the platform so he wouldn't miss Luisa in the crowd. As expected, there were a lot of passengers disembarking, but he recognized her right away. His heart swelled when she walked toward him. She was dressed for winter, wearing a black winter coat, long red scarf, and black boots. Strands of her auburn hair escaped her red wool cap.

They hugged and kissed. "How was your trip?" Andreas took her roll-away suitcase, put his arm around her and guided her to the exit. "Have you eaten? Are you hungry?"

"Everything went well, and yes, I treated myself to lunch and a glass of wine in the restaurant car, which was quite good."

When they got to the car, Andreas opened the door, and a very excited Pietro welcomed them. "He insisted on coming along," Andreas said. "He didn't want to miss out on welcoming a very beautiful woman."

Luisa petted Pietro who greeted her enthusiastically, obviously approving of his master's guest. Andreas had to finally pull him away before he smothered Luisa. "I used to have a dog until a few years ago," she said.

"What happened to him or her?" Andreas loaded Luisa's luggage into the trunk.

"It was a female, an Irish Setter, well a mix of Irish Setter and a few other breeds. It was old age. Lucy got to be thirteen years old."

On the way home, Andreas told her what they had planned for the next few days. "We'll have a get-together with Emilia and Peter, her fiancé."

"I'm looking forward to meeting him," Luisa said. "He sounds like a wonderful person."

"Yes, I'm very happy for Emilia. Peter is a great man. His parents own a farm nearby, and they're very nice people. In fact, you're getting to meet them tomorrow at one of our local restaurants. Somehow, we've all been quite busy the last few months. We've met a few times but decided it would be nice to have a little get-together to celebrate the engagement and your being with us." After a short pause. "I missed you."

Luisa smiled at him. "I missed you too."

When they arrived at Andreas' home, Emilia came outside next door. She waved at them, rushed over and hugged Luisa. Pietro snorted as if to say, he wanted a hug as well. Luisa petted his head. "He's a sweetheart," Luisa said. "I'm already in love with him."

"I hope not too much. Reserve some of those feelings for me," Andreas whispered to her.

After a dinner of roasted chicken, potatoes, salad, and red wine at Emilia's home, they sat in her den, a cozy room off the kitchen, enjoying a fire in the fireplace. It smelled of burning wood and pinecones. Emilia had lit the candles on the Christmas tree, which added to the festive atmosphere.

Luisa was surprised that they had real candles on the tree. "Aren't you afraid of fires?"

"We only light them for a short time, normally on Christmas Eve and Christmas Day and perhaps on Stephanstag … Saint Stephen's Day," Emilia explained. "The rest of the time, we use the Christmas lights." She pointed at the small electric lights on the tree. "I love the candles though. For me, that's part of the real Christmas tradition."

While sipping a glass of eggnog, Luisa told them about the busy time during the grape harvest in Vignaverde. She had brought along two bottles of Sangiovese from their last harvest. Emilia told a story about a rescue mission. A cat got stranded in a tree near the veterinary practice. Peter was busy taking care of an animal inside. People were standing around wondering what to do. Emilia spotted the cat and decided to rescue it. To the surprise of those around her, she grabbed a cloth tote bag and climbed the tree.

"The kitty was up quite high and complained miserably. At first, it was afraid, but I was able to calm it down, then put it into the bag and got ready to climb down. Suddenly I heard Peter from downstairs screaming 'Oh, my god, oh my god. Are you nuts?' He was afraid I was going to fall. When I got down, he was pale. 'Why didn't you call me? You could've been hurt.' Well, the cat was a happy camper. And for a little while, I was the heroine."

"I bet the kitty was happy," Andreas said. "You know it used to be your sister, the tomboy, who climbed every tree she could find as a kid."

"That's right, she did," Emilia said. "Well, it really wasn't such a difficult task. The lowest branches were strong, and they were easy to reach."

After finishing their after-dinner drink, Andreas noticed that Luisa was beginning to fade. "It's been a long day for you. We better get some sleep."

Chapter 37

It was another cold winter day when Luisa and Andreas took a stroll through the village of Andeer. It had snowed again overnight, but the sun was out. Fields and trees covered by white powder shimmered in the sun.

Wrapped in winter coats, hats, and gloves, they made their way to the veterinary practice where Emilia and Peter worked. It was a quiet day with only one woman picking up her cat that had been spayed. Andreas introduced Luisa to Peter, then kidded him about his near heart attack when he had discovered Emilia climbing the tree.

"It's true," Peter said. "I almost had a coronary." Then added with a smile, "Well, I'm glad Emilia and the cat are okay."

Emilia and Peter showed Luisa around the practice. It was a fairly small but clean and cheerful outfit. In one of the back rooms, they saw a few cages with a couple of rabbits in two of them. The little fellows were chewing away at some grass. They sat up on their hind legs, watching the humans eagerly. "They're recovering from bite wounds from foxes," Emilia explained. "We caught them just in time before their predators made off with dinner."

"They'll be released into the wild as soon as it gets a little warmer," Peter said.

Following the visit to the vet's office, Andreas showed Luisa the rest of the town. On their way through Andeer, they met Marianne, the librarian, who had helped Andreas with his

227

research. Marianne, lively and excited as usual, shook hands with Luisa, then turned to Andreas.

"Well, Mr. O'Reilly, I heard you not only found the mysterious Bella, but you also found love. How romantic." The young woman with piercings in her face and ears clasped her hands together and smiled widely.

Luisa looked at Andreas surprised, and he rolled his eyes. He turned to Marianne. "I can tell the village gossip is in full swing, but please call me Andreas." They laughed, then Marianne went on her way.

Next, they met up with Franz Suter, the police chief, and together with Franz, they went to visit Flurin Pitsch, the guide on the Swiss side who used to pick up refugees from Italy. They spent a few hours with him and his son, Bruno. Flurin was happy they had found Bella.

"So, this solves the mystery of the disappeared refugee. Too bad, I wasn't able to pick him up in time." The old man sighed.

"You shouldn't feel responsible," Luisa said. "From what I heard, you saved the lives of many people."

"We tried our best," was the humble answer of the old man. "You do what you can to help."

In the late afternoon, Tonio came by to welcome Luisa. Andreas invited him to join Emilia, Peter, Peter's parents, Luisa and him at one of the restaurants in town for dinner. Andreas had met Peter's family a couple of times since Emilia and Peter had announced their engagement, but he wanted them all to get together for a celebratory dinner at one of his favorite restaurants in the village, called Weisses Kreuz. It was an elegant but also homey restaurant, frequented by tourists and a favorite hangout for the locals.

As they walked the short distance to the restaurant, the sun was just about to set, and the temperature dropped. Luisa wrapped her scarf tightly around her. Andreas put his arm around her. "Are you all right? Is it too cold for you?"

"I don't mind. I enjoy all the snow. It's different from winter in Tuscany where we have a lot of rain. Snow makes the landscape more festive. But yes, I'd have to get used to long months of winter."

"Well, I wouldn't mind exchanging this cold weather for the milder temperatures in Tuscany," Andreas said.

"Aha," Tonio quipped. "You got yourself a beautiful girlfriend with a vineyard in Tuscany. Very sneaky, Dad." Tonio winked at Luisa.

"Hey, what are you insinuating? Watch it or you'll have to pay for your own dinner tonight." Andreas laughed and slapped Tonio's shoulder.

"Well, here we are," Emilia said. She opened the door to the restaurant.

An elderly waitress welcomed them and pointed to a table in the corner next to the window. "Your other party is already here."

Andreas saw Martha, Peter's mother, waving at them. Robert and Peter got up to welcome them. They shook hands, and Andreas introduced Luisa.

"Oh, my God," Martha exclaimed. "We heard from Peter and Emilia about your adventurous trip through Italy. What a story."

"It sure was," Andreas said.

"Yes, and one of the guides on the Swiss side still lives here in Andeer," Robert said. "That's quite something."

"That's true," Andreas said. "You know Flurin Pitsch, right?"

"Yes, we do," Martha said. "We had no idea though that he was a guide during the war. He sounds like a hero."

"Indeed," Robert acknowledged.

When the waitress came, they all ordered one of the restaurant's specialties — pork cordon bleu, filled with ham and alpine cheese, and french fries and vegetables, as well as a bottle of red wine.

Once the food was served, they quietly enjoyed the hearty but delicious dish. Andreas was happy to hear that the restaurant was also a favorite of the Walser family. He observed Robert, a quiet and friendly man, who seemed to have finally accepted the fact that his son went his own way and became a veterinarian instead of a farmer.

Just as they were getting ready to order coffee and dessert, Peter's phone pinged. He glanced at it and got up.

"Sorry about that, but I need to take this." He left the dining room and stepped into the corridor.

Emilia wrinkled her forehead and looked after him. "Must be an emergency," she mumbled.

Peter came back in and lifted his shoulder. "I'm so sorry, but we have a patient. A dog got run over by a car."

"Oh, no." Emilia got up.

"I think I can handle it by myself. Why don't you stay?" Peter said to her.

"No way, I'm coming with you. Sorry." She gave the others an apologetic look.

Andreas got up and put his hand on her shoulder. "Good luck. I hope the dog will be okay."

"I hope so too," Emilia said as she rushed after Peter.

Andreas explained the situation to Luisa. "Oh, no," she said. "Let's hope for the best."

"Let's go to the practice later and take them something for dessert," Tonio suggested.

"Good idea," Andreas said. "We'll take them some of the walnut cake."

Robert cleared his throat. "Lots of responsibility. I wanted him to take over the farm. I think it would've been less stressful."

"What do you mean?" Martha gave him a stern look. "You obviously forgot the situation with Hedy's birth."

Robert grunted. "Well, I guess so." He turned to Andreas, Luisa, and Tonio. "I was angry at him at first for abandoning the farm. We worked hard to make it successful, so we could pass it on to him. I just assumed that he, being the oldest, would take over." He shrugged. "I was disappointed when he enrolled in veterinary school without telling us, as if being a farmer wasn't good enough for him."

"You know that's not true," Martha said. "It just wasn't for him. He wanted to work closely with animals, help them."

"He could've helped them on the farm … I know." He lifted his hands in acknowledgement as Martha seemed to get ready to contradict him. "You're right. I realized eventually that he did the right thing."

"Well, took you long enough," Martha muttered as she smiled at him.

Andreas took a sip of his espresso. "I think as parents we always want what's best for our children. But sometimes what we consider good for them may not be their destiny." He glanced at Tonio who observed him closely. "And sometimes we have to accept we're wrong."

Andreas paused, thinking of his own turmoil when he first realized that Tonio was gay and wanted to go into fashion design, which Andreas at the time didn't consider a "manly" enough profession. He put his hand on Tonio's shoulder, giving it a friendly squeeze, then turned to Robert.

"I was also hesitant when Emilia decided to become a veterinarian because I knew how attached she can become to an animal. I was afraid not being able to save them all would break her heart and cause her too much stress. But I had to let her go and make her own decisions."

"Well, talk about Emilia," Tonio said. "Why don't we go by the practice and see how they're doing and bring them the dessert."

"Yes, let's do that," Martha said.

Andreas paid the check, fending off Robert's offer that they split the bill. "You can pay next time." He asked the waitress to pack two pieces of the walnut cake to take along.

They walked the short distance to Peter and Emilia's practice. "When they opened the door, Emilia was in the process of assuring a young woman in tears that her dog would be all right. Next to the woman stood a middle-aged man, who kept apologizing. "I'm so sorry, but the dog just ran into the side of my car. There's no way I could've avoided him." He gently put his hand on the woman's shoulder.

"I know," she said, sobbing. "It's not your fault. We just got him, and we're not used to him yet. He just pulled and took off running. He caught me completely by surprise. He's young and not well trained yet."

At that point, Peter walked into the reception area, pulling off his surgical mask.

"How is he?" The woman exclaimed, her voice shaking.

Peter smiled at her. "He's going to be all right. He has some bruises. He'll be sore for a while, but I didn't detect any fractures or internal injuries. We'll keep him overnight to make sure nothing crops up. You should be able to take him home tomorrow, though."

"Ah, thank God. Thank you so much." The woman hugged Emilia and Peter.

Relieved, the driver of the car wiped his forehead. "Thank God, indeed."

"He's an energetic young dog," Peter said to the woman. "He needs some guidance. I can recommend a good dog-training class."

"Thank you, that's what I need. Can I see him before I leave?"

"Yes," Peter said. "He's asleep right now. I gave him a sedative but come on back." The owner of the dog and the driver of the car gave each other a brief hug, then the driver left. The young woman followed Peter into the examination room.

A short while later, they came back outside. Her tears dried, the woman left, a smile on her face.

"A lucky outcome and a wonderful end to our get-together," Andreas said.

Tonio put the paper bag with the pieces of cake on the counter. "We brought you some dessert."

"Thank you," Peter said as he opened the bag. "My favorite." He smiled.

"Well," Robert cleared his throat and looked around the reception area. "This is a nice outfit, Son."

"Let me show you around," Peter said. "We have a few new animals in the back."

"All right," Andreas said to Peter's family. "We'll have to do this again."

Emilia and Peter took Peter's parents to the back to show them the facility. Andreas, Luisa, and Tonio left to go back to Andreas' home.

Andreas put his arm around Luisa as they were walking home. "I'm glad the dog is going to be okay," Luisa said. "And Peter's parents seem to be very nice people."

"Indeed, they are," Andreas said.

"The old man really had a change of heart about Peter," Tonio said. "That's good. It would've been sad if Emilia and Peter didn't have both families on their side."

Chapter 38

The night after the get-together with Peter and his parents, Luisa slept badly, in part because she wasn't used to the somewhat heavy and hearty food they had enjoyed in the restaurant. She also tried to come to terms with her feelings about the future of her and Andreas' relationship. The longer she was with him, the more she fell in love with him. She wondered how it would all work out. She couldn't simply move to Switzerland. She had a home and responsibilities in Tuscany. Andreas, on the other hand, loved Italy but was also very close to his family in Switzerland. Where would they live? Did their relationship even have a future? They had made plans for Andreas to spend the summer in Vignaverde, but then what? *I should just enjoy the time we have together.* Luisa exhaled deeply. After some tossing and turning, she finally fell asleep.

The next thing she was aware of was something wet on her nose. She opened her eyes and stared at Pietro's face. She heard Andreas chuckle. "Sorry about that. He insisted on greeting you first." Andreas lifted him down and hugged Luisa. "There is coffee, by the way, in case you're ready to get up."

"What time is it?" She yawned, raised herself on her elbows, and looked out the window.

"Nine o'clock and it's a sunny day and not as cold as yesterday," Andreas said. He lay down next to her. They snuggled and kissed. "Coffee can wait," he murmured as they were enjoying a leisurely hour of making love.

Later, they were eating a light breakfast of coffee, rolls, cheese, butter, and jam. Luisa groaned as she sat down. "If I stayed long enough, I'd have to buy a new wardrobe. How do people stay so slim here?"

Andreas gave a snort. "Have you noticed my midsection?"

Luisa laughed. "Yes, but there is nothing wrong with it."

"Well, first of all, we don't usually eat such heavy meals," Andreas said. "Yesterday was an exception. Besides, we get quite a bit of exercise, walking, hiking, swimming at the thermal pools, shoveling snow, and so on."

There was a knock on the door and Pietro barked happily. "It's open," Andreas called.

Emilia walked in. "Oh, it smells of fresh coffee."

"Hi there. Get yourself a cup," Andreas said.

Emilia came back from the kitchen, carrying a cup of espresso and joined them at the table. "How long are you staying, Luisa?"

"Only two more days ... unfortunately."

Andreas put his hand on hers and squeezed it. "I'll be in Tuscany soon. Can't wait to see you again."

"Well, I have a suggestion, but only if you don't have any other plans," Emilia said. "I have the day off tomorrow, and I really wanted to go and visit Lena and Luigi in the Ticino once again." She took another sip of coffee. "Papa has a few sculptures in some of the public parks and private residences, Luisa. You mentioned a few days ago that you'd like to see some his artwork."

Luisa nodded. "Yes, I'd love to, if that's possible."

"We could also visit the gallery in Locarno with ..." Emilia didn't continue, pressed her lips together, and gave Andreas a hesitant look.

236

Luisa picked up on the unsaid suggestion. She turned to Andreas. "Didn't you say your wife had a gallery with paintings of hers in Locarno?"

"Yes, that's right," Andreas said.

"Couldn't we go there as well?" Luisa asked. "I'd love to see some of her work too."

"I was going to suggest that," Emilia said, "but I didn't know how you'd feel about it."

"If it's okay with you, I'd love to see them." Luisa turned to Andreas, hoping she hadn't evoked any painful memories in him.

"Certainly, we can do that." Andreas sounded enthusiastic. "In fact, I just had an idea. You're leaving in two days. What if we drove to Locarno tomorrow and spent the last night in a hotel there? That way, I can take you to the station in Bellinzona or Lugano for your train ride back. The Ticino is a little more fun in summer, but it's warmer than here. Besides, there is plenty to entertain us. The old part of Locarno is quaint, and the city is next to the lake, the Lago Maggiore. It's a real tourist town but in winter most of the people there are locals, and it's not as crowded."

He turned to Emilia. "You could come with us for the day and then spend the night with Lena and Luigi. It's a short train ride to the Maggia Valley. We'll drop you off at the station and I'll come by the next day for a visit as well and take you back. How does that sound?"

"Sounds like a plan," Emilia said. "Peter owes me a couple of days off anyway."

Chapter 39

"No, Pietro, you'll have to stay back this time." Peter held the dog who was pulling on the leash, wanting to follow Luisa, Andreas, and Emilia as they were getting ready to leave for the Ticino. Andreas hugged Pietro goodbye and promised him an extra-large bone. His canine companion showed his disappointment for having to stay put with a sad face and pitiful whining.

"Goodbye, Pietro." Luisa hugged the dog as well. "I hope to see you soon in Italy."

"I'll take him for a long walk," Peter said. "He'll be very excited with all the animals at the practice. Come on Pietro, stop your pity party." He lifted Pietro up and put him in his car, then gave him a treat, which seemed to console the little dog for the moment. Peter then drove away, giving a goodbye-wave.

Emilia put a bag with bottles of water, some fruit, and other snacks for the road on the backseat. Andreas started the car, and they began their journey south. As Andreas told Luisa, they would be driving through the San Bernardino tunnel since the road across the mountain was closed in winter. The roads were cleared of snow, so they made good time. As they emerged from the tunnel, the sun lit up the fields and farther along the green meadows with patches of snow and the pine woods of the Ticino. Luisa tried to imagine what it looked like in summer. Andreas rolled down the window for a quick airing out of the stale tunnel air, and Luisa inhaled the scent of snow.

"I'll have to come back here during the warmer season," she said. "It's just difficult because of all the work at the estate and the vineyards, but I'll do it."

"Yes, you should take time off once in a while. We have some nice vineyards here as well. I know they can't compare with the ones in Tuscany, but we have a pretty good wine, a Merlot del Ticino. We'll have to try one for dinner tonight."

In the city of Locarno, Andreas maneuvered his car through the busy streets. At the hotel, which was situated close to the lake, Lago Maggiore, he parked the car in the reserved spots. Andreas and Luisa checked into their room, left Andreas' overnight bag and Luisa's suitcase, and together with Emilia, they went for a stroll through Locarno.

Since they were early, they stopped at a cafeteria, ordered espresso and croissants and admired the view of the lake and the mountains. It was somewhat damp so close to the water, but the sun was warm enough, and Luisa felt comfortable in her winter coat. Refreshed from the coffee, they walked up a few streets past fashion boutiques and small grocery stores that displayed their fare of fruit, cheese, salami, prosciutto, and other delicacies.

The old part of Locarno reminded Luisa of some of the smaller towns in Tuscany with their cobblestone streets and their picturesque houses. The gallery with Karla's paintings was in a street next to a small Romanesque church. Looking through the window of the art store, Luisa saw an older woman wave at them. It was Silvia, the owner of the gallery and the art store. She looked like an older hippie; she was dressed in a long, flowery skirt and a colorful woolen shawl wrapped around her shoulders.

She welcomed them with enthusiasm, kissing Emilia and Andreas and hugging Luisa. "You must be Andreas' travel companion. Tonio was here and told us all about your adventures." Then she turned to Andreas. "And, yes, she is beautiful."

Luisa felt the warmth rise to her face and Andreas chuckled. "Don't mind her," he said to Luisa. "We're all a big family and gossip is the modus operandi here."

While Silvia and Andreas chatted and teased each other, Emilia and Luisa went to look at a few of Karla's paintings. Luisa didn't consider herself an expert in art, but as she quietly observed the large, semi-abstract, colorful canvasses, she was deeply impressed. She knew from what Andreas had told her that his wife had been a successful painter, well known not only in Switzerland but throughout Europe and even overseas. These paintings showed her mastery of the craft and even more importantly, they expressed her passion and power.

"These are amazing," she said to Emilia, who agreed in a quietly reverential tone.

Luisa realized that Karla must have been such a powerful presence in Andreas' life. It worried her. What did Andreas see in *her*? She was a vintner, the host of a vacation estate. How could she measure up to his expectations? She knew these were ridiculous thoughts, but she couldn't help feeling insecure all of a sudden. Then again, he seemed to really care for her.

"What do you think?" a voice said next to her. Andreas put his arm around her.

"I'm amazed, overwhelmed." She exhaled deeply and looked at him. "These are beautiful. She truly was very talented."

"I know." He smiled but she noticed sadness in his eyes. They stayed for a while, then Emilia suggested they go look at a sculpture of Andreas' nearby.

They said goodbye to Silvia and walked down to the lake. Next to it was a small park with a garden area and a few sculptures by local artists, as Andreas explained. At one end of the park, one of his sculptures was displayed.

"It's a very early one, one of the first ones they allowed me to exhibit," Andreas said. It was made of Andeer gneiss, according to the plaque at the bottom, a green stone sprinkled with white and gray. It depicted a smoothly polished animal-like shape on a rugged base. The name of the sculpture was *Trapped*.

"That's a good description," Luisa said. "It looks like a trapped bird, trying to fly away."

"Yes, that's the feeling I tried to convey."

"Did you feel trapped at the time?" Luisa smiled at him.

"Something like that. I'll tell you the background of this sculpture some other time." He took her hand in his. They quietly observed the sculpture, then Andreas pointed out a few more artworks of local artists he knew.

"Let's have some coffee over there." Emilia pointed to a piazza nearby with a couple of cafeterias next to a few stores. "Afterward, I'll have to catch the train." She glanced at her watch. "I told Lena I'd be there by six o'clock."

"Fortunately, the train station is nearby," Andreas said. He grabbed Emilia's overnight bag. They walked to a coffee shop with a patio facing the lake and ordered coffee, water, and some pastries.

Luisa sighed. "You feed me too much. I'll have to go on a diet after all the holiday meals and the tasty pastries."

After finishing their coffee and sweets, Emilia got ready to leave. Andreas and Luisa walked her to the small train to the Maggia Valley which was already waiting next to a streetcar stop. Emilia kissed Andreas and hugged Luisa. "I hope to see you in Vignaverde again soon. Next time, I'll bring Peter too."

"That would be great. I'd love to have you and your fiancé visit. Say hello to him," Luisa said. "He's a very nice man."

241

"Yes, I know. I lucked out." Emilia boarded the train and waved at them as it pulled away from the train stop.

Chapter 40

Andreas and Luisa went back to their hotel for a little rest before going out in the evening for a last meal together. They would be dining early because Luisa's train was scheduled to leave at nine o'clock the following morning from Bellinzona, so they had to wake early to avoid rush hour traffic.

The restaurant Andreas had picked for their dinner was in the center of Locarno, close to the lake. Locanda Locarnese specialized in seafood, pasta, and vegetarian dishes. The friendly waiter brought them to a table next to the fireplace. In the evening, it got cold even in the south of Switzerland, so the fire added to the warm and cozy atmosphere.

They ordered their food and a bottle of wine, Merlot del Ticino, which Luisa praised. When the owner came by to say hello to Andreas, whom he seemed to know, Andreas told him that Luisa was the owner of a vineyard in Tuscany.

"Your wine is excellent," Luisa said to him.

The slightly overweight, elegantly dressed man was pleased about the compliment. After the waiter told them about the specials of the evening and they ordered their meal, Luisa asked Andreas if he came here often.

"Not that often. For special occasions, family celebrations, and for special people in my life." He lifted his wine glass, and they toasted each other. His verdigris green eyes sparkled while patches of light from the fire danced across his face.

The hotel Andreas had booked for them was a small but elegant building right at the lake. They sat by the window for a while, watching the sun set over the water. Andreas put his arm around her and kissed her. "I miss you already."

She smiled. "I'm still here though, and we have the whole night."

"You're right. What are we waiting for?" He led her to the bed and slowly removed her clothes while she did the same with his.

Lying next to him, satiated and relaxed after making love, Luisa thought of the days she had spent with Andreas and his family. The insecurities she had felt while looking at his former wife's paintings faded in the warmth of his presence. He had told her that meeting her and being together on their journey through Italy had given him a new lease on life. She, who had given up on romance years ago, was grateful for his love. Now, she felt that spark again. It made her spirit soar.

"I love you," she whispered.

He kissed her. "I love you too."

The night was over too fast. When she got up the next morning, she felt sad about the approaching separation. There was no time, however, for a lengthy goodbye. Traffic was heavier than they had anticipated; they made it to Bellinzona just in time for Luisa to board the train to Milano. Andreas accompanied her to her seat, hoisted her suitcase to the overhead bin, and got her settled. They kissed goodbye as the loudspeaker announced the departure of the train. Andreas had to almost jump off. He grinned and waved at her through the window.

Luisa took a deep breath and watched the industrial area and then the countryside zip by. She sent a brief text message to Andreas who sent back "Love you" and a few heart emojis. Luisa smiled. "Just like teenagers," she murmured.

As the train drove through Chiasso and reached the Italian side, an Italian customs official walked by, glanced at the passengers, then went to the next wagon. Luisa relaxed into her soft seat in the first-class carriage and thought of what was awaiting her in Tuscany. She had to change trains in Milano, and Julietta and Adam would pick her up in Florence and drive her to Vignaverde. She was excited, thinking about her pregnant daughter. Andreas had taken her shopping in Andeer where she had bought a few cute baby outfits. They knew by now that they were expecting a little girl. "I'll be a nonna," Luisa whispered and chuckled. "A grandmother in love."

Back in Bellinzona, Andreas felt bereft as he was watching the train leave the station. It became clear to him once again how close he and Luisa had become and how much he cared for her. The visit to the art gallery and seeing Karla's paintings again had triggered a quick pain in his heart, but the sadness had disappeared as soon as they had left. Being there with Luisa had in some way been a final letting go of Karla.

Now, however, he had to let go of Luisa as well, at least for a few months. What would happen afterwards? What would the future hold?

Even mature love was complicated, wasn't it? He chortled. "Silly old fool," he chastised himself. And yet, and yet, it was worth it, despite the confusion and heartaches. Love was worth it. It definitely was. For him and Luisa, for Peter and Emilia, and, yes, as painful as it had been, for Joshua and Bella as well.

Andreas walked to his car and drove out of Bellinzona toward the Maggia Valley to visit Lena and Luigi, and to pick up Emilia.

Chapter 41: June 2019

It was a sunny day in June after lots of rain during April and May. Wildflowers turned the green meadows into a cornucopia of colors—red, blue, white, and yellow. A light breeze cooled Andreas' face. He inhaled the earthy smell of an early summer day. While he checked the oil and water level in his SUV, Pietro marked and watered his territory in the yard, kicked his back legs, then looked at Andreas expectantly.

"Okay, ready to go?" Andreas opened the door of the car and lifted Pietro into his doggy seat in the back. He waved at Emilia, who stood in the open doorway of her house next to his. She waved back, and Andreas started the car. He was on his way to the train station in Bellinzona once more, this time to pick up Paulo who was coming for his promised visit. Paulo had decided to skip the busy Italian freeways in favor of a more relaxing ride on the train. He had wanted to take his wife Diana along, but as Paulo had told Andreas on the phone, Diana felt it was something he needed to do on his own.

When Paulo stepped off the train, Pietro welcomed him enthusiastically, jumping up at him and licking his hands. Andreas pulled him down. "I'm trying to stop him from doing this," he said. "Not everybody likes to be attacked by an enthusiastic pup."

"I love dogs," Paulo said and continued to pet Pietro, who not only wagged his tail but his whole backside.

Andreas noticed that Paulo had lost weight since he had seen him last. When Andreas commented on his slimmer figure, Paulo admitted a little embarrassed that he had felt the need to start exercising again since he was going to go hiking with a Swiss mountaineer.

"You know there are trains or cable cars to the top of most mountains in Switzerland," Andreas said. "There's bus all the way to the top of the Splügenpass, or we can drive by car."

"Oh, no. I want to hike, at least part of the way," Paulo protested as they walked to Andreas' car. "After you and Luisa left, I did some research on the area where my father's body was found and where he must have crossed into Switzerland. There are different routes where refugees were led by Italian guides across the mountains, all of them difficult and dangerous. And it was winter on top of it. It must have been so hard. Unbelievable. The least I can do is hike on the Swiss side in warmer weather."

Andreas put a hand on Paulo's shoulder. "Don't forget though, your father was a very young man then. We're a little bit older and not as tough."

"Yes, but still, hiking will do me good. I need all the exercise I can get. I have an office job and just don't do enough moving around."

At home, Emilia stepped out of her house and greeted Paulo. "You'll have dinner at my place," she said to Andreas.

"Thanks, hun," Andreas hugged her. "No work today?"

"I left early. It was quiet at the clinic. No sick or injured creatures."

Andreas filled Paulo in on his family. "Emilia is my youngest and an animal lover. That's why she became a vet."

"And how is Luisa?" Paulo asked.

"She is doing well." Andreas smiled. "I talked to her yesterday. I'm going to spend a few months in Tuscany this summer. In fact, you can drive back with me. That way you don't need to take the train back. It's only a little over two hours if we take the road across the Splügenpass to Bellano.

Paulo looked at him surprised. "Okay, that would be great, as long as it isn't too far out of your way."

"No, not at all," Andreas said. "It would be fun to say hello to your mother on my way to Tuscany."

"Very kind of you," Paulo said.

Andreas showed him the guest room and the bath, so he could freshen up. Afterward, they went next door to Emilia's for dinner. She had prepared a meal of chicken marsala, pasta, and salad. Andreas opened a bottle of wine and started a fire in the fireplace. Although the weather had been warm during the day, evenings in the mountains were still cool.

After dinner, they sat together next to the fireplace. They talked about Andreas and Luisa's trip through Italy to find Bella. Paulo told them about his early childhood. He was born during the last couple of days of the war. When he was little, his mother told him beautiful stories about his father. She told him that he was a good man and that he died during the war. She didn't go into any details of his demise, but she clearly wanted for Paulo to have loving feelings toward his father. Later, when he was older, he heard rumors from friends and a few relatives who suspected that Joshua had abandoned them. These were ugly rumors and his mother vehemently denied them, but Paulo had conflicting feelings.

"I was torn between idealizing my father and my increasingly suspicious and angry feelings toward him. When my mother married her second husband, who became my stepfather, I fully embraced him as my real father. He was a kind and generous man, and he filled the longing for a father in me."

"That's understandable," Andreas said. "You never knew Joshua. Your mother's second husband was your true father."

Paulo nodded. "But then you brought that love letter from him, and I can tell you that was a real shock for me. I had to reevaluate my feelings toward Joshua."

"I'm sorry, we created all this turmoil in your life," Andreas said. "Luisa and I talked about the effect this could have on Bella and her family. We were almost afraid of contacting you, but we knew we had to do it. You deserved to know the truth, however painful it was."

"Of course," Paulo said. "You did the right thing, the only thing you could've done. It brought heartache but also great relief and even joy to my mother and me, well to all of us. I'm so happy to find out that my father wasn't a coward or opportunist but a good, faithful husband, who looked forward to being a father."

They sat together for a while, looking at the fire. Andreas noticed that Paulo looked tired. "Well, I think we should call it a night. We need to be rested if you want to hike tomorrow."

"Yes, of course," Paulo said. He stretched himself and got up.

Andreas wanted to help Emilia clean up the kitchen, but she gestured for him to stay put. "I did most of it already. You two go and rest. I only have to work tomorrow in the afternoon. Are you going to take Pietro along or should I keep him?"

"We'll take him. He loves to hike and if he gets tired, I'll carry him." Andreas got up and he and Paulo went next door.

Chapter 42

Andreas and Paulo rose early the following day. After a light breakfast, they set out on their hike. Andreas drove to the village of Splügen where they left the car. They began their ascent to the top of the mountain along Via Spluga with Pietro running ahead of them. They stopped several times to rest. Like always when he hiked in this area, Andreas spent a moment enjoying the stunning view of the surrounding mountains. He pointed out the Weisshorn in the north and the Surrettahorn and Pizzo Tampoco on the border to Italy.

Paulo took a deep breath. "It's gorgeous here ... I wish my father would've been able to enjoy it more."

"It was winter, and up here it can be brutally cold," Andreas said. "But then for Joshua it was the end of a dangerous and strenuous hike. So even the cold and the snow-covered mountains promised freedom."

"A freedom he could never fully taste." Paulo's voice trembled, then he gave a shrug. "But at least for a moment, even a few hours, he was happy. That's what he expressed in his letter to Mother."

"Yes, that's true," Andreas said. He put his hand on Paulo's shoulder "Let's keep that thought in mind. He was happy."

Paulo nodded and they continued to wait quietly until Pietro became impatient and gave a quick bark to get the stragglers moving again.

When they arrived at the cave where Andreas had found Joshua's belongings, Paulo sat on a rock. He was out of breath and wiped the sweat off his forehead. "I definitely need to exercise more."

They looked at the different rocks inside and outside of the cave, trying to decide which one would be best. Andreas picked one that lent itself to carving. It was outside right next to the cave and Paulo liked it. While Paulo was relaxing and Pietro was running around sniffing out all the corners and crevices, Andreas took out his utensils from his backpack. He had made a drawing of the image and the text at home and Paulo had liked it very much.

The image showed the outline of a bird, lifting off in flight. The text was simple:

In memory of Joshua Goldman
Beloved Husband and Father
1918 - 1943

Andreas was invigorated by this work. It not only helped to bring closure to Bella and her family so many years later, but it was also liberating for Andreas. He could think of Karla with love but without the crippling grief that had prevented him moving forward and being fully engaged in life. Now, he saw new opportunities for his work, and he felt joyous again.

After the stone was carved, Paulo snapped a picture of it to show to Bella and the rest of the family.

"This is such an important experience for me, such a relief for all of us," Paulo said and gave Andreas a hug "You don't know how grateful we are to you and to the people who helped you."

They sat on the rocks next to the cave, relaxing and eating the picnic they had packed, prosciutto and cucumber sandwiches with apricots for dessert. Andreas watched as the shadows lengthened on the fields in the early afternoon. "Time to hike back," he said.

They hiked down to the village of Splügen and Andreas drove the car back to Andeer. After taking off his hiking boots at Andreas' house, Paulo did a few stretching exercises for his calves and rubbed his neck. "I'll be sore tomorrow, but the hike was wonderful."

"I know just the remedy for that," Andreas said. "You know, Andeer has a well-known mineral spa. It's great for relaxing your muscles."

"I didn't bring a bathing suit," Paulo said.

"I have an extra one you can try on." Andreas opened the front door.

They went inside, refreshed themselves with a glass of water. Andreas went into the bedroom, grabbed his new bathing trunks and handed them to Paulo. "They're new. I haven't worn them yet. Try them on."

"Thank you." Paulo held it up. "Should work."

Andreas put on his bathing trunks and a pair of pants over them. He grabbed a bag with some towels, his wallet, and a sweatshirt. Paulo came out of the guest room wearing jeans and a T-shirt.

"Did they fit?" Andreas asked.

"Yes. A little tight around the belly but they should do." He grinned. "Another reason to watch my weight."

"You're doing well," Andreas said. "But you better take a jacket or sweater with you. The days are warm, but the evenings can get cool up here."

Paulo grabbed a jacket and they walked to the spa since it was close by.

"Wow, that's impressive." Paulo admired the beautifully laid out mineral spa. Andreas used his pass to check them in. After taking off their clothes, they walked around and checked out the indoor and outdoor pools. Outside they relaxed in the water and admired the beautiful landscape of the Schams Valley.

"Heaven." Paulo exhaled and smiled.

"Not bad," Andreas agreed as he enjoyed the feeling of the whirlpool massaging his muscles.

An hour later, they dressed and walked back to Andreas' house. While Paulo called his wife to tell her about their hike, Andreas went into the kitchen and prepared a light supper of air-dried cold beef, called *Bündnerfleisch*, cheese, fresh bread from the town bakery, and a large mixed salad, which they enjoyed with a glass of Chianti. They sat on the patio, watching the sun set over the mountains. Andreas felt content, thinking back to their hike and the memorial stone he had carved. He hoped it had given Paulo a renewed feeling of gratitude toward his father.

Soon, the physical exertion and the relaxing bath took its toll and they both began to yawn. They went to bed early. Andreas' head barely touched the pillow before he fell into a deep, dreamless sleep.

Chapter 43

The following day, Andreas took Paulo on a tour of the town and introduced him to Franz, the Chief of Police, and to Marianne, Franz' daughter and librarian, as well as to Florin Pitsch, who used to guide the refugees from the border to the valley. Florin expressed his disappointment that he wasn't able to meet and save Joshua. Paulo, however, told him he was deeply grateful to anybody who had tried to help his father.

They also went on a few easy hikes the next couple of days. They visited the breathtaking Viamala gorge along Via Spluga between the city of Thusis and Andeer. The gorge was carved into the massive rocks by glacial ice and the water of the Hinterrhein thousands of years ago. As Andreas explained, the Romansh word "via mala" meant "evil road." In earlier times, the gorge offered the most direct access to the Alpine passes of Splügen and San Bernardino, but it was a narrow and dangerous path with the constant threat of falling rocks and turbulent water, hence the term. In modern times, it became one of the most beloved hiking paths and tourist attractions. Paulo was fascinated by the natural spectacle. He was pleased that his physical stamina had improved and the hiking had become easier.

A few days later, after packing the trunk of his van with his sculpting tools, suitcases, and bags, Andreas and Paulo said goodbye to Emilia and Peter. Andreas put Pietro in his doggy seat in the back.

"I'll see you in a few weeks," Andreas said to his daughter and future son-in-law. The newly engaged couple had decided to take a short vacation to celebrate their engagement at Luisa's estate in Vignaverde.

Andreas and Paulo waved and drove away, taking the road over the Splügenpass into Italy. The road connected the Swiss Hinterrhein region with the Valle San Giacomo and the village of Chiavenna on the Italian side. It was used as far back as the Roman empire and, as Andreas mentioned, was one of the highest paved roads of the Alps.

"I hope you don't mind narrow and twisty roads," Andreas said as they left Andeer. "It gets quite steep at times."

"No problem. As long as I don't have to drive."

Past the village of Splügen, they drove up the mountain on a well-constructed road, snaking along many serpentine curves. They were greeted by lush green fields with wildflowers and pine forests. Above the trees, the road passed a narrow set of hairpin turns. At the top of the Splügenpass, at a height of 2,115 meters, they stopped to enjoy the impressive vista of snow-covered mountains.

They continued their drive past the border into Italy. On the Italian side, the road was narrower and more challenging with lots of twists and turns. They passed narrow galleries and dark tunnels.

"I wouldn't want to drive here when it rains or at night," Paulo said.

Andreas agreed. "As beautiful as it is, it can get hairy during bad weather."

After about an hour, they drove by the lake of Monte Spluga in the Lombardy region of Italy.

"The scenery is absolutely beautiful," Paulo said. "I've been here before a long time ago, but it just makes me realize I should come back more often, take Diana along. This drive has been marvelous. This whole trip is so meaningful for me. Thank you so much for everything."

"Believe me, it was my pleasure and a great honor getting to know you and your family," Andreas said. "And you're welcome anytime at my place. As you can see, it's not really far, at least not in summer when you can drive over the Splügenpass."

They continued their drive to Bellano at Lake Como. They stopped for a quick visit with Bella who welcomed them with joy. She gave a hug to Pietro who greeted her with a happily wagging tail, then admired the photo of Joshua's memorial stone with the delicate carvings. "Joshua would love it," she said with tears in her eyes and a smile on her face. "I dreamed of him the other night." She hugged Paulo and Andreas. "He smiled at me."

After some refreshments, Andreas took Paulo home. His wife, Diana, invited Andreas for a late lunch, but he was eager to head on. It was still quite far to Tuscany, and he wanted to avoid rush hour traffic.

"I'll be back for a visit later," Andreas promised. "I also want to go to Quercia and tell the helpful people there that we found Bella. So, we'll definitely see each other again." He hugged Paulo and Diana, then called Luisa.

She answered her phone. Andreas heard some kind of agricultural machine in the background.

"Are you working in the vineyard?" Andreas asked.

"Yes, doing some checking on the grapes," Luisa said. "Where are you?"

"I just dropped off Paulo. He and Diana say hello. I'm leaving now and hope traffic won't be too bad."

"You should be fine. Just take your time."

"I will. Thanks. Love you. I can't wait to see you again."

"Love you too. Drive carefully. I'll keep the wine ready." Luisa gave one of her pearly laughs.

Andreas' mouth curved into a smile. Paulo and Diana smiled as well. "Your friendship with Luisa blossomed into love?" Diana asked.

"Yes," Andreas said, putting his phone into his pocket. "Our quest to find Bella and give her Joshua's love letter and finding you, the family, somehow stirred deep emotions in me, I guess in both of us." He hesitated. "I was depressed and still mourned the untimely death of my wife, Karla. I didn't expect this would happen, I mean, finding love again." He glanced at them. "It feels really good."

"We're happy for you," Paulo said, and Diana nodded. They hugged goodbye and Andreas picked up Pietro to put him in the car. "Ready for a fun time in Tuscany?"

Pietro confirmed this with a quick bark. Andreas started the car, waved at Paulo and Diana, and drove south, his heart soaring with joy and apprehension. What would the future bring? Joy and confidence, however, won out.

The End

Acknowledgements

The first persons I want to thank are my editors and proofreaders, Linda Cassidy Lewis and Lisette Brodey, my cover designer, Diane Busch, and my beta readers, LuAnn Strauser, Diane Busch, and Silvia Delorenzi for their excellent work and the many helpful corrections and suggestions. They helped me make this novel a better work.

I wrote the bulk of this novel in 2020 during the pandemic. I was fortunate to be able to stay home and use the "quarantine" as a time for my many creative endeavors. Not everybody was that lucky. What I couldn't do though was research the different locals of my book in Switzerland and Italy, in person. Although Switzerland is my first home country, I wasn't familiar enough with the specific area in the canton of Grisons or Graubünden near the Italian border that was the home of my protagonists. I had to depend on the internet and on maps and books, which though helpful are less than ideal. Fortunately, I have a friend who is familiar with that area and is a geography aficionada. Thank you, Silvia for not only being one of my beta readers but my research assistant and for your many suggestions about the geographical locations, customs, and culinary specialties of the Rhaeto-Romanic area and, of course, the Italian terms. You were a true and loyal help. Whatever I got wrong is entirely my mistake.

Some of my research, in particular with regard to the situation of the Jewish refugees in Italy during World War Two, are based on the wonderful book, *Benevolence and Betrayal: Five Italian Families Under Fascism* by Alexander Stille. Furthermore, the novels *The Magnificent Dappled Sea* by David Biro and *Beneath a Scarlet Sky* by Mark Sullivan served as inspiration for my own work.

Christa Polkinhorn, originally from Switzerland, lives and works as writer and translator in the Los Angeles area in California. She divides her time between the United States and Switzerland and has strong ties to both countries. She is the author of seven novels and a collection of poems. Her travels and her interest in foreign cultures inform her work and her novels take place in several countries. Aside from writing and traveling, she is an avid reader and a lover of the arts, dark chocolate, and red wine. She can be reached by email at cpolkinhorn@msn.com or you can visit her at her website www.christa-polkinhorn.com.

www.ingramcontent.com/pod-product-compliance
Lightning Source LLC
Chambersburg PA
CBHW020400120726
47904CB00002B/648